The Black Squall

The Black Squall

Lori Stone

Writers Club Press
San Jose New York Lincoln Shanghai

The Black Squall

Writers Club Press
an imprint of iUniverse.com, Inc.

For information address:
iUniverse.com, Inc.
5220 S 16th, Ste. 200
Lincoln, NE 68512
www.iuniverse.com

ISBN: 0-595-17485-X

Printed in the United States of America

For Mama

No woman is all sweetness;
even a rose has thorns.

MADAME RECAMIER

I

When I look back, it all seems kind of unreal. The murders, the car chase, the big con, the boat explosion. One day I'm living contentedly in Ohio, and the next afternoon I find myself in south Florida, running with the jet set, playing private eye, fighting off hoodlums and stealing just to stay alive. With a telephone call and a plane ride, I went from the tranquil life of a suburban professional to the random existence of an anxious fugitive.

It all started on the 12th, a Tuesday. My structured world had been spinning cozily along in the lazy, hazy, dog days of summer, and then everything changed, my entire life got rearranged, forever. I was minding my own business, tending pampered animals at my veterinary clinic, and looking forward to joining friends at an alfresco performance of the local Pops orchestra that evening. Borodin's *Polovtsian Dances*, timeless Gershwin show tunes, a medley of Scott Joplin ragtime. Some of my favorites. Streaks of platinum sunlight were lancing through cracks in the miniblinds, making the central air conditioner feel less effective than usual, and the mid-August swelter had reduced the chorus in the kennels to an occasional sharp yap. My attention was fixed on a fresh set of x-rays that were clipped to a fluorescent screen behind the broad teakwood desk that my husband, Peter, had given me to celebrate our second wedding anniversary, and the opening of my practice. The films provided full anterior and lateral views of the lower left foreleg of a three-year-old thoroughbred that had pulled up lame the day before. The problem was obvious, a condition called splints, and the treatment was simple. An injection, cold compresses, a tightly wound bandage, lots of rest, and the normally frisky colt would be jumping low rails in a month or so.

"Dr. Pearson," barked my assistant's voice on the intercom, "there's a Mr. Rehm for you, on line two, from Florida."

"Thank you, Angie," I replied, swiveling my lavender high-back chair to face the desk once again. "And while I have you, please tell Dr. LaRusso that I concur with his diagnosis of Ms. Poynor's gelding. Ask him to initiate a standard corticosteroid regimen as soon as convenient."

"Oka…" came the truncated reply as she released the key too quickly. It was an annoying little habit that I had tried more than once to have her correct, with obvious lack of success.

I removed a cloisonné, clip-on earring—pierced earrings can be dangerous when working with animals—and picked up the lightweight cameo handset. The stylish little phone was of Italian design. They do wonderful things with plastics.

"Hello, Mr. Rehm. What a pleasant surprise!"

"Good afternoon, Dr. Pearson," he began. "I trust that you're well?"

The sun-soaked, Florida drawl on the other end of the line belonged to an attorney with my father's bank in Fort Lauderdale. I didn't know him all that well, but the strain in his voice was obvious.

"I'm just fine. Thank you." I said as some dreadful premonition made a chill race down my spine. "How are things on the Mosquito Coast?"

"Well, I'm afraid that I'm calling with some rather unpleasant news," he said. "There's been an accident, you see. A boating accident. Early this morning. Involving your uncle's cabin cruiser. There was an explosion of some sort, and a fire. The Coast Guard is investigating, of course. They haven't issued a formal statement yet, but in a brief conversation with their Public Relations Officer twenty minutes ago I learned that the Search &

Rescue divers have recovered sufficient evidence to confirm that your father was aboard."

He took a long, ragged breath, then cleared an obviously dry throat. The suspense was unbearable.

"There weren't any survivors, Dr. Pearson," he finally continued. "I'm afraid that your father is... gone."

"Dad's dead?"

"It would appear so. I'm terribly sorry."

"And Uncle Bud?"

"I'm afraid that he's gone as well." The lawyer's voice was choked with emotion. "I don't know any more than that, and I'd prefer not to speculate. We've requested that the Coast Guard and Medical Examiner fax copies of their reports to the bank as soon as possible. We'll know more tomorrow. I assume that you'll be coming down to make the arrangements. When can I expect to see you?"

So I dropped everything, of course, left Dr. LaRusso in charge of the clinic, and caught the earlybird flight from Youngstown at 6:03 the next morning—not the sanitized, soporific boredom of jet travel, but real flying on a nineteen-seat Air Midwest Beech 1900 commuter. Its twin Garrett turboprop engines alternately hummed and roared as they clawed their way through the rain squalls that were troubling the upper Allegheny Plateau, and we flew so low over the iron gray ribbon of the Mahoning River that I could actually see the fruited orchards as we hedgehopped past New Castle and Beaver Falls. Then, after switching planes in Pittsburgh, I suffered a leg-cramping US Airways MD80 down to Lauderdale. I spent most of that time staring at puffy Stratus clouds, floating through wispy memories, and studying my reflection in the double-pane Lexan window, searching for echoes of Dad in my golden hair and Nordic features, or of Mom in my slender frame and level mouth. But try as I might, I couldn't find even a trace of their strength. Not then, anyway. I felt like a frightened little girl, all cold and hollow inside, and I flipped my compact mirror open over and over again to inspect every molecule of makeup. It was pristine, perfect, every time I looked. But cosmetics couldn't hide the tension in my tight-pressed lips, or the fact that my pewter eyes had dulled to ash. And I wept when I remembered that Uncle Bud used to call me handsome.

*   *   *

A split second after the big jet's tires thump-squealed on the runway, the reverse thrust deflectors flared on the engine exhausts, pitching me forward in my seat. Fighting the momentum, I pushed myself back into the narrow burlap cushion, pinched the bridge of my nose and yawned hard to break the residual pressure in my eustachian tubes, until my ears finally popped. Then, as soon as the sleek, aluminum Boeing came to a halt, I watched in wonder as the other passengers jumped to their feet in time-honored tradition, so that they could all stand still in cramped procession for another five or ten minutes. They never cease to amaze me. Lemmings, every one. Eventually, there came the mad stampede up the jetway, and the rude biological shock of Florida's summer heat: 103 degrees, 98 percent humidity. The terminal was somewhat cooler, but not a great deal more inviting, for the nape of my neck started itching, and that always means trouble. Somewhere, someone was watching me. The anonymous stalker made me feel menaced, hunted, so I hurried on my way. Little did I suspect that I'd soon be running for my life.

Next to television, airport terminals have become the great cultural levelers of our age. Atlantic or Pacific, north or south, they are all built to the same rigid specifications; of concrete slabs, exposed steel beams, acoustical tile ceilings, recessed lights, featureless carpets, and endlessly boring cattle chutes of perpetually exhaust-streaked glass. If you travel regularly, as I did, lecturing on equine gastroenterology, you soon discover that one terminal is much like any other. Regional flavorings have been assiduously purged by the architects of mass culture. Geographical cues have been carefully erased by the scions of globalism. A terminal punctuated by

IHOP, Pizza Hut, two newsstands, three bars and a video arcade can be found anywhere on the continent. In fact, it is. It's the same thing everywhere you go. And the passengers in their perpetual hurry to stand in unmoving lines don't give you a clue. There are ten-gallon Stetson hats in Portland, Rastafarians in Duluth.

The baggage claim area was crowded with sullen, steamy passengers, and I found that I really didn't want to be the self-sufficient feminist. I didn't want to elbow my way through the intransigent mob, and I had absolutely no desire to assert my independence by shouldering heavy luggage. Instead, I wanted to be pampered. I wanted to be cared for. So I caught the eye of a skycap, gave him my yellow FLL claim stubs, and asked him to meet me at the curb. A spotless Chevy Suburban from the Riverside Hotel was waiting for me there, its engine idling quietly, the air conditioner excreting a lazy stream of water which dribbled across the tarmac to the gutter. But as I made my way toward the Chevy a stringy-haired young man in faded bluejeans and engineer boots banged into me at full gallop. I saw the glint of stainless steel as he whipped a butterfly knife open and slashed my shoulder bag strap, then disappeared into the crowd.

The Suburban's Hispanic chauffeur tumbled out of the driver's seat. "Madre mio! Are you o-chay, Miss?"

"I'm fine, just fine," I lied, rubbing my undamaged shoulder, and trying to steady my knees.

"I'll call the policia!" he yelled in indignation.

"No," I insisted. "Don't bother. All he got was a cheap canvas bag, a bagel and copy of *Ms.* Let's just go, shall we?"

I wanted to get as far away from there as possible.

The chauffeur opened the side door for me, with a sweeping, solicitous flourish, and I gave three dollars to the skycap before climbing into the chilled luxury of crushed velour and tinted glass. Seconds later my luggage was loaded in the back, the tail gate bumped shut, and the van pulled smoothly away.

Coconut palm trees, multicolored stucco, and Spanish language business signs flitted by the windows as we drifted into town. I was the only passenger, so I asked the driver to swing down Seabreeze Boulevard, across the Brooks Memorial Causeway, and past the enormous yacht basin where Dad and Uncle Bud always kept their boats; but in the endless confusion of fly bridges, fishing poles, masts, rigging and antennas, I didn't see a single familiar thing.

So I checked in at the Riverside—it is a charmingly dignified hotel offering old world hospitality, warmth and elegance—and after the porter showed me how to open the drapes and turn on the bathroom light, I sat on the divan and kicked off my shoes. My knees still hadn't stopped shaking after the purse-snatching incident at the airport, so I pulled my ankles up underneath me to calm my legs, closed my eyes tight, and let my mind drift in a whirl of subjective reflection.

Somehow, none of it rang true. Dad and Uncle Bud were dead, or so I'd been told, and the very thought of it made me feel nauseous. I remembered that I had just sat there in my office for the longest time after Carl Rehm had hung up, stunned and silent, trying to fathom the imponderables of eternity, listening to the ghostly quiet of a dead telephone line. Then the earpiece crackled briefly, the dreadful smoothness of the dial tone returned, cybernetic life was restored, and I struggled through the swirling fogs of confusion to full consciousness. Yet the world was suddenly different, frightfully strange. It was smaller, less courageous, less virile. It was lonely. It was empty.

I remembered reaching out to touch the shiny brass nameplate on my desk. Dad had presented it to me right after I'd graduated from Ohio State's School of Veterinary Medicine. He'd been so very proud of me that carefree Saturday morning. It had shown all over his face. Tough old salt though he was, tears of joy had actually fallen from his gray, weatherworn eyes, and for the first time I had told him that I loved him. That had been five years ago. A lifetime ago.

"There I am," I'd heard myself mutter as I picked up the nameplate, and held it like a priceless jewel. "There I am, memorialized for all time in carefully etched metallic letters, filled with black enamel, and burnished to a fare-the-well. Dr. Jean Margaret Pearson, D.V.M. And now I can add a few more lines to complete this drab résumé. Twenty-nine. Widowed. Orphaned."

I heaved a painful sigh, pulled myself up from that bitter reverie, and changed out of my travel clothes into a simple black sheath and low heels. That's when I noticed that the tiny red message light on the bedside telephone was blinking.

"Hello, Dr. Pearson," said the digital recording. "It's Carl Rehm. Welcome to Fort Lauderdale. I'm sorry that you've had to come on such unpleasant business. I'm calling to confirm our appointment. I have prepared a few papers for your signature, and I've received a faxed report from the Medical Examiner. If you feel up to it after your flight, please drop by my office this afternoon, anytime after two. At your convenience, of course."

As he'd hung up, the recorder had caught Rehm saying, "I hate those damned voice mail machines." Then the phone clicked, twice.

    *   *   *

Though presenting the impression of stolid independence, Carl Rehm's legal firm was a wholly owned subsidiary of the bank. Thus, the offices of Marhead, Guyler, Rehm and Carp were on the twenty-first floor of one of those tall, mirrored monstrosities that define North America's postmodern cityscapes, and make you wonder what all of those conservative financiers are doing that they don't want people looking in on them. His executive secretary, Ms. Euladine Varga, showed me to the inner sanctum as soon as I arrived, and Rehm ushered me to a teal wing chair at the head of an oversized butler's table. The atmosphere was thick with elaborately structured pomposity—English walnut paneling, a Jacob Mallord William Turner watercolor, an intricate Kermanshah rug over antique red oak flooring, Shang dynasty bronzes, nicotine-stained meerschaum pipes in a scalloped delft rack, and oodles of smug self-satisfaction.

"Would you care for something to drink?" asked Rehm.

"Perrier over ice would be fine," I replied.

"Certainly," he said, signaling to Ms. Varga. "I can't begin to tell you how sorry I am about all this."

Rehm was a slight, fiftyish, balding man, who spent way too much time indoors. His freckled skin was almost pasty, his hands flacid. He peered over the half lenses of gold-rimmed reading glasses, pushed a pro forma letter across the little table, and handed me his personal Waterman fountain pen. I reviewed the letter carefully, and signed it in dark blue ink, establishing my claim to act as the executrix of Dad's estate. Then came the first surprise.

"As meticulous as your uncle was concerning matters legal and financial," Rehm said, "he made no recommendation in his will regarding the appointment of a contingent executor. He had stipulated that your father administer his estate, but that, unfortunately, is no longer practicable. An officer of the bank's Trust Department could step in to fill the void, of course, but such arrangements are somewhat impersonal, and rather costly to the heirs. By law, three percent of the estate's established net value goes to the executors as compensation for services, you see. Therefore, I have discussed the matter with Judge Holloway, and he has agreed to ratify a petition from you, should you choose to submit one."

I just stared at him blankly.

"Will you consider assuming this additional responsibility?" asked Rehm. He pushed another paper across the table in front of me. "It would mean arranging for you uncle's memorial as well."

"Yes, of course," I agreed. "Dad and Uncle Bud were the closest of friends. A shared funeral would seem particularly appropriate under the circumstances."

I gripped the fat Waterman pen once again, and the scratching of the 24K gold nib as it looped across the linen paper brought it all home like a thunderclap. Dad and Uncle Bud were actually dead. I felt the sudden heat of tears welling up in my eyes, but before I could reach for my purse Rehm produced a big box of Kleenex with practiced efficiency. Then Ms. Varga placed a small, open bottle of Perrier, and a crystal tumbler filled with quartermoon ice cubes, on crisp paper napkins in front of me. The napkins were neatly embossed with a Mylar impression of the bank's logo.

Rehm waited patiently for my sniffles to subside, and then handed me a stack of color-coded folders.

"The dark blue file contains a copy of your father's last will and testament," he explained, "and the light blue file has copies of stamped and sealed certificates of death. The dark and light green folders hold your uncle Bud's will and certificates, respectively. These will be useful when applying for life insurance and annuity disbursements, real estate transferals, boat and vehicle title changes, veterans benefits and the like. You'll want to review all of these documents at your leisure, of course, but you'll be interested to learn that you are named as the sole beneficiary of your father's estate, and as the primary beneficiary of your uncle's."

"Uncle Bud's?"

"Yes. Evidently, your uncle had no other family. Your father was listed as the principal beneficiary of the estate, but that point is now moot, so everything will go to you, with the exception of a few odd mementos that your uncle intended to leave to a friend here and there. However, since he resided aboard his cruiser it must be assumed that most of those things are irretrievably lost."

"And the red folder?"

"It contains copies of the Medical Examiner's preliminary reports on the post mortem examinations. I'm not at all certain that I should have had them faxed here. The certificates of death will prove quite sufficient for your needs."

"Is there something wrong with the M.E.'s reports?"

"No," Rehm hedged. "There's nothing wrong with them, per se. They are quite professional, and thorough. It's just that they're so… detailed. I would not recommend that you actually read them."

"I understand. But there is one question that I feel compelled to ask. Are the authorities absolutely certain that the bodies found on the boat were Dad's and Uncle Bud's?"

"It is a foregone conclusion. A pump attendant at Pier 66 observed your father and uncle leaving the gas dock together, aboard your uncle's cruiser, and the accident happened approximately thirty minutes thereafter. I spoke with the Medical Examiner about the identifications this morning. They were made on the basis of general physical characteristics, using drivers' license information in the data bank at the Department of Motor Vehicles. Additionally, to provide additional confirmation, she has contacted the appropriate dental surgeons and physicians, requested various medical records, and will compare specific histories, dental and skeletal x-rays to conclude the forensic analysis."

"And did they ascertain the cause of the fire?"

Rehm reached for his pen and avoided my eyes.

"The Medical Examiner has listed the deaths as accidental," he said. "It is the Coast Guard's responsibility to determine the precise cause of the fire, and they haven't returned our call as yet. However, your uncle's boat was rather old, and presumably not in the best repair. A Coast Guard investigator asked the bank about it, so I queried the computer files because your uncle had his cabin cruiser insured through our brokerage division. There was nothing unusual. Standard marine coverage. Let me see. I have the notes here somewhere. Yes. A thirty-one-foot Rawson cabin cruiser. Air conditioned. Recording fathometer. New Raytheon radar, GPS chartplotter, autopilot, and VHF/SSB radios. Two gasoline engines. Twin fuel tanks. Now, gasoline engines can be terribly dangerous, Dr. Pearson, because a gallon of gasoline has the same explosive force as ten sticks of dynamite. It is extremely volatile stuff. We have several gasoline explosions every year along the coast. If a fuel tank or line get leaky, or if the bilge isn't properly ventilated, a boat can blow up like a bomb."

There was a moment of absolute silence as I imagined what the end must have been like, and the horror of it made me shudder involuntarily.

"There is also this," Rehm continued as he handed me a white folder.

It contained a single piece of creamy bank stationery, listing the name of a local mortuary, and the name of another, thoroughly ambiguous corporation.

"These are two of the very finest firms in town," he said by way of explanation. "Stanek's is a respected and reasonably priced funeral home. They offer compassionate, traditional services, and they are able to provide you with their best parlor. I am certain that you will find their facilities to be more than satisfactory. On the other hand, Ebb Tide Inc. is an exceedingly discreet concern, which operates a state-of-the-art crematorium just west of Coral Springs. Given the nature of yesterday morning's accident... that is to say, the condition of the remains..."

His voice trailed down to a guttural whisper.

I nodded in agreement once again.

"Is there anything else?" I asked.

"Just this," he said. "Now that your father's and uncle's identities have been officially confirmed, followup stories about the accident will air on tonight's television newscasts. Also, Fort Lauderdale's *Sun-Sentinel* and the *Miami Herald* will run feature articles and stock obituaries in the morning papers. There is no way to avoid it. Boating fatalities are big news along the coast. So I decided to capitalize on the publicity. I took the liberty of having Ms. Varga inform the media that the family will hold calling hours at Stanek's tomorrow evening, and that a memorial service would be held the following day."

"So soon?"

"Well, you see," he postured, avoiding my real question while staring at his shoes, "the crematorium operates on a very limited schedule; only two nights per week, and then only between the hours of one a.m. and dawn.

South Florida has a large, retired Jewish population, you see, and the sight of crematory smoke is, well, quite undesirable. It's an extremely sensitive issue for the community, as I'm sure you can understand. At any rate, since the remains are utterly unviewable, I took it upon myself to have them scheduled for cremation this evening."

"You did what?!"

"The next date of cremation is four days away," he explained defensively. "I was merely trying to expedite matters—to be helpful, that is—so that you can complete your obligations and return home as soon as possible. Of course, you are absolutely free to alter these arrangements if you wish, but I'd need to know that now in order to alert the media."

I just sat there, angry, but silent. Everything was spinning out of control. Events were moving too fast, too impersonally, as though they were happening to someone else, not to me, and I could feel my anxiety growing.

"There's one other detail," he continued.

"What's that?"

"Your father and uncle each had a safe deposit box."

"And?"

"As executrix, you must inventory the contents of those boxes prior to filing the probate audits with the court."

My head was beginning to ache.

"If you'd like," he offered, "we could compile the inventories tomorrow morning. I'll be more than happy to assist you, of course. Would ten o'clock be convenient?"

"Why not?" I replied testily. "It would appear that I have little else to do."

My petulance was showing, and I really didn't care.

"Tell me, Mr. Rehm. What of my own account?"

"Oh, yes, of course. I'm terribly sorry. I looked into that this morning. I should have mentioned it earlier. As you know, your father established a restricted trust some years ago, for the purpose of funding your education and appropriate related expenses. Both he and your uncle were named as trustees. By law, the bank will now assume those duties. However, one condition of the instrument dictates that the trust be dissolved, with all principal and accrued interest being delivered directly to you, upon the attainment of your thirtieth birthday. That will be next April, I believe. You will find a copy of the trust agreement, along with a current statement of balance, in the orange folder. The current balance is inconsequential, but when you study your father's will, you'll notice a codicil which directs that all liquitable assets be transferred to your trust fund in the event of his death. This will have the effect of obviating certain estate and inheritance tax liabilities. In the case of securities, state and federal capital gains taxes may also be avoided. We will request that the Internal Revenue Service draft a letter of determination, establishing whether or not we can transfer your uncle's liquid assets into your father's estate prior to transferring your father's estate into your trust. It is an arcane and somewhat convoluted point, based on the legal theory that your uncle probably predeceased your father by a microsecond, but the potential reduction in tax liabilities could be highly significant. I have an accountant and tax law specialist working on it now."

There was a long, awkward pause in the discussion, and then he asked, "Is there any other way in which I can be of service?"

"As a matter of fact, yes. Would you please send all of these files to my attention at the Riverside Hotel? They're rather bulky, and I'd prefer not to carry them around with me."

"Of course. I'll have them delivered by messenger first thing in the morning. If there is anything else that I can do, please don't hesitate to let me know."

"Oh, I think that you've done quite enough already," I said before I could stop myself.

I was more than a little upset, but if Rehm was stung by my outburst, he didn't let it show. He merely thanked me and stood up, ending the meeting.

We said all of the obligatory parting words on the way to the elevator, and before I knew it the big doors thumped shut in my face. I pushed the plastic L button, enjoyed a smooth, uninterrupted descent, and it gave me a moment to think.

Was I being paranoid, or was something out of kilter? A virtual stranger had just scheduled the funerals of my father and uncle without even asking my opinion. Was that helpful and supportive, or highhanded and presumptuous? I wasn't sure, but I didn't like it. I didn't like it one bit. It made me feel manipulated, abused, and more than a little off balance. Was my wounded sense of ego appropriate, or had the purse-snatching incident simply rattled my cage? And was it my imagination, or had Dad's attorney just given me the bum's rush?

The elevator slowed to a stop, and as the burnished steel doors swished open the evening sun blinded me. Carl Rehm's north-facing office had been cool, and relatively dark, but the lobby of this temple of financial chicanery was lined with twenty-foot-high glass curtain walls, and polished pink granite covered every sizzling surface. It was like stepping into the nucleus of a monstrous solar oven. Then, while fumbling in my purse for my sunglasses, a gigantic, hulking darkness overshadowed me.

2

"D r. Pearson?" the mammoth specter asked.

"Yes?"

"I am sorry if I startled you, Miss," said a deeply resonant voice. "Please allow me to introduce myself. My name is L'Ouverture. Toussaint L'Ouverture."

"So, you're free at last," I challenged, in a weak attempt to gain some sort of advantage. "A bit far from Haiti, aren't you?"

"Ah, ha, ha!" came the easy, laughing reply. "So, Miss. You know your Caribbean history! But no. I am not that long-dead Haitian revolutionary whose epitaph was borrowed by the martyred Dr. King. I am a Lieutenant Commander with the United States Coast Guard here in Fort Lauderdale, and I am investigating the untimely deaths of your father and your uncle. I would like to speak with you for a moment, if I may."

Dark glasses now in place, I held one hand up to shade my eyes as I tried to make out the details. He was well over six feet tall, quite broad in the shoulders but narrow in the hips, weighed slightly in excess of two hundred pounds, and had the deceptively aloof stance of a Clydesdale. It struck me as odd that, given the exceedingly torrid weather, he was dressed in a Class A uniform, complete with tie, jacket, braids, service ribbons, and a stiff-brimmed officer's cap.

"Here now, Miss," he said with a lyrical accent, "the afternoon sun has you at a disadvantage. Let's go somewhere more pleasant."

"Why?"

"Because I wish to discuss the circumstances of your father's demise."

I started to argue as he took me gently by the arm, and led me out of the bank into the sticky tropical heat, but curiosity got the better of me. And besides, I've always been a sucker for a handsome man in uniform. We walked around the corner to a cramped little side street, and ducked into a hole-in-the-wall coffee shop that reeked of caffeine, black beans and Jimmy Buffett. It was only marginally cooler in there, so he took off his jacket and cap as we sat down on opposite sides of a narrow plywood booth, which was painted in vivid hues of Biscayne blue and Flamingo pink. That gave me a chance to take a closer look at my host. He had a long, rectangular face, chestnut skin, teriyaki eyes, and black, curly, closely cropped hair. It was a pleasant countenance, cunningly offset by an upper central incisor of solid gold that sparkled when he smiled.

"Coffee?" he asked.

"No. Something cool."

"Two iced coffees with chilled cream," he cooed to the waitress. "And just a touch."

"A touch of what?"

"If I say it out loud, the owner might lose his license." He grinned as though we were sharing a confidence. "They make it up quick in the bath-tub, after they wash the pigs."

I was uncomfortably aware that I was in a strange place with a strange man whom I'd met only moments before, so I stiffened my back and said, "If you've got something to tell me about Dad's death, please get on with it."

"Look," he said, suddenly all business. "You made a big mistake in the bank just now. Listen to a friendly word of advice. Never take anyone in South Florida at face value, much less at his, or her, word. You must be more careful, Miss."

"It's *Mrs.*," I barked with authority.

"Yes, but poor Peter died nearly two years ago. Ah, such a pity for so beautiful a woman to be widowed so young. So now *Miss* is a more appropriate title. No?"

I'll give him this. He'd done his homework.

"Just who did you say you are?" I demanded.

"Ah, yes, Miss. That is much better now." His smile returned just as quickly as it had disappeared. "You should always ask to see some form of identification. Here is mine."

He reached into his shirt pocket, pulled out a miniature wallet, and flipped it open. It contained a light green Coast Guard gate pass, and a laminated Coast Guard picture ID, complete with prismatic, holographic seal.

"The concierge at the Riverside tells me that I can buy these in Miami for two hundred bucks apiece," I bluffed. "Twenty bucks more, and they'll throw in the cheap little plastic case."

"Yes, Miss, but can the little hustler get you these?"

He lay a sheaf of 8x10 color glossy photos on the table.

It only took me a moment to realize that they were pictures of a wooden-hulled boat lying on its keel on the bottom of the sea. It was Uncle Bud's cabin cruiser, or what was left of it. What little remained above the water line was badly charred, like the logs in a burned-out campfire, and the transom had clearly smashed into the bottom, the weight of the engines having drawn the boat down by the stern. The hulk was sickening, grotesque, like a moldy old coffin, and it took a great deal of effort to keep from turning my eyes away.

The waitress brought two tall glasses of foaming, tawny brew, and I sipped at mine slowly as I sorted through the pictures. Each one had a label affixed to the lower right-hand corner. Interior, main cabin. Bent prop shaft. Hole near keel, starboard. Damage to hull, port. Evidence of fire, cockpit. Damaged fuel tank, starboard. Broken engine mount. Location of HR #1.

"HR #1?" I asked.

"Human remains," he stated without emotion.

I looked him straight in the eye and said, "Whose?"

He didn't flinch a bit as he answered, "Your father's."

"So why show these dreadful pictures to me?" I sighed, while sipping at the heavily creamed coffee.

"Take a second look at the damaged fuel tank, starboard, if you will. Do you notice anything peculiar?"

I turned the photograph around at 90° intervals, studying the tank from all angles.

"My attorney, Carl Rehm, said that there had been an explosion; that such things are not at all uncommon. It appears as though the starboard fuel tank ruptured, violently. The metal is badly torn. Is that what you mean?"

"Ah, yes. Very good. Now, look at the tank more closely. But this time, think of it as an aneurysm."

I glanced back at the photograph, and my blood turned instantly cold. The skin on my arms and neck had turned to gooseflesh.

"An aneurysm is a thin spot in the wall of a blood vessel," I declared as though lecturing a student. "It balloons, like a blister, and can rupture in times of stress. Any discharge, therefore, flows outward. But the torn metal of the starboard fuel tank bends inward."

"Now look at the damaged hull, starboard, where the fuel tank was located."

He fished through the pile of photographs and placed another one in front of me.

"The planking splinters outward," I said in wonder.

"Conclusion, Doctor?"

"The starboard fuel tank didn't rupture on its own. Something else must have exploded. Something powerful. Something located between the tank and the hull."

"Bravo!" he exclaimed. "Muy bueno."

"A bomb?"

"It certainly looks that way. An incendiary device of some kind. We will know for certain after the Navy's forensics team finishes the chemical analysis of the debris. And there is one thing more. We also found a solitary, insulated wire leading from the area of the fuel tank up through the hull. The other end of the wire was freshly stripped, and attached to a partially melted swivel bracket which had held the frame of the weather canopy."

I looked at him without comprehension.

"An unsophisticated but highly effective antenna," he explained patiently. "You see, Miss, the canopy frame was made of aluminum tubing. It is an excellent conductor of electromagnetic impulses; of radio waves. Therefore, it appears that the bomb was set off by radio remote control."

"Then they were murdered!"

"The evidence is undeniable."

"But why?"

"That is my question," he said through gritted teeth. "I want to know *why*, Miss, and more importantly, I want to know *who*. Your father was an old-style buccaneer, a soldier of fortune, a rogue, and he made his share of enemies along the way. But your uncle never met a stranger. Everyone liked him. He was kindly, agreeable. Yet the bomb was placed on his boat, so he must have been the target. And it must have been placed on board by someone with both skill and access. So you see, Miss, this was no accident. This was a premeditated, engineered, cold-blooded assassination."

It took me a minute to respond.

"The town where I grew up is often called the Mafia capital of the Midwest," I said, "so I've heard a lot of strange stories over the years. You make it sound as though this were a professional hit."

"Anything is possible, but I do not think that La Cosa Nostra was involved. It is not their style. They like to get up close, and personal. A .22

caliber bullet in the back of the head would be more typical. Bombs are too anonymous, too uncertain. No, Miss, it was not the Mob."

"Then who?"

"With all of the electronic equipment available today, anyone could have done it," he lamented. "Why, a child could make a radio trigger from the remote model airplane controls found in any hobby shop. Listen to me, Miss. I have just started piecing this together. My divers are still collecting evidence. But when I am done, it will not matter who did this. I will find him, and he will pay."

"I try to keep up with the news," I said. "Do you mean to tell me that with all of the problems the Coast Guard is having with drug smugglers and illegal aliens, you've really got time to investigate the unheralded murder of two hapless boat bums?"

He looked me straight in the eye, and I nearly came unglued. I had seen that expression once before, in the eyes of a Bengal tiger that I was feeding at the Cincinnati Zoo. It had looked right past the twenty pounds of raw beef dangling from my pitchfork, and made eye contact with me in a mystical kind of way. It neither growled, nor moved. It simply emptied its thoughts into mine. "I'll eat that sissified steak," it had said, "but I'd rather chase down something live, and crush its neck with my teeth, and feel hot blood in my mouth." And I had known without the slightest doubt exactly what that big cat really wanted on the menu, and I'd had terrifying nightmares for weeks.

"I met your father several years ago," L'Ouverture said. "An interesting chap. I liked him. He was one straightforward fellow, but fair. You must have inherited your cynicism from someone else."

I frowned indifferently, but looked away.

"The answer is," he continued, "that I will spend all of my personal time, and most of my professional time on this."

"Why?"

"Because your uncle was special. Because when my illegal alien parents landed on the beach they had no clue how the system worked. Oh, they had big hopes for the American Dream, but no savvy. So your uncle took an interest in them. Why does not matter. He helped them to get started, to set up a business, to become citizens. And he helped them to invest in things that really matter. Things like a good piece of land, and a house, and their children's educations. Now their oldest son is a commissioned officer in the United States Coast Guard. I have a journalist sister who is raising three beautiful girls, one brother who is a systems analyst with NOAA, and Washbelly is studying for the Bar. Yes, Miss. Your uncle was a saint, and he remained a good friend of our family all these years. Last month he advised my parents on the purchase of a retirement condo on Cape Perdi. Mama is old island, you see. Very superstitious. The project is named for her favorite blossom; a passion flower."

"Washbelly?" I asked with a raised eyebrow.

"Washbelly is Jamaica-talk for a woman's last baby."

He took a long pull at his iced coffee, then put it down hard.

"Listen," he declared. "My family came here with nothing. Nada. Now, we have everything. And the man who made it all possible…"

He choked up momentarily, as though he were going to cry.

"…the man who made it all possible was blown to kingdom come yesterday morning by some faceless, cowardly, son-of-a-bitch who is going to be very, very sorry. Oh, yes, Dr. Pearson, I have time for this."

I wanted to apologize for the crack that I had made about illegals, but there are times when an apology, no matter how sincere, is nearly profane, so I just sat there quietly and waited for him to go on.

"I did not seek you out this afternoon for the sheer joy of making your acquaintance," he finally said. "I need your help."

"Anything."

"I want you to keep your eyes and ears open, Miss. I want you to pay attention to everything that you see and hear. Listen to what people say, but do not ask a lot of fool questions. You are a veterinarian, after all, not an investigator. Just be observant. You are trained for that. Look for anomalies. If you learn anything interesting, or if you need help, you can reach me at the Coast Guard HQ, any time, day or night. If I am not there, and in all likelihood I will not be, they will patch you through to my cell-phone."

He took a business card out of his wallet, circled a telephone number, and slid it across the table.

"I'll be happy to cooperate," I said, "but what am I looking for?"

"If I knew that, we would not be talking."

I was beginning to like this man. He was intelligent, well-spoken, sensitive, and I detected a sardonic sense of humor lurking behind his tough, male bravado.

"Listen, Miss," he said, softening a bit. "I am sorry about your uncle and your father. I know that this is not a good time for you, that having to bear your sorrow alone is extremely difficult, but I want you to know that you have at least one friend in South Florida. Someone who cares very much about what happened to your people yesterday. Someone who desires to help make things right. Your family's pain is my family's pain. I would like to help in more obvious ways, but I think that it would be best if we are not seen together after this."

"You don't want to scare off the rats, do you?"

"They are far easier to kill when they are out in the open."

There was a protracted moment of silence, and then he said, "I assume that you were familiar with your uncle's cabin cruiser. It must have been a comfortable old tub."

"It was more like a junked-up old scow," I said. "Uncle Bud had all kinds of papers jumbled absolutely everywhere—books, navigational charts, annual reports, newspapers, prospectuses, journals, magazines—and there were dozens of drinking glasses filled with No. 2 pencils. You've never seen such a mess in your life; but an organized mess, like you'd expect to find in a professor's office. It just looked so out of place on a boat. It's no wonder that it burned, with all of that paper, and gasoline fumes and stuff."

"Gasoline fumes?"

"Yes. From the engines."

"Oh, no, Miss. You are mistaken. That boat had twin diesel engines."

"But I thought..."

Some primal instinct told me to shut my mouth, while my subconscious started grinding away.

"I understand that you are a first rate veterinarian," L'Ouverture said, "but if you do not know gasoline from diesel, you should be very careful around boats."

He reassembled his photographs as we said our goodbyes, and then he ordered another iced coffee, with just a touch, as I stood up to leave.

"By the way," I asked. "What's *a touch?*"

"It is a homemade banana liqueur. Me fahder, e make zeet down in de basemen."

"This is your family's shop?"

"The first of seven," he answered with pride. "Your uncle was one very shrewd fellow when it came to selecting prime business locations. You should see this place at lunchtime. It is a regular gold mine. Papa and Mama are relaxing at Chautauqua this month, soaking up culture and avoiding the summer heat. I received a note from them yesterday. Kissinger is lecturing at the Hall of Philosophy. Yo-Yo Ma is performing in the Amphitheater."

I could understand why his parents found upstate New York so appealing as I stepped back into the street. Thick, gelatinous heat waves were shimmering up from the pavement, making the bank's foundations appear to quiver, the shriek of rutting tomcats echoed down a garbage-strewn alley, and an overwhelming stench of overused frying grease hung in the air like smog.

Turning to walk back toward the main street, I was nearly run down as a gang of rollerblade commandos shot past me in a whirling confusion of dayglow helmets and elbow pads. I barely had time to trip back into the doorway. Then the questions that had been sloshing around in my subconscious clarified themselves. If Carl Rehm had looked into Uncle Bud's marine insurance at the express request of the Coast Guard, then why the confusion about the engines? And if L'Ouverture had no idea who had murdered Dad and Uncle Bud, then what made him think that I'd stumble across anything useful?

Those thoughts made my stomach feel queasy, and then I got that itchy feeling again. Someone was watching me.

I started looking for a cab.

3

After walking around for twenty minutes, I eventually found a taxi in front of a glitzy hotel—the kind with a fountain out front, and a covered plaza made from polished bronze and Plexiglas. It was a gypsy cab, a Mercury Mystique with customized electric magenta paint, and a dozen layers of clearcoat which had been buffed to a laser finish. In full noonday light the glare might have caused serious injury to the optic nerve.

The driver was an exuberant young man of such diverse ethnic parentage that the physical characteristics of his cocoa-colored face defy description. He was lounging on one of those uncomfortable-looking, wooden-beaded seat covers, and his tightly knotted dreadlocks were hanging halfway down to the floor in the passenger compartment.

"Whah to, Mees?" he asked through a gap-toothed grin.

"Home," I said reflexively.

"An' whah's dat, Mees?" came the amiable reply.

I had to think a few seconds before saying, "The Riverside Hotel."

Without warning, that taxi jerked away from the curb like a bottle rocket, to the inevitable reggae musical accompaniment of Bob Marley, and we quickly accelerated to warp factor nine. The windows were all wide open, so I had to hold the hem of my dress down in the hellish storm of hot air.

"Can you turn on the air conditioner?" I yelled over the wind.

"Yes, Mees," he yelled back. "We have a veddy good air conditionah now. A fow six-tee. Fow windows down at six-tee miles an ow-ah!"

He tilted his head back, and laughed uproariously at his Chumbo rendition of redneck humor, as Lauderdale flashed by in lurid streaks of neon.

Imagining that further conversation was pointless, I stuffed my hems under my legs, and grabbed my shoulder-length hair to keep it from slapping me in the face. That's when I noticed that a black BMW 740i sedan was following us, turning whenever we did.

"I've changed my mind," I yelled. "Take me to the marina."

"Wheech one?"

"Bahia Mar."

He shrugged and took an impossibly fast left turn, but the mystery car stayed right with us, about half a block behind.

"You hev friends!" my gap-toothed driver frowned.

"Friends?"

"De car behind oos. He stays weeth oos like a cat on a mouse."

His choice of similes made me wince, and for no clearly definable reason I started fearing for my life.

A block or two later we turned onto a broad, palm-tree-lined boulevard. Then the BMW accelerated rapidly, pulled alongside the cab, eased in close and started pacing us. Two heavily tanned young men were sitting in the front seat, wearing expensive-looking dark blue suits, glossy ties, and black, bug-eyed sunglasses. They had the muscular necks of football players, and no-nonsense mouths. The one on the passenger's side leaned out of his window, and hollered something unintelligible. He pointed vigorously at our back wheel, motioning for us to pull over.

"Is there something wrong with the rear tire?" I yelled.

"No way, Mees. I have brand new Meechelin Radial XGTs. Extra wide. Made for racing at LeMans, Eendianapolis. I checked dee air in dem just thees afternoon."

"Then what do these guys want?" I asked with a trace of fear in my voice.

"Nothing good, that's fer hell-damn sure. They could be carjackers, maybe. Or keednappers. Or steekup men. De driver, he has a big peestol on dee dash." `

"Can you lose them?"

"Yah-hoo! Amerika!" young Gap-tooth cried with glee. "Burt Reynolds! Steve MahGueen! Dees is why I come here. Dees ees why I am in Lauderdale. I watch all dee great movies back home. *Boolet. Smookee en de Bandito.* Jus watch me, lady. You better hang on!"

He wasn't kidding either. At the very next corner Gap-tooth stood on his brakes, snapped left behind the BMW in a maneuver that would have made Richard Petty wince, snapped left again onto a side road, and then right as he dropped it into forty-second gear. Somewhere in all of that lunacy he ejected Bob Marley from the tape deck, and inserted a home-made cassette with just one song repeated over and over—the Sixties' rock anthem, *Born to Be Wild*—and with his mammoth, rear-deck-mounted, chromium-plated speakers turned up to max plus ten, I'll bet that they heard us all the way to Havana.

Caught completely off guard, the driver of the BMW flew past us. But he pulled a quick spin turn, shot through a used car lot, and was back on our tail in no time. He drove with abandon, like a Hollywood stunt man, floating his car around corners with the easy grace of a skier cutting schusses in freshly fallen snow.

Glancing backward, I saw that the blue suits had removed their sunglasses, and were glaring at me with unbridled ferocity. Worse still, the passenger now held the pistol in his hand, next to his shoulder, where he could thrust it out the window in an instant.

Meanwhile, clouds of blue smoke pouring from his XGT Extra-Wides on every turn, Gap-tooth jinked and jagged his cab around, taking us further and further into an increasingly foreign landscape of squat little houses and barefoot children. His driving was unconventional, but effective, and even though we didn't manage to lose the BMW, we increased our lead to a block and a half. Incredibly, young Gap-tooth knew just how to use that meager advantage.

Taking a sharp right that nearly threw me to the floor, we skidded down an old shell road alleyway, between dilapidated garages vintage 1930, where we got bounced around like seeds in a maraca, kicking up a storm of dust that I thought Gap-tooth had conjured to cover our escape. But when we got to the end of the road he threw out the clutch, locked the handbrake and snapped the wheel around, sending us into a 180 degree skid. When the cab finally skittered to a stop, a bare inch from the lip of a drainage canal, we were facing back in the direction from which we had just come.

That last bit of mayhem slid me across the back seat so hard that I smacked my head on the door frame, and I decided that it was time to get out, but before I could reach for the handle the back of the cab jumped up a good two feet. Then the front end popped up. The back end abruptly sank all the way to the ground, followed by the front, and then the back rose all the way up again.

"What the hell's going on?" I screamed in exasperation.

"Low riders, Mees!" My champion grinned excitedly, turning half way around to share his joy. "Pneumatic peestons. Great big ones. Low ride or high water, we can do eet!"

Before I could think of anything to say, he dropped the clutch and we were off again, back end high, front end nearly scraping the ground, into the boiling cloud of dust. And suddenly, there was the BMW, directly in front of us and closing fast. The blue-suit men were still glaring at us, but now they wore masks of fear. Their unbelieving eyes grew as round as saucers, and the driver jerked hard to his right, with not a microsecond to spare, leaving us barely enough room to pass by. Young Gap-tooth never missed a beat.

With my dress now flapping up above my hips, I spun around and glanced out the rear window just in time to see the BMW hit a utility pole dead center. The force of the impact snapped the pole in two like a pencil, knocking the electrical transformer loose. That pudgy, gray tank separated from the transmission lines as it plummeted, threw a huge shower of white-hot sparks, and crashed onto the hood of the sedan. Its top broke open, hot oil flew everywhere, and an orange fireball exploded into the sky, igniting the leaves of an ancient persimmon tree nearby. The last thing that I saw was the dark blue suits as they wriggled out of the driver's side window, scrambling to get away.

"Hot sheet! Geeve 'em Hell!" young Gap-tooth cried with glee. "I am Mel Geebson! I am Jedi Knight! Death to the alien invaders!"

A few seconds later, we popped out onto a busy avenue. Gap-tooth lowered the back end, leveled the frame, changed tapes again, and we cruised along like any other cab on a hot summer's eve.

"Ees good driving; no?" Gap-tooth asked, glancing at me in the rearview mirror.

"Is good driving; yes," I confirmed with a quaver in my voice.

My stomach was in a knot, and I was badly shaken. In fact, I was close to tears. But I was also strangely elated as I sat in that breathtaking rush of tropical air, trying to stop my knees from quivering, remembering those four preposterous saucer eyes, and listening to Gaptooth's stereo as Willy Nelson warned mothers everywhere not to let their babies grow up to be cowboys.

*   *   *

The sun was going down in a splendid tantrum of scarlet as I got out of the cab and said a heartfelt goodbye to Gap-tooth, whose real name turned out to be Norman Alfons Nakita de Zavala—a modern Renaissance man. After paying the fare, I handed him a hundred dollar bill, which he accepted with the kind of smile that you usually see on a little child who has just received a new puppy, and he responded by giving me his business card. I nearly threw it away as he peeled off, but I thought better of it, and tucked the card in my purse as a souvenir.

I had been to the marina many times before, of course, but after sign-
ing in at the security desk, and walking past the first bustling pier, I felt
altogether lost. Long purple shadows transformed the usually friendly
yacht basin into a frantic maze of nautical traps and trolls. My mental
charts were smudged with tears, and my navigation was off. My homing
beacon was no longer there. Dad was gone for good. I trundled back to
Security, got a blurry Xeroxed sheet of directions and started out again.
Past the too-loud parties and the ever-smoking grills. Past the nonsensical
excitement and the fevered gaiety. Past the blasé owners and their euphoric
guests—the haves and the wanna-haves. Through the scintillating realm
of perpetual motion that defines the lives of yacht people.

Yacht people. Boat people. The two extreme ends of southern Florida's
unique societal spectrum; opposite poles in the Sunshine State's peculiar
American Dream. It's Horatio Alger in the brave new world. From rags to
riches. Or maybe now it's Jorge Alegro, and from rafts to reechez. Yes, this
is truly America—the way it is today, the way it's always been—pulsing
with the constant influx of those miserable failures and castoffs from far-
away places, who couldn't make it where they were, and who come here
with nothing more than a hope and a prayer. And they all manage to prosper somehow, too, because if you can't make it in America, you can't make
it anywhere.

Then suddenly, she was lying right there in front of me, secured bow-
first to the weathered pilings. Fifty-some feet of somber, inanimate houseboat, straining gently at her taut mooring lines in the wash of passing jet
skis, as grim and disconsolate as an Old Testament mourner. Somehow,
she knew. She knew that Dad was gone for good, that he was never going
to return. Perhaps she'd heard the death rattle of Uncle Bud's cruiser when
it sank to the bottom in agony, the way that whales hear each other's bel-
lowing a thousand miles away. Or perhaps she'd overheard the whispered
gossip on the docks. No matter how she'd divined the news, it had had its
mournful effect. She looked morose, lonely, unloved. She bore the solemn

countenance of a faithful old hound lying on her master's grave, and she needed help.

I lifted the spring latch on the inside of the railing, swung the gateway open and stepped aboard, but my weight didn't bother her at all. She didn't groan, or even list. It was as though she didn't even know that I was there.

I put my hand on her railing in a reassuring way. I petted her freshly varnished mahogany, brushed a spider web from her sun deck ladder, smoothed the ensign where it had wrapped itself around the staff, and gazed at a familiar place gone strange. A crisp new tarpaulin was furled along a pole, the creases from its factory packing still evident. The free end of a spring line lay coiled neatly on the deck, its terminus wrapped in black electrician's tape. A pair of folding canvas deck chairs were lashed to the aft bulkhead of the lounge, against the absolute certainty that one of those blustery little rainstorms that dart about the Florida landscape would sweep them into the water.

Dad was everywhere I looked—in polished brass and new fittings, in shiny paint and clean windows. I halfway expected to hear him laughing at a joke that Uncle Bud had just told, but the only sounds were the creaking of nearby boats as they rocked back and forth in their slips, the clapping of dirty harbor water from a dozen incoming wakes, the braggadocio of half-drunk sport fishermen as they returned to port for the night, and the relentless, echoed droning of drive-time traffic ricocheting along Las Olas Boulevard.

I walked over to the big sliding glass door, rattled it, found it predictably locked, reached to find the hidden key that Dad always kept behind the old Schwin 10-speed bike that was chained to the aft bulkhead, and then stopped in my tracks. With the interior of the boat darkened, a reflection of the stern showed in the glass door, and I bit my lip as someone stepped aboard behind me. I could see very little in the gloom, but whoever it was stood stock still in the shadows, waiting.

There's an overhang on the boat, where the top deck extends aft beyond the glass door to the lounge. The joists are exposed, and against one of them Dad had mounted a collapsible boat hook—an aluminum pole with a stainless steel point and barb on one end. It resembles a harpoon, and makes an ugly but effective weapon. So, dropping my purse, I reached up, snapped the boat hook loose from its clamps, and then, gripping the pole tightly in both hands, I spun around and assumed a semi-crouching position.

The shadowy figure didn't move a millimeter.

Several long seconds passed in absolute silence, and then a throaty feminine voice said, "Really now! Is that any way to greet an old friend?"

"This hasn't been a good day for friends," I growled. "Who are you?"

A disgusted sigh filled the night air. "My business is that I've come to visit a sweet ol' gal who's just lost her father. And my name, since you seem to have forgotten it, Sugar, is..."

"Delsie?"

"Tis I," she replied, with a twinkle in her voice.

The boat hook clattered to the deck as I ran forward to embrace her, and for the first time since leaving Ohio I let myself go. I wept like a lost child come home. It's a good thing that she was wearing a simple cotton windbreaker, because I would have ruined the shoulder of anything nice. She stroked my hair gently, but didn't say another word until I had calmed down to where I only had the sniffles.

"So what's with the jolly welcome?" she asked, pulling back far enough that I could see her face.

Yes, it was really, truly her, my girlhood friend of many tantalizing, spring break vacations—long raven hair, oval face of flawless complexion, and almond-shaped eyes that shone like onyx. Women spend hours painting their lips to achieve the seductive, pouty shape given to her by nature, and all of that beauty was poised on an exquisitely sculpted neck, like on that statue of Nefertiti. Her mixed Anglo-Mexican heritage gave her a visage that most women would kill for, and her status as one of the richest heiresses in America made her the envy of nearly everyone. She was, in fact, the only woman alive of whom I was truly jealous.

"It's just been one of those days," I groaned.

"I don't believe that I've ever had one," she replied haughtily. "Would you care to tell me about it?"

"Yes, I would, but not here."

"Of course not here, you silly girl! Come on. Put that obnoxious little toy away, pick up your things, and let's go get spoiled on the big boat."

"Your father's?"

"Not anymore. He's mine now."

"He?"

"Yes, *he*," she explained. "Men are always calling their boats *she*, and *her*, and giving them raunchy names like *Foxxy Girl*, *Fannie May*, and *B.J.*, so I turned the tables on them. I gave mine a masculine name."

"Which is?"

"*Jerome.*"

"Not after that lunkhead wind surfer?"

"You remember!"

"Remember? Wasn't he the idiot who was showing off one day, and ran into the side of a tugboat?"

"I prefer to remember him for his outstanding character."

"Oh, he was a character, and it stood out, all right. He got drunk and surfed naked one sunny afternoon, after some bimbo from New Jersey helped to get his motor running. I remember because you made me watch!"

"Just broadening your horizons, Sugar."

We smiled briefly at the memories, and then I asked about her parents.

"Daddy has finally retired from the sea," she said, "and he's taken Mother with him. Doctor's orders. Oh, they had a good, frolicsome run at it, and they have absolutely no regrets at all, but there's too much smog and humidity here for his emphysema, and Mother prefers wildflowers to wahoos, so now they live on a big spread an hour north of Taos. It's dry as dust, and boring, boring, boring, but they still throw the occasional party for whoever can manage to wheel themselves up the ramp."

She took me by the hand as we ambled along the docks, turning far more heads than when I'd minced through there alone, and then we walked down the broad private pier to her "big boat" as she called it.

The massive bulk of the *Jerome* had always intimidated me—Delsie's father had converted it from a World War II Navy Minesweeper—but she had managed to soften its lines by painting the superstructure a delicate cream, and the hull a rich buttermilk. Two bold and slightly tapered stripes traced down the hull from stem to stern; one royal blue, and the other a warm maroon. They made the yacht look eager, playful, as though it were straining at the leash, even when the engines were stone cold. Delsie always did have a waggish sense of style.

After climbing up the gangway—the main deck must have been twelve feet above the water—Delsie sat me down in a cotton-rope chaise, gave me a tall Bloody Mary, stiff with Absolut 100 proof vodka, and said, "Now give with the details."

So I told her about my day. She asked questions at all of the appropriate places, frowned at the apathy of Carl Rehm, scowled at the saga of Norman the cabbie, mixed me another drink, and then sat on the end of my chair.

"Okay, Sugar," she said, "you do a pretty fair impression of Katie Couric, but you haven't told me anything important."

"Not important?"

"Not a bit. All you did was give me the facts, like Jack Webb, that funky old fart in *Dragnet*. 'The facts, ma'am; just the facts.' What I want to know is how you *feel*."

"About what?"

"About losing your Dad, for starters."

"What are you," I complained, "some kind of therapist?"

"I'm not board certified, but what the heck. We're friends, Sugar. Just tell me what you're feeling."

"I really don't know."

"What comes to mind when you think about your Dad?"

I took a long pull at my drink, ran into a slug of Tabasco, and sucked in an ice cube for relief.

"Delsie, I hate to admit it," I finally said, "but what comes to mind is that I really didn't know Dad all that well."

"Okay. Go with that."

"It's funny when I stop to think about it. Dad and I spent so little time together. A few days at Christmas, or New Years. Things like that. I spent my summers working a remuda on a dude ranch out in Colorado, or interning at the zoo. And I spent even less time with Dad after I met and married Peter. But when Peter got killed in that dreadful traffic accident, Dad invited me to stay with him for a while. We took the boat out, and followed the sun, and drifted, and fished, and swam whenever it got too hot, and we just lived for a month with neither rhyme nor reason. I caught Dad looking at me every now and then in a wistful kind of way, and I knew that he was remembering Mom. I suppose that I look a lot like her. And although Dad was getting older—he was in his middle 60s then— there was still enough of the male animal left when he pulled in the anchors, or muscled the bows across the waves, that I could see why Mom had fallen so desperately in love with him all those lonely years ago.

"We'd sit in big canvas chairs on the top deck at night, under a canopy of stars like I'd never seen before, and grill thick, juicy steaks, and slabs of potatoes and onions, and wash it all down with humongous glasses of gin over cracked ice. Then Dad would tell me fantastic stories about the sea, and the islands, and the dying river of grass. Those were his stories, too— his own personal yarns about outlandish people, and exotic places, and stranger-than-fiction events—and I never once questioned whether those tales were fact, or fiction, or some inventive combination, because I really didn't care; because his stories supplied me with a remarkable kind of escape. That's what Dad was offering me, that was his special gift to me, and that was exactly what I needed. Yet even so, even with Dad letting his guard down like that, I don't think that I can tell you anything really important about him, like how he managed to surround himself with such curious friends, or why he chose the peculiar life he led."

The damn had burst, and I started crying again, but quietly this time, weeping.

Delsie took one of my hands in hers, and as I dried my eyes on a cocktail napkin she asked, "So what can I do to help, Sugar?"

"I don't know," I sniffed. "Carl Rehm has arranged for the cremations, and he's scheduled calling hours for tomorrow evening at a place called Stanek's. I guess that the legal and financial stuff will take care of itself in time."

"And what about the disposition?" she asked tenderly.

"What?"

"The ashes, Sugar. What are you going to do with the ashes?"

"Oh, I don't know. Consign them to the briny deep, I suppose. I really don't want to think about it. I really can't think about it. Not now."

The vodka was having the desired effect, and all I wanted to do was sleep.

"Sugar?" Delsie asked. "Will you let me take care of that li'l detail for you? Will you let me plan the sprinkling?"

I suppose it was the word *sprinkling* that did it.

"Sure," I said sarcastically. "That would be a big help, Delsie. I'll keep an eye on the lawyers, spy for the Coast Guard, fight off the bad guys, wrestle with the little man who isn't there, and you're in charge of... sprinkling!"

I sat up then, pulled a pillow to my face, and cried and cried until I thought that I was going to be sick. And when I finally stopped to wipe the tears from my eyes, Delsie was sitting there, looking at me with that knowing, sympathetic smile that Aunt Rita used to affect when I told her about failing grades, or boy troubles.

"Sugar," she said, "I didn't like the car chase story that you told me earlier, so I think that you ought to spend the night right here. There's plenty of room as you know. I'll have the crew hoist the gangway, and I'll ask Raul to post a guard. We'll both sleep better that way. No one knows that you're here, so you can forget about things and get a good night's sleep. In the morning we'll have a positively sinful breakfast, then get an early jump on the day. What do you say?"

I said, "Um-hmm," and watched through bleary eyes as she pushed a doorbell button mounted underneath the rail. Like magic, three impressively fit-looking young men appeared on deck, dressed in stiff white shirts, shorts, socks, deck shoes, and hats.

The rest was kind of a blur, but I remember thinking that the Plaza Hotel had nothing on the *Jerome* as I drifted off to sleep on satin sheets.

4

Delsie let me sleep late, and after a cool, invigorating shower with eucalyptus and cucumber bath gel, I joined her on the fantail—I in an aqua robe, she in a mango sarong. Cleopatra never looked so good.

"That must improve crew morale," I remarked.

"The boys?" she said. "They're all gay."

"You're kidding!"

"Sugar, I may kid about a great many things, but never about sexual preferences. The boys love me dearly, but their tastes run in other directions. Actually, I prefer it that way. They are all exceptional seamen, they know how to cook, tend bar and cater, and they are extremely protective. As a result, I sleep very well at night. And Raul brings a little something extra to the mix. He used to be a Navy SEAL; a highly trained warrior. Since he signed on as captain, no guest has been obnoxious more than once."

Breakfast was positively scrumptious. As it turned out, Geoffrey, the first mate, was not only a fine sailor, but an omelette chef extraordinaire. After one of his 2-egg, cheddar and sauteed mushroom specialties, with sliced beefsteak tomatoes, grapefruit sections, croissants with lemon marmalade, and two cups of hazelnut-vanilla coffee, I felt like a renewed woman.

"The calcium is good for you," Delsie proclaimed, handing me a bottle of Tums. "I've got my day all planned. What about yours?"

"Well, I start with safe deposit box inventories at ten," I said, "followed by a little prying and snooping, then dinner somewhere, and I end it all with the dreaded reception of long-faced mourners from seven until."

"Snooping?"

After telling her about my afternoon errand, Delsie asked if I had brought a cell phone with me.

"Yes," I said. "It's on Travel Link. Why?"

She explained her plan, and we swapped numbers, adding each other to our speed dial lists. Then she asked Geoffrey to drive me to the Riverside Hotel for a fresh change of clothes.

*   *   *

Carl Rehm was waiting for me at the safe deposit queue, a pair of bright yellow sign-in cards in hand. He offered a simple, "Good morning, Dr. Pearson," as he handed me a cheap ballpoint pen. I smiled at him briefly, and crammed my signatures right on top of his. It was a surly, childish gesture, but I wanted him to see me that way. I wanted to appear upset, spiteful. It was my turn to lead him around by the nose.

"Judge Holloway approved both of your petitions," he announced, "so you are now the legally appointed and duly enfranchised executrix of both your father's and your uncle's estates. I'll send the cover letters and the signed original paperwork to your hotel this afternoon. You'll want to keep those documents in a safe place, but I'll put a set of notarized copies in the bank's files, just in case."

His cold, patronizing attitude was getting under my skin, so I merely nodded.

"With your permission," he said, "the crew can start drilling."

"Drilling?"

"Safe deposit boxes work on a two key system. Each box has two separate locks, both of which must be disengaged in order to operate the bolt. The bank retains one key, which fits the master cylinder, and the patron keeps the other key, which fits the second cylinder. One cannot open a safe deposit box without both keys, and since your father's and uncle's keys were not recovered with their remains..."

"I understand." I cut him off sharply. "Please proceed."

He nodded to a blue-uniformed workman who was kneeling on the floor of the vault, and a moment later a heavy, portable drill started grinding away on the keyway slot of one of the brass cylinders which punctuated a thick, dull, stainless steel safe deposit box door. The mechanic's assistant sprayed a continuous mist of thin white oil on the bit to keep it cool as it cut through several layers of pins and springs, and in five minutes the door was open. The workmen repeated the process on a second door, and then an armed bank guard stepped in, pulled the black metal boxes from their niches, and took charge of them.

Rehm led the way to a quiet little conference room with an antique cherry table at its center. He unrolled a thick piece of blue felt, and spread it across the flawless wooden surface before stepping over to a sideboard where he picked up a supply of yellow legal pads and freshly sharpened pencils. Only then did the guard set the boxes down.

"Wait," I said to the guard as he turned to leave. "Please stay."

The guard looked questioningly at Rehm, received a grudging shrug, and sat down on a chair against the wall. Rehm was visibly annoyed by this. The guard was quietly amused. My plan was working just fine.

"Which is which?" I asked, as I took a seat at the head of the table.

"Number 133 is your father's."

"Then I'll start with the other one."

The process was simple, and went smoothly enough. I opened the hinged lid of Uncle Bud's safe deposit box, and removed things one at a time. As I identified each item, Rehm recorded the inventory point for point on one of the legal pads. He started to write the list in pencil, but I stopped him, insisting that he use a pen instead.

Uncle Bud's safe deposit box contained all of the typical items that one would expect to find. The title to his cruiser, along with some maintenance warranties. Life, property, and casualty insurance policies. Some structured annuities. The deed to one hundred and sixty-seven acres of farmland in Nansemond County, Virginia. A copy of his will, his living will, and a healthcare power of attorney, all of them witnessed by my Dad. Bearer bonds, debentures, brokerage account statements and the like. Three recent federal and state income tax returns. A gold railroad watch, with a heavy double chain, from which hung a Phi Beta Kappa key. A handful of tarnished Liberty Dollars. A plastic box filled with old-fashioned shirt studs, tie tacks, collar stays and cufflinks.

As soon as we had cataloged everything, I took the legal pad from Mr. Rehm, and instructed him to put the entire lot back in the box while I checked each item off the list. When he finally closed and latched the lid, I signed the pad, Rehm signed, and I asked the guard to initial it as well. Rehm didn't like that at all.

It was then time to delve into Dad's box, a task that I wanted to postpone, but could not avoid. Its contents were somewhat different. The titles to his houseboat, his runabout, and his old, blue, pickup truck. A small bundle of letters wrapped with a crusty rubber band. A birth certificate. An honorable discharge from the U.S. Army. A clear plastic box containing a stack of family photographs, including those of my Mom, Dad's parents, and Dad's brother, all of whom were deceased, and none of whom I had ever met. Some yellowed newspaper clippings heralding Dad's brief career as a tight end in the American Football League. A theater ribbon from the Korean War. A Purple Heart. A Good Conduct medal. A Distinguished Service Cross, with citation. Forty thousand dollars in bearer bonds. Ten thousand dollars in cash. A 9mm Luger pistol with an eagle and swastika stamped over the receiver; nine rounds in the magazine, one in the chamber. A plain, white, #10 envelope with the word *Jean* handwritten across it.

I held that envelope gently, and sat staring at it for the longest time.

"It's perfectly permissible to read it," suggested Rehm.

Reaching into my purse, I opened the miniature Swiss Army knife that Dad had added to my key ring years before. "No woman," he had said, "should ever be without a sharp knife, no matter how small."

The paper made a soft hissing sound as the keen little blade sliced through the crease along the top edge of the envelope. Inside lay a simple piece of typing stock in a neat, business trifold. I removed the memorandum with care, smoothed it out tenderly, and studied Dad's last bequest. The note read simply, "Alice in Wonderland II."

I smiled at the memories, and it all came flooding back. It was almost as though Dad were standing there beside me. I could smell his Bay Rum, his Ben Gay, and that red, medicinal mouthwash he favored. There was the scent of fresh salt air, machine oil, metal polish, propane cookstoves, kerosene lanterns, conch chowder...

"If you don't mind my asking," Rehm queried, "what does the note say? Is there anything that we need to be concerned about, from a legal perspective, that is?"

The magic of the moment had been shattered, the phantom nearness dissipated, and I wanted to scream. But I held my temper in check one more time, and handed the paper to Rehm. He read it carefully, then looked strangely relieved.

"No offensive surprises," he stated, giving the paper back to me. "Just a curious puzzle. You'd be astonished at how often we find shocking notes in these sessions. Last minute changes to wills. Admissions of paternity, or bigamy, or both. Confessions of criminal behavior. Things like that."

"It's not a puzzle," I sighed. "It's more like a reminder. When I visited here after my husband Peter died, Dad and I went cruising for a month, north on the Intracoastal Waterway. It was the second time that we'd done that. The first was right after I met Dad. I told him that I felt like Alice in

Wonderland on the first trip, because everything felt so clean, and special, and different. The second trip was even better than the first, so we referred to those excursions as the Alice cruises. Dad stored some letters from my Mom in here, and pictures of my grandparents. Good family memories. I guess that this was his way of remembering me as well. He told me last winter that the second Alice cruise was one of the happiest times of his life. It was for me, too."

I sniffled a little bit then, but not very much, as Rehm repacked everything just the way Dad had left it. Well, almost everything. He pressed the thumb release and slid the magazine from the grip of the Luger pistol, ejected the round from the chamber, and slid the loose cartridge into the magazine. Then he put the pistol and the magazine into the safe deposit box, separately, explaining that it was against the law to store a loaded gun in a bank vault.

The workmen had gone by the time we returned to the vault, leaving shiny new cylinders in place of the ruined locks. The guard slipped the boxes into their tomblike cells, closed the doors firmly, then stepped aside. Rehm secured all four of the locks, handed the master key to the guard, put the patrons' keys in a tiny manila envelope, and gave the envelope to me. That done, the guard left us alone while Rehm took red plastic markers, which looked like elongated thumbtacks, and slid the tangs all the way into the keyways.

"You may keep the keys," he said, "but you may not remove anything from either box until after the wills have been probated. The red tags indicate that the accounts have been frozen by court order. We can Xerox the inventories at the clerk's desk, if you'd like. You can keep the originals, and I'll have typed copies prepared from the Xeroxes, for submission to the court."

There was a momentary pause.

"I guess that's it," he said.

"Thank you, Mr. Rehm," I replied, as flatly as I knew how. "You've been very thorough, as always."

"I'm glad to be of assistance, Dr. Pearson." he muttered, a troubled look clouding his brow.

I turned to go, but before I could step out of the vault he said, "Miss Jean, have I done something to offend you?"

This was the moment that I'd been angling for.

"No," I said. "Why?"

"Well, you seem so... distant."

"Oh, it's just all so very difficult."

"I understand." He nodded sympathetically. "But I get the impression that you're angry somehow."

"Angry? Enraged would better describe how I feel."

"Would you care to tell me why? Perhaps I can help."

It was time to go into my bereaved, widowed little orphan act. So I looked Rehm squarely in the eye, with the most hurtful, penetrating stare that I could muster.

"It's just that one usually has some place to go," I complained. "There's a corpse to view. There's something to say goodbye to. When a loved one dies in an automobile accident, the family at least has a place to visit. A place by the side of the road. A place to make contact. A place to leave a flowers. But I don't have that, Mr. Rehm! I don't have anything at all. I don't have a body to grieve over. There's no cold hand to kiss goodbye. There's no finality to it. There's nothing palpable. It's all so damned abstract. I talked with Dad on the phone a few days ago, and then, whoosh, he and Uncle Bud vanished into some kind of vacuous, Never-Never Land. It's like they never existed, or like they never left. It doesn't make any sense."

I snuffled a little, and wiped my nose with a tissue.

"I don't have a meaningful place to mourn," I continued, "but worse yet, no one has told me anything really important. No one has told me exactly when the accident happened, or where, or how. Do you honestly want to help me, Mr. Rehm? Do you? Then make this dreadful moment real. Make it materialize. Put flesh and bones on it. Tell me what happened!"

I hadn't planned to, but I started crying again, hard. They say that a good actress convinces herself first, and then her audience. I must have given a stellar performance.

For his part, Rehm was visibly shaken. Lines of anguish etched his face, and his lower lip started to quiver. He looked embarrassed, even guilty.

"Let's go back to the conference room," he said. He took me gently by the elbow, as though he were going to lead me back down the hall.

"No!" I shouted, twisting out of his grip. "No more coddling! I'm not a child, dammit! Just tell me straight out. Don't sugarcoat it. Forty-eight hours ago I lost my entire family, all that I had in the world, and I want to know what happened."

"Miss Jean, I'll be glad to tell you what I've heard. It wouldn't stand up in court, you understand. It's hearsay, after all, not firsthand. I wasn't there. But it's from good, reliable sources."

"Damn it all, Carl! I'm not asking for a ruling on the admissibility of evidence. Spit it out."

"It happened early in the morning, on the day before yesterday. Witnesses at the marina told the Coast Guard's investigators that your father and uncle departed together shortly after dawn. In your uncle's cabin cruiser. Just the two of them. Your father said something about going fishing in the Keys, though why they'd want to go there now I can't imagine. They'd just rounded the John Lloyd Jetty, and were running close inside when it happened. A surf fisherman saw the explosion from the beach. He used his cell phone; dialed 911. A Fire-Emergency patrol boat and a Coast Guard cutter responded, as did a handful of pleasure craft, but it was too late. There was nothing that anyone could do. Your uncle's boat had burned to the waterline and sunk."

"Okay," I said, dropping a soggy Kleenex in a stainless steel can beside the door, "that tells me where, and when, but what happened? Boats don't just burn for no reason, do they? What caused it, Mr. Rehm? Tell me. Make me understand."

"I don't really know what caused the explosion," Rehm replied, "but that was a pretty old boat. Twenty-five years, at least. As I said yesterday, I queried the insurance files. The declarations listed two gasoline engines. Perhaps a leaky fuel tank exploded. Gasoline can be dangerous, you know. Fumes can build up. An electrical spark from a servo, or from the starter motor, and..."

He paused briefly to compose himself.

"When the Coast Guard shares its findings with the bank, I'll call you right away, Miss Jean. But I don't know anything more just now. Honestly."

I put my hand on his arm to stop him. He was pretty rattled, but he'd told me what I'd wanted to hear.

"Thank you," I said. "You've been very kind, Mr. Rehm. I hope that I haven't seemed rude or ungrateful."

"Nonsense," he exclaimed, puffing out his chest, and once again assuming the role of the custodial attorney. "This is a frightful time for you, Miss Jean, and you're doing just fine. Truly, you are. Why, I'd like to think that I'd do half as well under the circumstances."

He showed me upstairs to the bank's main entrance, and escorted me to a cab which was offloaded a harried-looking Ms. Varga. Balancing one of those stiff plastic grocery baskets filled with soft drinks of all descriptions, and a white paper bag which containing a dozen or more deli sandwiches, she looked positively miserable. Rehm offered to carry the paper bag, and she followed him back inside.

"The John Lloyd Jetty," I told the cab driver as I crawled into the lingering aura of hot pastrami on rye. "But first, can you take me to a flower shop?"

*   *   *

The maintenance warranties in Uncle Bud's safe deposit box had been for a series of engine refits performed at Curlee's Boat Yard, so I had the driver take me there after visiting the John Lloyd Jetty, where I whispered a muddled eulogy, and dropped a pair of crimson roses in the water. The taxi driver was most obliging. They usually are when you pay them to sit still for forty-five minutes with the meter running.

Like most establishments that specialize in heavy work, Curlee's was a jumble of broken equipment and fractured debris. Rusty gray would describe the color of the place. Grim would do for its atmosphere. The gravel drive reeked of used engine oil, and I was thankful that I had worn flat shoes. But when I walked up to the shed a pleasant surprise awaited me. The interior was brilliantly lit, the concrete floor was painted with glistening gray enamel, and I couldn't see a speck of dust anywhere. Even the Lexan skylights were sparkling clean. Three classic motor sailers rested in stout wooden cradles, and a small cadre of mechanics was working on them feverishly, each man dressed in smart, pressed overalls.

I found Sigmon Curlee in a spacious office that was positively crammed with nautical keepsakes from a lifetime of boat work. I could hardly walk through the place. The plank-covered floor and walls were festooned with propellers, portholes, binnacles, bells, and an eight-foot, spoked oaken helm. There were only a couple of places to sit—a squeaky swivel chair where Mr. Curlee held court behind a stubby wooden desk, and a lumpy leather couch on the opposite side of the desk, its faded, maroon cushions having given way to natural tan through years of heavy use. I sank into lopsided comfort at one end of the couch.

A big, muscular, balding man of congenial disposition, Mr. Curlee became almost courtly, in his own way, when he discovered who I was.

"I was terrible sorry to hear about your daddy," he began with an overly serious frown. "He was one helluva man. Oh, yeees, sir. He helped my uncle to get his master's papers back years ago. Helped a lot of other people with their problems, too. He was a real man's man. Tough, honest, and smart. Shrewd, too. Yeees, sir. He could catch 'em, clean 'em, and cook 'em up for dinner. That's for sure! I'll miss that old boy. I truly will. But you know what I'll miss the most, little lady?"

"What?" I asked with real interest.

"I'll miss the way that your daddy always thought about things," he replied as he scratched at the stubble on his chin. "Now, most people just go around doin' things. You know. They run around doin' stuff all the time, and they never think a lick. But not your daddy. Nooo, sir. He was always thinkin' about something. About the way things work. About why people do the crazy things they do. He was always tryin' to make some sense of it all. I reckon that's why folks 'round here liked him so dang much. 'Cause he made a difference; you know? He brought a little sense to the madness. Why, I heard one fella call your daddy a windward philosopher once. I guess that's about right."

"My Dad?"

"Why, yeees, ma'am. Oh, yeah. I remember now. You didn't grow up around here, did you? You stayed up north somewheres. Weeell, we won't hold that against ya. Nooo, sir. But you know, Miss Jean, you should maybe oughta stay 'round here a spell, and listen to some of them stories about your daddy. They'd make you proud. Yeees, sir. Right proud."

"Thank you, Mr. Curlee. I'd like that. I'd like that very much indeed. Perhaps after the funeral. But I stopped by on another matter this afternoon. I'd like to learn about my uncle's boat."

"Your uncle?"

"Dad was on Uncle Bud's boat when he died."

"Oh, sure, that's right," he said with a dismissive wave of his big, rough paw. "You know, I never knew that them two boys was related. I liked 'em both, and I'm right sorry about your uncle, too. He was a real nice fellow, mind you, but a book-learned man, if you know what I mean. Kind of hard to understand sometimes. He talked about money and numbers like he was in church or something. Now, if you're interested in fixing that old boat of his..."

"It's on the bottom with a broken keel."

"Aw, that's too bad. Insurance?"

"I'll submit a claim on behalf of the estate."

"Insurance company will demand the salvage rights. Here, little lady. Give them my card, if you don't mind." He handed me several neatly printed business cards from a thick stack on his desk. "My middle boy, Sonny, is a natural-born, scuba divin' fool, and he's right good with tools, too. Yeees, sir. He can pull them engines out, and we can rework 'em maybe, if they ain't hurt too bad. Make the insurance company back some of their money."

"Well, that's why I'm here, Mr. Curlee. About the engines."

"Goooood engines," he said with feeling. "I put 'em in myself."

"Well, yes, sir. But, you see, I just don't understand about the faulty engines, the explosion, and the fire."

"They saying my engines exploded?" he yelled, sitting bolt upright in his chair. "They saying that? They saying it's *my* fault? Who says so? Them damn Yankee Coast Guard college boys? I'll set them straight. Yeees sir! They was new engines, not some ol' rebuilts. They wouldn' 'a' blowed up in a million years. Wouldn't even 'a' blowed a gasket. Hellfire, good as they are, I never have trusted them factory mechanics. Paid by the hour. What do they care? So I took the heads off both 'a' them engines while they was still in the shippin' crates, turned the shafts manually, checked the seats and seals on all of them valves, found one that was slightly out of spec, retooled it smooth, put on new gaskets, and torqued them bolts down myself. Here. Wait a minute."

He got up, dug through the files, and came back with a copy of the papers that I'd discovered in the safe deposit box. Then he sat down close beside me on the couch, and held out part of the maintenance record.

"Look here," he said. "Ya see? I torqued them heads down to factory specs. Both of 'em. Exactly 115 foot pounds on bolts one through twenty-six, then retorqued one through twenty-six to 205 foot pounds, then set interior bolts twenty-seven through thirty-three to 20 foot pounds.

Blowed up? Like Hell they did! Let 'em say that to my face and I'll put some arm on 'em!"

I waited a few seconds, to let him calm down.

"It wasn't the Coast Guard, Mr. Curlee," I said. "They haven't finished their investigation yet. It was one of the lawyers at the bank. He said that it was probably a leaky gas tank. A gasoline explosion."

"A lawyer!" he snorted. "What would a fool lawyer know about marine engines? Had one out here last month. Wanted us to fix a little 15 horse-power piss-ant pusher for his rinky-dink sailboat. Motor was all burnt up and froze solid 'cause the idiot didn't know enough to mix 2-cycle oil in with the gas. Ran it too rich. No lubrication. Fool didn't know nothing at all. I'll bet that bank lawyer is the same way. Couldn't put his finger up his... ah, ear... without a funnel."

"Probably."

"Besides, ma'am." he went on. "Your uncle didn't have no gasoline engines. Not anymore anyway. Oh, that ol' cruiser had come with 'em, all right, as original equipment, maybe thirty-forty years ago, but they was plumb wore out. Weren't worth nothing at all. Tolerances all shot to hell. No compression, hardly. So we decided to switch to diesels 'cause they're cheaper, and safer. Fuel oil don't cost half what gasoline does, and it don't get fumey and explode like gas neither. Let me show you the paperwork."

He pulled another maintenance sheet from the file, along with a glossy sales brochure.

"Here now," he said with pride. "I finished that job eleven days ago. Two brand new, out-of-the-box, Caterpillar 582 horsepower electronically controlled 3176B inline 6-cylinder diesels. Hell, ma'am, I was worried about the integrity of them old mounting timbers, so I went the extry mile, built a brand new rack, and bolted both of them engines in on com-pression-resisting Iroko-cored bearers. Them old fuel tanks were okay though. Made of heavy-gauge aluminum, like the Navy uses. We flushed 'em out real good, and installed new feeder lines with flexible joints so there wouldn't be no leaks, no how.

"No sir, little lady," he said, wiping his forehead with a big, red western bandana. "If somethin' exploded on that boat it wasn't them brand new engines, or them fuel tanks, neither. More than likely, it was a leaky cookstove. Or a gas lantern, maybe. Bottled gas, both Butane and Propane, is heavier than air. It can settle down in the bilge, stay there for weeks, and then, BOOM!"

"I'm very relieved to hear that it wasn't the engines, Mr. Curlee, and I'm also glad to know that you did all of the work personally. It gives me great peace of mind."

"Well, nearly all of it." He stuffed the papers back in the folder. "Me and my crew do every bit of the mechanical work. Never let no one else touch it. But I hire other folks to do the cleanup. You've seen my shop."

"It's beautiful."

"Yeees, ma'am. Thank you, ma'am. We do beautiful work here, too, but it's real dirty work, so I hire other people to clean up when we're done. First we refloat the boats, give them a little test run, redistribute the ballast if necessary, tune them up sharp, put them through a real sea trial, and then they get a thorough scrubbing down. It's real good customer relations, 'cause people tend to have a lot more confidence in what they *can't* see if they like what they *can* see. And that's why I always make sure that every boat that goes out of this yard is as clean as Granny's kitchen."

"Uncle Bud mentioned that his boat looked awfully good when he got it back," I lied. "Who cleaned it up? I'd like to thank him, too."

"Well, he's gone now, ma'am. Ya see, the guys I hire for cleanup work are kind of transient like. I never ask about their lifestyles, 'cause they'd probably lie, and if they did tell the truth I probably wouldn't hire them anyways. The guy that worked on your uncle's boat showed up the day we finished the sea trials. I remember 'cause your uncle's boat was the only one he cleaned. Anyway, I hired him late one evening 'cause I needed someone real bad, and I let him sleep out in the dock shed 'cause he didn't have no place to stay. When I got here the next morning he was already hard at work, and he did a right smart job, too. But he quit at dinnertime.

Said it was too much trouble for the money. So I paid him out of petty cash, and he left."

"Where did he go?"

"I don't rightly know," he responded, scratching at his chin. "Oh, yeah. I recall he said somethin' about needin' enough money for bus fare to Key West. Funny sort of guy. Name was Sandy. He was clean enough. Clothes were kind of tattered, but he didn't smell nor nuthin'. He seemed too smart for scut work, but he'd seen rough times. He had a pretty rough scar on his jaw, and he was missin' his right earlobe. Probably had one of them earrings in it, and got it ripped off in a fight or something. Why these young guys want to wear women's jewelry I'll never understand."

I glanced at the folder that Mr. Curlee held open on his lap. Taped to the inside front cover was a checklist of clerical and maintenance tasks, with a bright red X in the box next to a notation that read "insurance notification."

"What does this mean?" I asked.

"Well, ma'am, it's another value added service we provide. Whenever we do an overhaul that's got insurance ramerfications— 'specially if the overhaul means a drop in insurance rates, like in your Uncle's case where we substituted diesel for gas—we notify the insurance company at the start of the job. Now that's right good public relations, too, 'cause when you hand some guy an invoice for $20,000, it's smart to give him a memo showing how you saved him $400 a year on insurance premiums. Customers just love stuff like that."

Maybe it was his boyishness, or his candor, or his openness. I'm not really sure. But I found that I was developing a real sense of affection for this rough-hewn walrus of a man. He reminded me of a block of old-fashioned rock candy—all hard, sharp edges on the outside, but sweet, and pure, and clean. And yet, there was a disturbing undercurrent, a darker element of his persona that I couldn't quite identify.

"Mr. Curlee," I said. "I really do appreciate your taking the time to talk with me this afternoon. I guess I just want to know everything that I can, because the more I learn about things, the more peace of mind I find. I sleep better that way."

"Yes, ma'am. I understand. I truly do."

He looked at me kind of funny then, with just the faintest hint of lasciviousness, and I suddenly felt uncomfortable as he took my hand in his big, rough mitt.

"I surely am glad you came by to see me, Miss Jean. It's been right nice. Yeees, ma'am. And I want to tell you something else, too. Your daddy was one of the real ones, one of a dying breed, and he must 'a' been right proud of you, 'cause you're as pretty as a speckled pup. Listen here. If you need anything, anything at all, you just let me know, ya hear?"

He flashed a toothy grin in my direction, and squeezed my hand with a little too much zeal. What could have been an awkward moment was salvaged by the crunching sound of a fast car braking on loose gravel, followed by the blare of a multi-tone car horn.

"Maserati," Mr. Curlee declared.

"How's that?"

"The horn. It's a gen-u-ine Maserati. Pure Eye-talian. I've got one. Not the car. Just the horn. It's on an old '83 pick-em-up truck."

We both smiled at that, and then he showed me to the door.

As it turned out, this particular horn had come with a flaming red Maserati Spyder as standard equipment. The umber top was folded down, and a stunning brunette lounged behind the hand-sewn leather wheel. Wearing designer sunglasses and a gold silk scarf, Delsie looked like a young Elizabeth Taylor, but considerably riper.

Now, I've heard some pretty strange remarks about the sexual predilections of automobile mechanics, and I don't really know if they apply to boat mechanics as well, so I couldn't tell if Mr. Curlee's men were staring at the car, or at Delsie, or both. One thing was certain, though. Every head in the yard was straining to get a better look.

"You're right on time," I said.

"I got all of my errands done," she announced as I climbed in and tied a green babushka over my hair. "How was your day, Sugar?"

"Taxing, but very instructive."

"So let's swap stories," she suggested as the sports car raced toward the highway and dinner.

5

Delsie swung by the Riverside Hotel, so that I could change into something more appropriate, and while there I called the Coast Guard HQ.

"Communications," said a sternly professional female voice.

"I'd like to speak with Commander L'Ouverture, please."

"Your name, ma'am?"

"Dr. Jean Pearson."

"Aye aye, ma'am. Checking your authorization. You're approved, ma'am. Patching you through now."

I heard the distant warbling of an electronic phone, and then a firm, male voice answered, "L'Ouverture."

"Good evening, Commander. It's Jean Pearson."

"Well, hello, Dr. Pearson," he replied, his voice softening. "To what do I owe this honor?"

"I just thought that I'd touch base."

"I am so pleased that you did. How are you doing?"

Not wanting to sound like a victim, I decided to skip the saga of Norman, but I told L'Ouverture about the diesel engine refit, about Sigmon Curlee, and about Sandy, the cleanup man who had worked on Uncle Bud's boat.

"The pieces are starting to come together," he said thoughtfully. "By the way, the forensics report is back from the lab, and the chemical analysis of the debris confirms a bombing. Mass spectroscopy indicates that a common form of plastique was used. C4. Not much to go on there. Microscopic investigation shows that there were no taggants in the residue, so there is no way to trace the source of the explosive. But C4 is so common that identifying the manufacturer would be of little help in any event. Whoever destroyed your uncle's boat knew his stuff, though. The Navy munitions technical staff reports the use of a dust initiator to enhance the blast and cause an implosion. Other than that, I am afraid that there is nothing much to report. Was there anything else of interest in the safe deposit boxes?"

"No."

"Well, please keep me informed if you come across anything interesting. In the meantime, I'll run a background check on Sigmon Curlee, and ask the Highway Patrol to help us locate the cleanup man.

"Oh, yes," he added. "I spoke with my parents earlier today, and they asked me to convey their deepest regrets."

I thanked him, he wished me well, and we hung up.

Delsie took me to an atmospheric restaurant called Yesterdays, where we sat on an air conditioned deck, and watched as an endless parade of pleasure boats plied up and down on the Waterway. We ordered Shrimp Salads Louis, and then arrived at Stanek's about thirty minutes early. I wanted to get a feel for the old mansion-turned-mortuary before having to deal with a horde of strangers, and it felt precisely the way I expected; subdued, prim and lifeless. But it was reasonably homey, rather than institutional, and it was comfortably lit. Thankfully, there was no piped-in, electronic organ music. No *Beautiful Dreamer*.

Ms. MayBelle Dickson, a very sweet, 70-ish, white-haired woman, pointed out our station in the north hallway, and then led us to the parlor where the guests would be assembling. Three gorgeous stained glass windows, the broad central one so tall that it stretched from baseboard to ceiling, stood in triptych on an outer wall. Warmly lit by soft exterior floods, they depicted a mangrove brake at low tide. The subtleties of the layered glass were so sublime that one could almost feel the sharpness of the oysters which clung in bearded bundles to the spreading, cane-like roots.

"Tiffany?" I inquired.

"Louis Comfort," our hostess replied quietly. "They were commissioned for The Winter Palace, one of the luxury hotels of St. Petersburg, in 1916. But when the Great Depression came, The Winter Palace closed for lack of patronage, like so many of the grand resort hotels, and it sat derelict for years and years. Hurricane Donna did such serious damage to the structure in 1960 that it had to be razed, so Father rescued *The Mangroves* and installed them here. He thought that they should be exhibited in a public setting, as was originally intended, so that people could derive some pleasure from them. I like to think that they bring serenity to a room perpetually troubled by sorrow. If you don't need me, I'll leave you two alone now."

The room was filled with flowers, and I started sneezing.

"Who sent all of these?" I asked.

Delsie held her hands up defensively. "Not from me, Sugar. They're from friends."

She looked at me quizzically, as though she knew a great secret, and I started reading the tags. There were sprays and bouquets from a lot of Dad's and Uncle Bud's associates, from old friends and neighbors at the marina, from people whom I had never heard of before. In fact, I found myself surrounded by sweet, well-wishing thoughts from people all over Florida; all over the country. It's hard to put it into words, but that raft of flowers brought me a strange brand of comfort; a peace I simply cannot describe. And I had to smile just a bit when I discovered the magnificent arrangement from Commander L'Ouverture's parents, Jean-Pierre and Isabela.

Then I gathered my courage and looked at the focus of the room. Instead of a pleated bier and open caskets, a simple table stood at the far end, it's rectangular top and square legs painted in glistening white lacquer. On it sat two foot-square cubes. Each was wrapped in stiff white paper, and both were tied with broad, snowy ribbons. One had a coral rosebud caught up in its bow. The other had a yellow-bee orchid.

"The rose is your father," Delsie explained. "The orchid is Uncle Bud. This is part of my contribution, Sugar. I gave it a great deal of thought. They were fine men—I knew them both from childhood, you know—but neither one had any specific denominational affiliation. So I came over here first thing this morning, and viewed the urns, every style that they have, and they were all plug ugly. Then I called a Japanese friend of mine. She took me to see her family's mortician, and I made a bold decision."

She paused briefly, gesturing toward the boxes.

"This is the manner in which the Japanese Shinto honor the bones of their dead. The sandalwood boxes are handmade, and dovetailed. They are plain and unpainted, but really quite lovely. The wrapping is sun-bleached rice paper, and the bows are watered silk. Everything white to indicate purity and renewal. I hope that you approve. If not, there's still time to..."

"Oh, Delsie, it's perfect," I sighed, hugging her and feeling the pressure of tears welling up in my eyes.

We found a padded bench, and sat alone with our thoughts for quite a little while, reflecting on life, lost loves, departed friends, Uncle Bud, Dad and mortality. Then it was time to take our places for the receiving line.

So Delsie and I stood side by side, and I guess that we made quite an impression. At least that's what I heard later on. The daughter: tall, svelte blonde, black cotton dress, seamless hose, calfskin shoes, a simple gold choker. The friend: luscious brunette, black lamé gown, silk stockings, patent leather heels, the palest of pink pearls.

The first to arrive were Chet and Berdie Kissack, who said very nice things about Dad, and who asked me to visit them sometime. Next were Carl and Ingrid Rehm. She observed that I looked a great deal like Dad, which I do, and said that he'd spoken of me often, which I hoped was true. Sigmon Curlee introduced his wife, JoBeth, who had absolutely nothing to say, but who said it anyway while giving me the once-over but good. He held my hand in both of his the entire time, applying pressure in a friendly but unnecessary kind of way, and gave me another business card for the insurance company before she dragged him off. A lot of other couples came as well. I cannot remember all of the names, but there were Richard and Brownie Hamilton, Kev and Peggy Rice, the Molinas, Judge and Mrs. Holloway, Celia Woods and her husband Buck, the Garrisons. The singles included Jim Foley, Levi Bloch, and Rosa Garelli, who'd flown all the way in from Hawaii.

About half way through the evening, a quiet, wiry little man named Arte Peebles took my hand. He had warm blue eyes, but very pale skin.

"My wife sends her condolences and regrets," he offered. "Laura's doing kind of poorly these days, and she don't get out much, but she sure did love your daddy. A lot of us did. She's got Lupus, just like me. Has to avoid the sun, you know. That's why I run the bait shop now. I still get to work by the water, smell the salt air, and see the big fish when they hoist 'em over on Charterboat Row. It keeps me in touch with myself, if you know what I mean.

"But listen here, Miss Jean. I've got something that belongs to you now, I reckon. Your daddy was a mighty keen hand around boats, and he liked to do most of his own maintenance, but there was one thing that he hated like thunder. He detested working on reels. He didn't like all them little gears, and free-spool, and level-wind and such. And worse than that, he despised stripping off old lines and winding up new, much less eight or twelve reels at a time. But that's one of Arte's specialties, ya see. So your daddy'd bring 'em all down to me once a year. I'd open 'em up, flush out the gunk, polish up any corrosion with rouge, not emery, lubricate 'em real good with sewing machine oil, put 'em back together tight with an axle grease seal, and see that they were spinning free and true. Then I'd wind 'em all up, firm and level, with whatever kinds of line your daddy wanted."

I waited, but he didn't say anything more.

"I'm sorry," I finally admitted. "I don't understand."

"Well, of course not, Miss Jean," he replied sympathetically. "Your tiller can't be tracking too straight now, can it? The reels, hon. Your daddy's. I've got 'em. Finished rewinding 'em this afternoon. They're wrapped in florist paper, just a'waiting for you. You come on down to the bait shop any time you've got a mind to—it's on the landward side of the gas dock at Pier 66—and pick 'em up. They're yours now, ain't they?"

"Dad's fishing reels?"

"Every last one. It was like a ritual with your daddy. Once a year he'd bring 'em by, and let ol' Arte fix 'em up."

"Thank you, Mr. Peebles." I tried to smile, but didn't quite pull it off. "I'll drop by one day soon. I promise. It was very nice of you to visit with us this evening. Please give my best to your wife. I hope that she'll be feeling better soon."

"Yes, ma'am. Thank you, ma'am." He grinned, as he shook my hand once again. "I'll be certain to pass that along. She sure did love your daddy."

As the evening dragged along the line began to dwindle, and as it dwindled the guests became increasingly single, and the singles became increasingly female, and the females were all weepy, and clingy, and sad. So I spent the better part of two long hours commiserating with a clutch of whimpering spinsters, and it left a stale taste in my mouth.

"I take it Dad was popular with the ladies!" I commented.

"Well," Delsie replied, "when your mom disappeared, it just shattered your dad's big, romantic persona. Oh, everyone at Bahia Mar knows the whole tragic story, Sugar. Star-crossed lovers, and all of that. Your daddy could heal other people's broken spirits, but no one could ever touch his. Not completely, anyway. And, you know what men do when they're broken-hearted."

"Rebound?"

"Like jai alai."

Just when it looked as though there were going to be no more visitors, a great bulldozer of a man surged down the hallway, his oily seersucker jacket flapping in the breeze, a limp Panama hat perched over a too-red face. He stopped directly in front of me, not a finger's width separating his stomach from mine. His stench was like that of a slaughterhouse fog, and he stared me right in the eye.

"Lieutenant J.D. Okun," he announced with the sour breath of a life-long boozer. "Monroe County Sheriff's Department. You look just like him."

"If that's a compliment, I'm pleased," I replied, resolving not to breathe too deeply again.

"Well, it sure-fire ain't. I knew your daddy, little girl. Smart-ass wise guy. Liked to go around people. Liked to work behind their backs. Thought he was smarter, or better, or somethin'. Well, I hear he's done passed now, and I'm rotten glad to be shed of him!"

I was shocked, and angered, but whatever I wanted to say, it just wasn't worth inhaling.

"You plannin' on stayin' long?" he demanded.

"Why?" I croaked. "Am I suspected of something?"

"Already convicted, if'n you're his daughter," he snickered. "The lemon don't fall far from the tree."

Having run out of pleasantries, he spun heavily on his heel and stormed back up the hallway.

Delsie grabbed my wrist and dragged me into the parlor, where the heavy scent of freshly cut flowers provided a most welcome reprieve.

"Whewie!" she said, the purple draining from her cheeks. "I didn't know that I could hold my breath that long. I'll have to think of that fat slug the next time that I go snorkeling."

"What do you suppose that was all about?" I asked.

"Beats me. Bad blood, I guess. An old grudge, maybe?"

"I wonder if the Chamber of Commerce has approved his little welcome-to-Lauderdale schtick."

"Oh, he isn't from around here, Sugar. This is Broward County. Very cultured. Very civilized. He said Monroe County. That's all the way south and west of here. As far as you can go and still be on dry land. Well, sort of. The Everglades."

"And he came all the way up here just to gross me out?"

"At least he wasn't wearing a hood and toting a cross."

"That's not funny, Delsie."

"It wasn't meant to be, Sugar. But don't you worry your pretty little head. I'll take care of him. I dated an IRS agent from Miami last year. Marvin just adores me. He even asked me to marry him, but it was one of those different age things. I'm living in the Age of Adventure. He's living in the Age of Tranquility. It was a bad mix. Anyway, I'll give Marvin a call and see if we can arrange a surprise audit for Lt. J.D. Okun. A deep audit. Six or seven years back. That should keep him busy for a while. If he's as dirty as he smells, he might even get fined."

"Delsie! I didn't know that you were such a witch."

"Why, Sugar," she purred, twisting back and forth ever so slightly. "The only magic I have is what you're looking at."

Brownie Hamilton came up to me about then. She had terrific legs for a woman her age—dancer's legs—and a cheery smile to match. She said that she had known my Dad for over thirty years, for longer than almost anyone, and she knew that I had hardly known him at all, and she asked if I would like to hear a few stories about him. It was a very kind offer and I accepted without hesitation, so we found a couple of folding chairs, and sat down opposite *The Mangroves*. Some thoughtful person provided us with glasses of Mimosa, a charming cocktail made from orange juice and champagne, and Brownie positively enthralled me with her personal rendition of the life and times of a renegade maverick, my Dad. I gasped, and I wept, and I even laughed a little, until sometime just after midnight.

"Thank you, Brownie," I finally said, giving her a long, heartfelt hug.

"No, Sweetie. It is I who thank you," she replied in a voice suddenly tight with emotion. "You are a lovely and very apt young lady. Your daddy was quite proud of you. He boasted about you all the time."

Then, with a slight tremor in her voice she added, "It's so nice to know that he left something of himself behind."

But as I gazed at the dozens of names in the registration book that Ms. Dickson presented to me, and at the hundreds and hundreds of flowers, I realized that Dad had left even more of himself behind, in a great many places, with a great many people.

*   *   *

Delsie and I argued in the car. She wanted me to return to the *Jerome*, but I suddenly wanted to be alone with my grief, and insisted on spending the night at the hotel. I eventually won out, so she dropped me off, grudgingly but with a hug, then roared away in her hot little Italian bomba.

I was halfway across the lobby when it hit me that I was too keyed up to go to sleep. A little Benadryl would fix that, and it would help the allergic reaction that I'd had to the flowers as well, so I decided to look for a drugstore. The desk clerk told me that there was an all-night pharmacy two blocks east, on the corner. It was pretty late, but I really didn't care, so I set off down the street, glad to be out in the open air, and grateful for the exercise. An LED bank clock showed that it was 12:57, and a cool 78 degrees.

I have traveled enough to know that there are three kinds of cities in the South: those that are stuck in time, and haven't built anything new since the Second World War; the so-called New South Cities, which obliterate everything historically meaningful as they erect skyscraping commercial fortresses that are devoid of human scale and value; and those enlightened few which retain the best of the old, allowing the worthy survivors of the past to live on with dignity, while building contemporary structures around them. Those last cities are very much like the rare families that encourage grandparents to live with their progeny, inspiring and enlightening younger generations while still making small but honorable contributions.

It was that sane philosophy which had permitted the Grove Drug Store to endure, surrounded though it may have been by modern shoebox towers. The exterior brickwork was of a fanciful, geometric design, a blue-and-white tiled sidewalk announced an offset, corner entrance, and the beveled glass windows in the cypress doors sparkled with Olde English inscriptions rendered in 24 karat gold. The interior, however, was a freakish hodgepodge of outdated Edwardian fussiness and contemporary kitsch. A grayish tin ceiling cluttered with hanging paddle fans hovered over a decrepit vinyl-asbestos floor and worn-out formica shelves, while a splendiferous, marble-topped, mahogany lunch counter reigned supreme next to a line of squealing video games.

The stock was the same aspirin and antacid, toothbrushes and tampons that you'd find in any drugstore from Boston to Baja, so I shopped quickly, and left with a crinkling plastic bag in my hand. Then my neck started itching, and that panicky feeling returned with a vengeance. Someone, somewhere was watching me. I was sure of it. But when I glanced around nervously I saw absolutely nothing, and so I started back to the hotel.

The streets were absolutely deserted, the doorways mostly dark. No pedestrians. No cops. No people of any description. But I picked up the pace just the same. I couldn't see very far, but I sensed that something was out there. Something powerful. Something close. Or perhaps my nerves were just shot. I couldn't be sure. Was it my imagination, or did I hear footsteps? I took another quick look around. Still nothing.

The city was gloomier than before, and I found myself walking on a black stretch of sidewalk where glass from broken street lights crunched loudly beneath my feet. Then a tidal wave of anxiety overwhelmed me as I realized that the shattered glass hadn't been there fifteen minutes earlier. Someone had shot those lights out with a pellet gun. Alarms went off in my brain, like searing, red-hot flares. I had just graduated from being a target of opportunity for a common mugger, to being the specific trophy prey in a deliberate and orchestrated hunt. The odds were now clearly against me.

I heard footsteps again, glanced over my shoulder, and saw one of the dark blue suits from the BMW, not fifty feet behind. Adrenaline surged through my veins like fire. I pulled my hem up and started running, as best I could in low heels, but an Oldsmobile zoomed by and screeched to a halt against the curb just ahead of me. The passenger door flew wide open, blocking my escape, and the other blue suit slid across the front seat. He jumped out, grinning, as massive as a Grizzly.

"We're gunna have ourselves a little chat," said the driver as he opened the back door. "Get in."

"I'll scream," I threatened.

"You'll die," he countered, tapping a heavy bulge under his jacket.

The other thug caught up with us just then, and he shoved me hard in the small of my back. I stumbled toward the door, went down hard on one knee, and then I heard the hollow, piercing scream of an eagle, only much, much louder.

From out of nowhere came a knotted mass of muscle in a black silk exercise suit. All I could think of was Batman. He kicked the guy who had pushed me, smacking the side of the bad guy's knee so hard that his leg buckled like a stalk of celery. You could hear cartilage ripping like sail-cloth. A definitive chop to the throat, a crushed larynx, and blue suit number one was down for good. Then Batman did a flying spin kick, caught the driver's wrist as he attempted to pull out a pistol, and flipped the weapon into the night. But the driver had not been caught off guard like his partner. He clamped his brawny hands on my would-be rescuer's throat, thumbs pressing into his trachea. In a flash, my hero brought his arms down low, made a rockhard double fist with his hands, and banged them up between himself and his adversary. He broke blue number two's grip, throwing his arms high and wide, and then slammed his own fists down again like a giant pair of sledgehammers. The twin blows fractured both of the bad guy's clavicles. They sounded like tree branches snapping, and he howled in agony.

Frisking both of the goons and finding nothing, the stranger took my hand, lifted me gently to my feet, and said in an appallingly conversational tone, "Well, Dr. Pearson. Shall we finish our stroll?"

It was only then that I recognized him.

"Raul?"

"Miss Delsie didn't like the story that you told about yesterday's taxi ride," he explained as we walked across the street to the Riverside, "so she asked me to keep an eye on you."

"Since when?"

"Since you left the hotel this morning."

"But I never saw you. I never even suspected."

"That's the general idea. Covert operations require stealth. Find 'em, flick 'em, and flee. That's our motto."

"Whose?"

"My old unit. Navy SEALS. I'm sure that Miss Delsie told you. She just loves to brag about me. Our mission was simple. Locate and liquidate."

"And those two back there?"

"Incapacitated, that's all," he said as though discussing the weather. "A few days in the hospital, a couple of weeks of therapy, several months at the gym, and they'll be almost as good as new."

"Almost?"

"Well, they'll never be quite the same. It's psychological, you see. They were playground bullies, not warriors, so this little fracas undoubtedly shook their confidence. They won't mess with you again; believe me."

"Who were they?"

"I have no idea. Neither one carried any form of ID, and there weren't any plates on the car. Just a bumper sticker that read 'R&S.' There wasn't time to conduct even a cursory interrogation, and I think it best that we avoid involving the police. Miss Delsie called me on my cell, you see, and told me about Lt. Okun, so I don't know who we can trust. But one thing's for certain."

"What's that?"

"Your little car chase yesterday evening wasn't a case of random street violence. For reasons unknown, these guys were targeting you specifically, and that means that this isn't over. Whoever hired them will come at you again, from a different direction."

Raul's analysis scared the wits out of me. I felt violated, victimized, anything but safe, and I found myself wishing that I had never come to Ft. Lauderdale.

6

"I'm going to pack," I announced as Raul followed me into my hotel room. "I'm going back to the *Jerome*."

"An excellent decision, Doctor," he agreed. Raul pulled back the edge of one of the drapes, and peered out the window. "Will Belgian Waffles and fresh strawberries be suitable for breakfast?"

It was his deadpan delivery that made me smile, spontaneously, if idiotically. I guess that I need the relief. The tension all day had been frightful. But then I noticed that the little red message light on the phone was blinking, again.

"Hi, Dr. Pearson. It's Angie," squawked the digital recording.

It was my assistant in Youngstown.

"We're all fine here. The animals are okay, too. But there's a problem, a pretty big one. I really think that you should call me just as soon as you get in. I know it might be late, but that's okay. I'll be up watching Leno. If you get in later than that, please call me anyway, and wake me up. It's really, really important, Dr. Pearson, and I don't want to leave a message about it. I hope that things are going well. Oh, dear. I mean... You know what I mean. I'll be waiting for your call. Bye now. Oh, yeah. My number is area 330-314-7662."

I dialed the number, and after seven rings got a sleepy, "Hedd-oh?"

"Hi, Angie. It's Jean Pearson."

"Oh, hi. I must have fallen asleep. You okay?"

"I'm managing. What's so important that I'm getting you up in the middle of the night?"

"Someone broke into your townhouse," she yawned.

"What?"

"The police came to see me at the clinic this morning. Whoever it was cut your phone lines. Disabled the alarm system, too. A neighbor saw your lights on, knew you'd left town, called 911. But when the cops got there, the place was empty."

"Empty? They took everything?"

"Oh. No. Sorry. They didn't take anything. Not that I could tell anyway. What I meant to say was that nobody was there when the cops arrived."

"Did they do any damage?"

"Not really." She yawned again. "They picked the locks. Quieter that way, I guess."

"So why did they break in?"

"I don't know. They went through your desk; through every drawer in the house. They even went through every box in the attic. It's a real mess up there; like a bomb went off. Your Macintosh was turned on. Your correspondence and document files were open. The FIND FILE window was on the screen."

"But I unplugged the surge protector before I left, Angie. That computer system was dead. And there's an AfterDark screen saver with a ten-digit security code. You can't even access the welcome screen without entering that code."

"I know, Dr. Pearson," she replied sleepily. "I installed that screen saver for you; remember? Whoever it was either knew your security signature, or had the back door to the program."

"The back door?"

"People are kind of stupid. They're always forgetting their codes, and locking themselves out of their own computers. So the software designers leave a back door in the program. Another way to provide access."

"Wonderful! Do the police have any idea who did it?"

"Kenny, one of the detectives, dated my cousin Sherry for a while last summer. You remember Sherry. She's the trim little redhead who fell off that roan mare just as she got to the downhill privet hedge during the steeplechase this spring. Broke her left radius. Anyway, Kenny stopped by, and told me that the only fingerprints at the townhouse were yours, Peter's, mine and the cleaning lady's."

"So they used surgical gloves."

"Looks like. Oh, and another thing."

"Wait a minute," I said impatiently. "Hold on."

A muted beeping announced that someone was trying to reach me on my cell phone. Fishing it from the bowels of my purse, I said, "Yes?"

"It's me, Sugar," Delsie huffed in exasperation.

"Listen," I interrupted her, "I'll have to call you back. My assistant is on the hotel phone. Someone broke into my townhouse."

"Then you're two for two."

"What?"

"Marina security reported to me as soon as I parked Emillio."

"Emillio?"

"My car, Sugar. Listen up. Security says that they ran someone off your dad's boat earlier this evening. Attempted break-in. They didn't make it, though. Never got through the door. Whoever it was grabbed a trash bag from the garbage can on the dock, and threw it into some kind of motorized canoe when he took off. Security thinks that it was probably a junkie looking for something to sell. Must have read the obituary in the paper, and knew that you'd be at Stanek's. That happens a lot. Sugar, have you seen Raul by any chance?"

"He's here with me now."

"Do tell! Trouble?"

"More than a little."

"Okay, Sugar," she said as though ordering a deck hand to weigh anchor. "This isn't a request. I want you to..."

"I'm already packing."

"Good. When can I expect you?"

"Thirty minutes."

"I'll be waiting with a fresh pot of coffee. We've got some talking to do." She hung up, and I grabbed the other phone.

"Angie, are you still there?"

"Here," she yawned.

"What's the rest of it?"

"They broke into your townhouse mailbox, too. Ripped that beautiful brass faceplate off with a crowbar. It's too badly bent to repair. I checked. It will cost you $237.00 to have it replaced."

"The mail's gone, I suppose?"

"Everything except the fall catalog from Neiman Marcus. I asked the Post Office to hold your mail until you get back."

"Well, that sure puts a cap on it!" I said angrily.

"Not really."

"There's more?"

"Yesterday morning's clinic mail was stolen, too, and America Online froze our corporate account because someone tried to hack into our e-mail."

"What the hell is going on?"

"I don't have a clue, Dr. Pearson. I kinda hoped that you'd tell me. It's getting a little scary up here, so I called Wells Fargo, and hired a night watchman for the clinic. I was concerned about the animals. You know. And I also hired a roving security patrol, for both the clinic and your townhouse. I hope you don't mind."

"Mind? Angie, bless you! That's great. You just earned yourself a bonus."

"Not necessary, Dr. Pearson."

"Oh, yes it is," I insisted. "You went way beyond the call of duty, Angie, and I want you to know that I appreciate it."

We swapped a few quick notes about clinic operations, said goodbye, and I told Raul about the break-in as I finished packing.

"Black bag job," he grunted.

"How's that?"

"Professionals," he said. "Locks picked, communications cut, alarms deactivated, computer hacked into, no fingerprints, and they probably had police frequency scanners. That's how they knew to bug out before the police got there. A black bag job. Straight out of the covert ops manual. Classic super spy stuff. So it had to be people with solid training— Quantico, Langley, or Special Forces maybe—but whoever's behind it, they're not with the government, because if the Feds had hatched this operation, the FBI would have picked you up by now."

"Operation!" I wailed. I suddenly felt weak, and sat on the edge of the bed. "What are you talking about?"

"Listen," he said, "I don't know what the hell's going on, but I can tell you this much for sure. Whatever it is, it's private. The crews are uneven. The guy who hit your townhouse was a pro. Real skill. But those pukes on the street tonight were lame. Strictly schoolyard. If government spooks had been in charge, there'd be a consistent approach, a pattern, and they'd have hit everything hard, at the same time."

"You see a connection between these events?" I asked. "They're a thousand miles apart."

"Yes, and Berlin and Tokyo were on opposite sides of the planet in the 1930s."

"I see your point. So what do you suppose they want?"

"Damned if I know. Information, most likely. They probably think you know something, or that you have something. Documents, cassettes, zip disks, perhaps even film or video. They're looking everywhere. In your mail, in your computer, even in your dad's trash."

"The purse-snatching fits, too," I muttered angrily.

"What's that?"

So I told him about the incident at the airport, and he just stared at me, like a geometry teacher waiting for a new theorem to sink in. I hadn't felt quite so stupid since eighth grade math.

"Okay," I asked, "what now?"

"We vanish, Dr. Pearson. We get you aboard the *Jerome,* ASAP, and set up a security perimeter. You and the boss gotta talk this through."

"Delsie says she'll be waiting up with hot coffee."

Raul smiled appreciatively.

"She's not a bad skipper," he allowed as he pulled a small digital phone from his pocket.

Raul called the *Jerome* while I called the front desk. I told the night clerk that I was going to visit a friend in Coconut Creek, and I asked her to leave my account open. Then I grabbed a few things, stuffed them into my overnight bag, and we left. Raul had parked his van in a public lot around the corner, so he took my cell-phone number and made me wait in the ladies room off the hotel lobby until he called. When my cell-phone rang I ran out to the curb, jumped into the van and we were gone. Twenty minutes later an electrical winch ground heavily as the *Jerome's* crew raised the gangway behind us.

"Everything set?" asked Raul.

"Mikey is up on the fly bridge with the Excalibur night vision glasses and your H&K," Geoffrey reported. "All of the hatches are dogged down, the infrared deck lights are burning, and the IFR minicameras are on. I'll activate the ultrasonic alarm system and hydrophones as soon as you're safely below."

"H&K?" I asked as we tumbled down the companionway.

"Heckler & Koch," said Raul. "An MP5SD submachine gun. Nine millimeter. Very sweet. This one's fitted with a suppressor; what you civilians call a silencer. The Navy thinks that I dropped it in the Med."

$*$ $*$ $*$

Good to her word, Delsie was waiting in the dining saloon with a gallon of hot coffee in a trendy Thermos pitcher. Geoffrey had managed to whip up a tray of pastries as well. Heavy velvet drapes covered the portholes, and several closed circuit television monitors displayed pictures of the entire rear deck, the foredeck and the pier. For added security, Raul tuned the Wave Radio to an all-night Spanish language station that was hosting a Calypso festival, "to confuse any long-range microphones," he said. "Just in case."

"There will be rumors flying tomorrow," Delsie sighed.

"What?"

"I can hear it all now, Sugar. Bereaved daughter slips out of hotel in wee hours with Latin Lothario."

"You're right," complained Raul. "This will ruin my reputation. Now, if you ladies will excuse me, I have some security details to check."

"All right," I grumbled as he left the room. "Let's get down to business."

"Right," said Delsie. "What do we know for sure?"

It took me thirty minutes to lay out all of the pieces—the explosion aboard Uncle Bud's cruiser, the purse-snatching incident, the meetings with Rehm, L'Ouverture and Sigmon Curlee, the taxi chase, Lt. Okun's threat, my attempted abduction, the break-in at my townhouse, the computer trespass, the missing mail, the thwarted looting of Dad's houseboat; everything.

"So what can we conclude for certain?" asked Delsie.

"Well, there can be little doubt that Dad and Uncle Bud were murdered," I said, "and Raul speculates that parties unknown believe me to be in possession of some kind of information, or documents, or film, or something. He's pretty certain that it's not the government."

"Sounds reasonable. Do we call the police?"

"And tell them what? That the Blues Brothers attempted to kidnap me twice in the last two days? That the first time I was rescued by the Caribbean Road Warrior, and then by the Phantom of the Drug Store? And why? Because two local characters whose deaths have been listed by the Medical Examiner as accidental were assassinated in some bizarre conspiracy to steal my mail? Yeah, right! I'll report it, then you can visit me in a padded cell somewhere, and push Jello down my feeding tube."

The room fell deathly quiet for a couple of minutes, and then Delsie broke the silence.

"All right, Sugar," she said. "I'll buy that. But we can't call the police for a more important reason. We can't call them because we can't afford to trust them. We have to assume that Lt. Okun didn't just happen to show up at Stanek's tonight. He's clearly not leadership material, so someone else must have sent him. But we don't know who, and we don't know who's connected to whom. In fact, we don't know much of anything."

There was another long moment of silence.

"Delsie," I asked, "do you really think that my life is in danger?"

My legs felt like jelly, and my throat was so tight that I couldn't even manage to swallow my coffee.

"Sugar," she said in a reassuring tone, "let me ask you a question. Have you ever been to New York, walked from a restaurant to Broadway to see a musical, then walked back to your hotel after stopping at Sardi's for dessert and coffee?"

"With Peter."

"Well," she smiled, "you're far safer here than in Manhattan; believe me. You're on an ex-Navy warship, with all of the hatches battened down, security measures in force, and with a small but elite private army watching over you. In fact, you're more secure here than anywhere you've ever been in your life."

"Thanks," I said, feeling a little better. "Now let's look at this thing again. We must be missing something."

"It would help if we knew what the bad guys were searching for."

"Whatever it is, it must have something to do with Uncle Bud and his work. Like L'Ouverture said, the bomb was on Uncle Bud's boat, so he must have been the target."

"And he and your dad said that they were going fishing?"

"Yes, but they couldn't have been. Dad left all of his fishing reels behind. That nice little man, Arte Peebles, told us so tonight. Remember?"

"That's right!"

"And Carl Rehm said that he didn't know why Dad and Uncle Bud would want to go fishing in the Keys anyway."

"In the Keys? Shallow water fishing? This time of year? I wouldn't go there now for love nor money. Well, not for money anyway. There are huge clouds of bloodsucking mosquitoes everywhere, the lovebugs are swarming all over the place, splattering up your windscreen, and the gnats will drive you mad, if the bottle flies don't eat the hide off you first. And besides, that fat old cruiser of your uncle's drew too much water."

"So if they weren't going fishing, where were they headed?"

"South, at least," said Delsie.

"How come?"

"You said that their boat exploded just after they'd rounded the John Lloyd Jetty; that people saw the explosion from the beach. Well, there isn't anything north of the jetty but hard rock breakwaters, and the only beach is to the south, so that means they were headed south."

"Okay, but there's a lot of territory south of here."

"Not nearly as much as there is to the north. It narrows things down a bit. But let's get back on point. If someone murdered your Uncle Bud, then there must have been a reason."

"Yes, but everybody liked him," I insisted. "He didn't run with the bad boys, he didn't play around with married women, he never cheated anyone, and he didn't gamble or owe anyone any money. He had a way of putting people at ease. Dad used to say that Uncle Bud attracted friends the way that blue serge attracts lint. And he did, too. So with no enemies, where's the motive?"

"It must have had something to do with his business. He must have been working on something important. Any ideas?"

"Not a single one," I sighed, slouching back in my chair. "He always had several projects under way at any given moment. Research, consulting, planning, auditing, cost accounting. Things like that. And Uncle Bud was ever the circumspect professional. He never said very much about his work, except in private, insisting that discretion was the hallmark of his vocation. He lived and he worked aboard that old cruiser, so between the explosion, the fire and the sinking, there won't be anything useful there. I know, Delsie. I've seen the photos. Terrible images. Total wreckage. And there was nothing in his safe deposit box that will help us either."

"Too bad," said Delsie. "So you don't have any idea what he was doing these days?"

"The only thing that I know for certain is that he researched a retirement condo for Commander L'Ouverture's parents several weeks ago."

"Not much to go on there."

"No."

My eyes were starting to get droopy, and I was having a hard time staying awake.

"Where was it?" asked Delsie.

"Where was what?"

"The retirement condo."

"Some place called Cape Perdi, I think."

"Cape Perdi?"

"Something like that," I yawned. "L'Ouverture said that his mother was interested in it because she was old island. But I wasn't paying that much attention to his parents' retirement plans. My mind was on other things."

"Cape Perdi," Delsie said thoughtfully. "That doesn't sound right at all. A cape is a peninsula. Why would an island woman find a peninsula attractive?"

"I don't know." I yawned again. "I think that's what he said. It's probably some form of Caribbean French. Some kind of provincial dialect, maybe. Some sort of local, idiomatic patois. L'Ouverture's family is Haitian, after all. Cape Perdi? Possibly from the French *perdrix*, meaning partridge. Cape Partridge? But partridges aren't shoreline birds; are they? On the other hand, *Perdrix* came from the Old French *perdis*, which came from the Latin *perdix*. The partridge's genus is *Perdix*, and the Latin derived from the Greek, also *perdix*. Like so many things, it goes back to the Greeks. To the prehistoric Minoans, actually. From ancient Aegean mythology. Perdix, the nephew of Daidalos, who invented of the pottery wheel. He fell from a great cliff by the sea, but the goddess Athena loved him, and changed him into a partridge so that he wouldn't crash on the rocks."

"You're drifting," chided Delsie.

"Um-hmm," I replied sleepily.

Delsie sat at the table with her head in her hands, a glazed expression covering her face, staring into sheer nothingness. Then she smiled thinly.

"Oh great swami madam veterinar-rian," she teased in a sing-song manner as she shook my arm.

"Hmmmm?"

"Wake u-up," she crooned. "You're on the wrong side of the wor-rld."

"Mmmmmm..."

"Wake u-up, thou classically trained and erudite Doctor of Veterinary Medicine, and confounding speaker of the French tongue, whose weird intellectual ramblings are marginally entertaining but entirely wrong. Wake u-up."

"Why?" I complained.

"Because I know where they were go-ing."

Sing-song or not, she said it with such confidence that I was wide awake in an instant.

"Where?" I demanded to know, rubbing my eyes.

"Your medical training is excellent, your knowledge of literature impressive, and your French passable in a bourgeois sort of way, but you don't know very much about Spanish, do you?"

"I can order chalupas at Taco Bell."

"Pay attention, Doc," she ordered. "*Cayo* was the Spanish Conquistadores' word for a sandy, low-lying island. In the Caribbean *cayo* got shortened to *cay*, and in their Anglicized form, the *Cays* are called the *Keys*. Also, the Spanish word for green is *verde*. You know, like verdant. Like the Italian composer of *La Traviata*, Giuseppe Verdi, more commonly known to light classical lovers as Joe Green."

"Where is this multicultural analysis taking me?"

"Taking *us*," she corrected. "L'Ouverture probably didn't say Cape Perdi, Sugar. It doesn't make any sense. I never heard of the place. So what I think he said was *Cay Verde*; Spanish for Green Key."

"One of the islands?"

"Yes, ma'am!"

"I want to go there, Delsie. Have you got a map, or a chart or whatever? Can we figure out where it is?"

"We don't need a map, Sugar. Take a look at this."

She got up from her chair, pulled an oversized copy of *An Illustrated Guide to the Florida Keys* from the bookcase, and began thumbing through it.

"It's not Green Key like the color," she announced. "It's Greene Key, with an *e*, like the family surname. It says right here in this cute little inset box with the grapevine border—I just love the way that they design these things; don't you?—that Greene Key was named in honor of William Zebediah Chilton-Greene, a British traveler, naturalist, and contemporary of Charles Darwin, who discovered seven unique species of flora and fauna which were endemic to the island. Most are now thought to be extinct. Humph! Too bad."

"Delsie, I want to go there," I repeated.

"I know, Sugar, and we will. It's as good a starting point as any. But first, let's get some sleep. We've got a memorial service to conduct tomorrow evening."

"You mean later today, don't you?"

She frowned, nodded silently, and led the way to our sleeping quarters. The eastern horizon had the pale look of impending dawn as I stumbled off to my stateroom, and I honestly don't remember climbing into bed.

7

It was nearly half past twelve when I finally crawled out of bed, and shuf-
fled to the shower, but I felt strangely optimistic for the first time since
arriving in Lauderdale. I still had the memorial service to suffer through
that evening, but Delsie had insisted on taking charge of those arrangements, and I was more than satisfied to let her wrestle with the details.
Anyway, I had something different planned for the afternoon; something
very personal, almost spiritual, that I felt compelled to do.

Corn flakes, skim milk and coffee would have suited me just fine, but
Geoffrey wouldn't hear of it. He sat me at a table under the aft deck
canopy, and served up a big platter of Belgian waffles with fresh, sliced
strawberries.

"Raul insisted," he announced with a wink.

"You know," I said as I speared a thick chunk of waffle for my first delicious bite, "under other circumstances I might just fall in love with that
man."

"I feel the same way," Geoffrey sighed.

Delsie joined me about twenty minutes later, and after we had thoroughly gorged ourselves we retired to her suite. I needed to borrow some
old clothes so that I could pay a visit to Dad's boat. As it turned out, she
didn't have any.

"Just help yourself to whatever you need," she offered. "If you get them too dirty, we'll simply throw them away."

After cutting off a dark blue pair of Harley Davidson jeans, which I had to draw in at the waist with a length of white cotton rope, I knotted the tails of a pink Victoria's Secret blouse at my midriff to tame the excessive bust. Then I stared at my image in the mirror, and groaned.

"I look like Elly May Clampett," I groused.

"Not true, Sugar. Elly May fixed her hair in pigtails, and she was much more buxom than you."

"But not more than you," I said with a trace of envy.

It was a scorcher of a day, and I was thankful that Delsie had made me trade my cheap, plastic flip-flops for a pair of cork sandals, because I could feel the heat reflecting up from the floating concrete docks as I walked along.

The marina was already growing noisy with the clamoring and clanking of too many weekenders, few of whom treat the yacht basin with the basic courtesies expected in a public hotel. Dad used to say that it would be fun for the residents of the marina to take the name of the worst offender, drive out to his house in a dozen cars one Tuesday afternoon, park on his lawn for a couple of days, throw wild parties, play loud music, smoke dope, get drunk, raise all kinds of hell, hump in plain view, throw condoms in the flower beds, and leave mounds of leaking garbage bags behind. Oh, well. Certain things get sacrificed by those eccentric souls whose homes make small dents in the sea, and at the very top of the list is quietude.

There she was again, fifty-some feet of vintage, barge-type houseboat, somewhat less forlorn in the blistering light of day, but still resembling a sorrowful mortician in one of those drab old movies about Victorian England. Well, if there were ever a suitable day for mourning, that one certainly qualified, but I was determined not to let her wallow in it. She deserved better. Much better. And besides, I needed to follow through on Dad's instructions.

The key was right where Dad had always hidden it, in a chink in the bulkhead behind his arthritic Schwin ten-speed. Nearby, I opened the spring-loaded weather cover on the security keypad, and was relieved to find that the alarm system still responded to my personal code, 19031911—the years in which Marie Sklodowska Curie had received the Nobel prize for physics and chemistry. A little green light flashed faintly, announcing that the primary system had been disarmed, and the LED readout displayed the message WELCOME HOME, JEAN. I checked the sliding glass door. It was secure and unharmed, except for a broad, shiny scratch on the weathered aluminum frame where the previous night's intruder had tried to jimmy the latch. Then I unlocked the double-catch safety mechanism, slid the glass panel open, and stepped into the darkened lounge. What I had expected to find were the fusty smells of stale beer, soiled laundry, dust and aftershave. The spoor of the bachelor. What assailed me instead was the oven-hot stench of mildew. I retreated right back into the sun.

A quick visit to Security told the tale. Learning that Dad had passed way, some maintenance idiot had shut off the dock power, and padlocked the circuit breaker box for good measure. Security was happy to restore the power, but only after I signed a form stating that I would accept financial responsibility. Then I opened every hatch, unbolted every porthole, turned on every ventilation fan and set the air conditioner to run at full blast. Even so, the wooden structure of the boat had heated up like the bricks in a kiln, and I found myself perspiring, regardless of the steady onshore breeze that was blowing through from stem to stern.

The first thing that I did was check the wet cells. They were down to half an amp, the bilge pumps and alarm system having thoroughly drained them, but now that Security had restored the dock power, the automatic charging system was taking over and building them back up. It would take twenty-four hours to give the batteries a full charge, but that wouldn't matter with the dock power on.

Then I checked for spoiled food, but Dad had cleaned out the refrigerator and vegetable bins before leaving on his ill-fated adventure. All of the
trash cans were empty too, except the one beneath the paper shredder
under his desk. It still contained a sizable wad of multicolored confetti, so
I pulled out the plastic bag, knotted it shut, and tossed it on the chair
beside the door.

I didn't have the heart to go through Dad's personal things yet. I just
couldn't bring myself to touch them. I thought about lightening the mood
by playing some of his music—he had left a couple of CDs on his Pioneer
5-disc player; remastered copies of George Van Eps guitar, and the
Modern Jazz Quartet on Blues at Carnegie Hall—but I couldn't do that
either because something stopped me; warned me. Now, I don't believe in
ghosts, but there was a presence on that boat, or at least it felt as though
there were. Whatever it was, it prevented me from feeling like the rightful
owner, or even like the deceased owner's legally enfranchised daughter. It
made me feel like a hireling; like it was okay for me to tend to maintenance items, but not to sit on the bed. So I contented myself with a childish look-but-don't-touch routine, and I felt kind of silly. I stared at one of
Dad's little paintings, a Syd Solomon shorescape. It was full of crashing
beauty and raw energy, all frothing aquamarines under roiling gray skies,
but it reminded me of Dad's death, of fouled waters and acrid smoke, so
my mood plunged from silly to sullen. Helping myself to one of Dad's
Heiniken Darks made me feel a little bit better, and then I remembered
why I'd really gone there.

Alice in Wonderland II. A clue in a game played by a middle-aged man
and his college student daughter. A game Dad invented, or so I believe,
because I've never met anyone else who's ever played it. He called the game
Namivia, a conjunctive of Name Trivia, and it had just two rules. First, the
clue had to be a recognizable name. Second, the name had to evoke a specific quotation, which would be both obvious and meaningful to the
recipient of the clue.

It all started right after I met Dad. He invited me to move in with him on the boat for a while, and when I was out on the beach one day Uncle Bud dropped by and asked Dad to accompany him on an errand. Dad hadn't had time to get an extra key made for me, he hadn't shown me where the spare key was hidden, he didn't want to leave the boat unsecured, and he didn't want me to feel slighted if I came back and found myself locked out. So he left a yellow Post-it note on the lounge door, reading simply, "MacArthur." I came back, took one look at that note, and knew exactly what it meant. General Douglas MacArthur: "I shall return." Next came a monogram in response to my bitter complaint about the inadequacy of a government pre-med scholarship that I had received. "JFK." The message was clear as a bell. John Fitzgerald Kennedy: "Ask not what your country can do for you. Ask what you can do for your country." I stopped whining and hit the books.

Over time, Dad invoked other distinguished names. "Oliver Hardy," when I ran the boat aground during our first Christmas vacation together.[1] "Rhett Butler," when I informed Dad that Wilson Phillips had broken up.[2] "FDR," when I admitted that I was terrified of taking my veterinary boards.[3] And my all-time favorite, "Bugs Bunny," which I often found waiting on my answering machine.[4]

And now, "Alice in Wonderland II."

The story that I had told Carl Rehm while inventorying the safe deposit boxes had been one hundred percent, Grade A, U.S. Prime hogwash. Dad and I had never called any of our excursions the Alice cruises. The actual meaning of "Alice in Wonderland II" had been instantly apparent, but the

---

1 Oliver Hardy. Comedian of early cinematic fame. "Here's another fine mess you've gotten us into."
2 Rhett Butler. Fictional hero of *Gone With the Wind*. "Frankly, my dear, I don't give a damn."
3 Franklin D. Roosevelt. 32nd President of the United States. "The only thing we have to fear is fear itself."
4 Bugs Bunny. Wisecracking Warner Brothers cartoon rabbit. "Eh, what's up, Doc?"

contents of Dad's note to me was none of Rehm's damn business. He never should have asked me about it. He'd been overbearing in his handling of the cremations, pushy in his management of legal affairs, and I very much resented his intrusion into family matters that were both personal and painful.

I walked into the head, following Dad's clue.

The British mathematician and writer, Charles Lutwidge Dodgson, made two lasting contributions to English literature under the pen name Lewis Carroll: *Alice's Adventures in Wonderland,* and its sequel, *Through the Looking-Glass, and What Alice Found There,* or, Alice in Wonderland II.

With its great sunken tub and marble fixtures, the bathroom was the showpiece of the boat. Directly across from the doorway, on the windowless outside wall, there was a framed, 3-foot wide, full-length mirror which ran all the way from the baseboard to the ceiling; a height of nearly seven feet. I stood directly in front of that looking-glass for a moment, admiring my hillbilly couture, and then pressed the lever so cleverly hidden in the frame. Like magic, the mirror swung silently toward me on silicone-lubricated piano hinge, revealing a shallow closet of sorts, big enough that even Dad could stand up in it.

Dad had shown me his secret closet on one of my early visits. Something peculiar had been going on, so he'd said that if there were any kind of trouble I should step inside the closet, pull the mirror door quietly closed, and stay there. He'd slept on the couch in the lounge during my entire stay, with a Model 1911 .45 caliber Colt semiautomatic pistol under his pillow. There'd been a second .45 hanging in a military holster on the left-hand wall of the closet, and a .30 caliber M-2 carbine sat in a rack on the right-hand wall. The short-barreled carbine was of the folding shoulder-stock variety favored by the Rangers during the Korean War. It had a 30-round magazine locked in its breech, and a second magazine was bound to the first with black electrician's tape, upside-down and side-by-side, doubling the gun's ammunition. Dad trained me in the use of both weapons during our longer boating expeditions, because he insisted that the people most likely to survive life's many unpleasant challenges were those who had the most varied skills at their command.

I looked into that pitch-dark closet now. The pistol and the carbine were in their usual places, and on the floor was another #10 envelope with the word *Jean* handwritten across it. Opening the envelope, and unfolding the enclosed bit of paper, I found that the message read, "the smuggler's secret." It wasn't a person's name, and it didn't make any sense at all. What was Dad trying to tell me?

I'd hardly had time to address this enigma when I heard the flat *bong!* that the alarm system makes whenever anyone steps on the welcome mat at the inboard end of the boarding ramp. Then I heard heavy footsteps as two men started yelling, "Hello! Hey! Anyone aboard?"

Since the days of the Phoenicians, three thousand years ago, rule number one of marine etiquette has dictated that one never board another person's vessel without first asking for, and getting, their permission. Therefore, whoever the intruders might be, they were either extraordinarily uncouth, or up to no good. Then, too, there was something peculiarly unnerving about their voices; some distinct but unrecognized quality that filled me with dread. So I stepped into the closet and pulled the mirror-door closed.

I couldn't hear as well anymore, but I could see beautifully, because the mirror was one of those thick, two-way glasses that police departments use in their interrogation rooms. I heard a lot of indistinct mumbling, more muffled "hellos," and I felt the rumble of heavy, approaching footfalls. Then one of the men strode right past the bathroom, and proceeded to the master stateroom. He wore white deck shoes, white cotton socks, white cotton slacks, a white web belt, a white knit shirt. Very natty. His companion appeared next, and stepped into the bathroom. Beige deck shoes, no socks, khaki slacks, pale blue shirt. Clean cut, but second rate. He glanced around and hollered, "As long as I'm here," lifted the toilet seats, and proceeded to empty his bladder in a thundering torrent.

Whitey came back a minute later and said, "Step aside," as he prepared to take his turn. It was then that I recognized him. It was Lt. Okun.

Khaki-pants shook his little toy before putting it away, then pulled a comb out of his pocket and stepped in front of the mirror.

"I still don't get it," he said, holding his face less than two feet from mine while straightening his hair. "What do you want with this old barge, anyway? It looks like a reject from the Spanish-American War."

"Shit," answered Okun. "I don't want this friggin' boat. All I want is to git the daughter the hell outta town; back up north where she belongs. The memorial service is tonight, and I figure the only other business she might stick around for is to sell this old junker. So if I offer her a decent price, and if she takes it, then she's back home with her kitty cats, and the hell out of my hair."

"Or," said Khaki-pants without any emotion at all, "we could stuff her in an oil drum with some used engine parts, and sink her out in the Gulf Stream like them Wise Guys did with Manny the Lip."

I was beginning to perspire, heavily. The mirror-door was gasketed to prevent vibration, and the rubber seal was preventing me from getting any air. The inside of the closet was beginning to heat up. I was rapidly running out of oxygen.

"Listen," said Okun, "let's go have ourselves a beer. We'll find that Yankee bitch sooner or later. Then just let me do the talking. They ain't no need for muscle. I'll just make her an offer she can't refuse, close the friggin' deal, and we're done. Ya hear?"

"Hey!" Khaki yelled. He was leaning so close to the mirror that his breath fogged the glass, his nose not six inches from mine. "Look at this."

My heart all but stopped.

"I got a pimple on my lip where that broad the other night..."

"Oh, shut up," Okun barked disgustedly. "Let's get out of here. It stinks on this tub."

Leaving the toilet seats up, they turned and retreated from the head, without even flushing.

A few seconds later, after I'd heard the alarm system *bong* once again, I fingered the mirror door's interior release lever, and tumbled out onto the floor, gasping for air and positively dripping with sweat. Then, glancing in the vanity mirror over the sink, I discovered an odd creature staring back at me. She was panting like a collie after a hard run, her hair was matted like a well-ridden pony's, and Delsie's silk blouse was stuck to her chest like a tattoo. She was a fearsome-looking creature, stern and intense. But what unnerved me was the glacial intensity of her eyes. They held menace. And then I noticed something that really frightened me. The .45 was in my hand, locked and cocked.

*   *   *

After closing up the boat I walked back to the *Jerome*, sporting a dish towel turban, and a chartreuse tube top that I'd rummaged from a drawer under the guest bunk. I was carrying my little plastic bag of paper shreddings, and I must have looked like a wet bilge rat, because Geoffrey didn't recognize me at first when he intercepted me at the top of the gangway.

"Don't ask," I threatened as I swept past him and headed for the luxury of a warm shower, body soap and hair conditioner. It was one of those rare times when shaving my legs actually felt good; like I was scraping off something nasty.

I told Delsie about Lt. Okun and Khaki-pants, without mentioning the envelope, and we agreed that Raul's assessment had been on the money. We were up against some very determined people, and it was clear that we couldn't afford to trust anyone. Next came a light snack of lemon tea and crumpets, followed by a much needed nap.

Delsie was busy, so she had Geoffrey wake me up around six, which was a bit disconcerting since I had slipped out of my clothes and was sleeping in the buff. But I came to appreciate why Delsie felt so secure with her crew. It must have been like that in the Oriental harems. The wives, the concubines and the eunuchs. Total trust. No threat of sexual invasion.

When I arrived topside I noticed that the crew had expanded dramatically. A half dozen deckhands in crisp white uniforms were setting up tables and chairs, and a catering crew was organizing floral arrangements, ice sculptures, a well stocked bar, and platters of cold hors d'oeuvres.

"Are we expecting many guests?" I asked Delsie, not sure how I'd hold up under the strain of playing hostess.

"After a fashion," she said. "But there's nothing to worry about, Sugar. I've got everything under control. Just leave it to me."

I didn't have much choice in the matter, so I decided to order a martini and relax. The bartender was a magician. That first drink went down like water, so I decided to have another.

The evening air was just beginning to cool off when a Cadillac limousine arrived from Stanek's. Two chauffeurs dressed in black from head to toe got out, and solemnly carried the white boxes of ash up the gangway. Delsie showed them to a table beside the bar, where they deposited each box in the middle of a wreath woven from dark green, palmate leaves.

As the limo drove off, a charter bus pulled up. Leaving the diesel engine running in characteristic style, the driver got out with a dozen eager young men, and opened the luggage gates. The young men immediately unloaded a large number of battered black boxes of various shapes and sizes, and started hauling them aboard.

"Those healthy specimens are from one of the fraternities at Florida International University," Delsie said. "I've hired them to tote our guests' luggage and. Then, while we're at sea, I've arranged for them to be fed and entertained at a strip club down the boulevard."

"Delsie!"

"Don't get your panties in a wad, Sugar. They're all of age, and it's a very classy club. I've been there a time or two myself. Nothing too risqué. More like the highbrow showgirl revues in Vegas. Art rather than porn. The music is first rate, and since these bright young fellows are all music majors, they found my offer most appealing."

"You expect them to listen to the music?"

"Sugar, who ever said that you can't have your cake and eat a slice of pie too?"

The luggage was being carried to the aft upper sun deck, behind the bridge and stack, and the fraternity boys seemed as happy as colts.

Then I noticed that the driver was helping a covey of tuxedoed septuagenarians off the bus, one at a time. Assisted by the music majors whenever necessary, the elderly men made their slow way up the gangplank. The first to gain the deck was a sprightly old chap who gave Delsie a big hug and pecked her on the cheek.

"Good evening, Ms. Delsie," he said.

"I'm so happy that you could come!" she replied.

"Well, that cushy, air conditioned bus that you sent made it all possible, and the assistance that these fine young men are providing is very much appreciated."

"Bob, you know that they love you," she purred. "They wouldn't have missed this for the world."

"That's nice to hear, Ms. Delsie, and I'm sure that it's true, but the rumor on the bus says that these young fellows are going to see the show while we're out. Some things never change. Thank goodness for that."

Delsie smiled and turned to me.

"Jean," she began the introduction, "I'd like you to meet my favorite musician, Mr. Bob Roberts. Mr. Roberts, this is Dr. Jean Pearson."

Mr. Roberts greeted me with the gentlest of smiles.

"Much though I enjoy Ms. Delsie's company," he said, "I'm terribly sorry that we have to meet under such sorrowful circumstances, Ms. Jean, and although I didn't know either of them personally, I'm certain that your father and uncle were fine men. You must miss them terribly. Please know that the boys and I want to do whatever we can to lighten your burden this evening. We'll do our level best, and if something special should happen to strike you, please let us know, and we'll try to accommodate your wishes."

"Thank you, Mr. Roberts," I replied. "Your condolences are very much appreciated, as is your kindness. I'm honored to have you all aboard with us this evening."

"You all?" he said with a grin, taking my hands and squeezing them gently. "Down South we say *y'all*, Ms. Jean, so you're clearly not from around here. But then, neither am I. We'll just make that our little secret."

He released my hands and looked at Delsie once again.

"What did you decide?" she asked.

"We're going to use Benny Goodman's 1934 arrangement," he answered, "but we'll have to slow it down and tailor it a little because Ms. Lilly wants to use the vocal stylings that she worked out for Ella's 1955 recording with Sachmo."

"It should be wonderful."

"I see that Ms. Lilly's van is here," he said excitedly. "If you ladies will excuse me, I'd like to go down and greet her."

"Of course."

When he'd gone about half way down the boarding ramp I took Delsie by the arm and whispered, "Who *is* he?"

"Cretin," she sniffed haughtily. "He is a Florida institution—what they call a living national treasure in Japan—Mr. Bob Roberts, of the Bob Roberts Society Band. His is a group of gifted elderly musicians who are keeping the music of the Big Band Era alive. They play irregularly, often outdoors in orange groves, and they draw crowds like you wouldn't believe. For the fun of it. For the music. For the love. They've organized something special for this evening, and that's all that I'm going to say."

The driver of the van and Mr. Roberts helped a tiny, ancient, but very animated black woman into a wheelchair, and escorted her up the ramp.

"Ms. Delsie, Ms. Jean," Mr. Roberts said when they were safely on deck, "I have the high honor and tremendous personal privilege of introducing Ms. Lilly Lane Cordele. Ms. Lilly..."

"Which one of you beautiful young girls owns this great big ol' boat?" Miss Lilly interrupted him.

"I do, Ms. Lilly," Delsie said. "Welcome aboard."

"Umm, uum, um! It's sho 'nuff perty," Miss Lilly declared, taking Delsie's hand in her left. Then she reached for mine with her right.

"So child, you must be Ms. Jean," she said in the most compassionate voice that I'd ever heard. "Hunny, the good Lord gives, and the good Lord takes away from all of us. Don't matter if you're black or white, rich or po'. Times like this hurts our hearts to the root. I knows jus' how you feel, child. I surely do; 'cause I's done lost all my folks, too. So hunny, I'm 'a' goin' to pray for you some, and sing for you some, and cry with you some, too, and you and me is goin' to be sisters."

I was so touched that I hardly knew what to say, but that didn't matter because Miss Lilly went right on with other concerns.

"Mr. Bob Roberts, where do I..."

"Up there." He pointed to an area behind the bridge.

She gave the aft upper sun deck a long stare and shook her head.

"I sho hope you got a strong back for haulin' old ladies," she scolded.

"Not to worry, Ms. Lilly," Delsie cut in. "Mama had a chair lift installed for Daddy when his emphysema got bad. When the time comes, I'll be happy to take you up myself."

"Child, you're a blessing to me," said Miss Lilly. "You truly are. Praise the Lord for you! Now I've got one more question to ask."

"Yes, ma'am?"

"I want y'all to know that I'm a God-fearing woman, and a servant of the Lord; always have been, and hope always to be. But I'm a Methodist, not a hardline Baptist or Evangelical. And I ain't no Holy Roller, neither. So if you children would be so kind as to direct me, where are the libations?"

"Ms. Lilly," chuckled Mr. Roberts, "it will be my pleasure to accompany you there."

"You come too, child," Miss Lilly said to me.

"I'll be happy to join you in a minute or two," I replied.

When Mr. Roberts had Miss Lilly happily ensconced at a table near the bar, I turned to Delsie.

"Give with the details," I demanded.

"Not everyone with great talent or skill makes it to the top," Delsie said. "In Ms. Lilly's case, she lacked the flexibility to succeed in the music business of the 30s and 40s. What that means is that she had a husband and five children, and refused to travel from club to club on the back roads, leaving her family to fend for themselves. So she sang in small country churches, and nearby roadhouses mostly. Yet she an extraordinary gift. She had a lush set of pipes, but she also had the ability to stylize, to improvise, to bend notes in ways that no one had ever thought of before. Grown men cried when they heard her sing. Women swooned. Her music went straight to the core of their souls. Something like that can't be hidden, any more than you could hide a Shania Twain or a Kenny G. So she became a kind of folk legend, and the great ones came to visit Ms. Lilly at her farm in south Georgia. Some came to listen. Still others came to learn. Billie Holiday. Mahalia Jackson. Sarah Vaughn. Lena Horne. And she sang with them, and they were good to her. Now she lives in a retirement home outside Pompano Beach. Why don't you sit with her for a spell? The stories you'll hear!"

A number of guests now arrived on foot, having left their cars in the parking lot. Most had been at Stanek's the night before. I was relieved to see that Carl and Ingrid Rehm were not part of the crowd, and extremely pleased when Arte Peebles introduced his wife, Laura. She was unsteady on her feet, and appeared terribly fatigued.

"I wouldn't have missed this for the world," she wheezed.

*   *   *

The crew was busy casting off lines, and Raul was using the side thrusters to ease the *Jerome* away from the pier, so I invited Laura Peebles to join us at Miss Lilly's table. As it turned out, Miss Lilly hailed from Albany, Georgia, the home of that unfortunate woman who had been killed in the Olympic Park bombing in Atlanta. But Miss Lilly did not want to dwell on that, because Albany had an illustrious musical history.

"Ray Charles was born there," she informed us. "So was Harry James."

While I listened to her captivating stories about the heyday of Jazz and Big Bands, the sky began to take on the tangerine pinks of sunset, and I noticed that a lot of smaller boats were getting under way as well. But I paid no attention to them because it was officially the weekend, after all, and in calm weather boat people do like to boat.

As we passed the sea buoy, and crossed from the shallows to the deep water, where the waves turned from aqua to azure, Delsie came and escorted Miss Lilly to the elevator.

"It won't be long now, Sugar," Delsie said upon returning. "I wish that I could have stayed here with you, but I had to play the dutiful hostess. Tell me about Ms. Lilly's wonderful stories."

So we chatted for a little while, until we felt the engines die off.

"Now?" I asked timidly.

Delsie nodded sadly.

Panic suddenly enveloped me like a thickening arctic mist. My hands turned cold and clamy, I felt disoriented, and I started shaking.

"Delsie, I don't even remember what I'm supposed to do," I protested. "I feel kind of numb; kind of nauseous."

"Not to worry, Sugar. You only have to do one thing. I'll take care of everything else. Just stay right beside me, and I'll tell you when it's over."

We walked to the aft rail, and I got a terrible fright. Fanned out behind us, like the spreading feathers of a peacock's tail, were the soft navigation lights—all green, and red, and white—of sixty or seventy boats, each crammed absolutely full with well-dressed people standing still and facing us in reverential silence. A thousand mourners or more, gathered on a quiet, darkening sea, to wish Dad and Uncle Bud farewell.

Delsie saw the fear in my eyes, the whiteness of my knuckles as I grasped the iron railing, and whispered, "It's all right, Sugar. Come on."

The crew had attached a heavy chrome ladder to special cleats on the stern of the vessel, and Delsie eased down it in the murky half-light of dusk as the band began to play a melancholy tune that I knew, but could not name.

A muted trombone took the lead, supported by a tenor saxophone that cried with every note.

I inched down the ladder next, followed by Raul, and found myself standing on a slatted, teak swim platform, just inches above the water. Then Geoffrey passed the first of the white boxes to us as a lonely clarinet took the melancholy tune, improvised an octave above the score, spiraled down, oh, so gently, and handed it with tender affection to Miss Lilly.

With steel brushes swishing a plaintive rhythm on a snare drum, mellow brass weeping a soft counterpoint in the background, and the clarinet backing the melody like a mezzo-soprano, Miss Lilly began to sing.

We lived our little drama...

Raul handed Uncle Bud's ashes to me as Delsie untied the ribbon and rustled the stiff rice paper off the box. I glanced up toward Miss Lilly, then looked at Delsie with a questioning expression.

"The way Mama tells it," she said, "your father was walking along the dock one day, whistling this tune, and so Daddy invited him aboard for a drink. That's how they met and became friends. *Stars Fell on Alabama* was always Daddy's theme song. It was one of your dad's favorites, too."

I nodded in appreciation, and got swept away in a tidal wave of memories. Then, sliding the lid off the box, I said goodbye to Uncle Bud as Miss Lilly's words came to me like a kiss.

I can't forget the glamour,
       your eyes held a tender light...

Raul offered us the other box, and Delsie helped me to unwrap it. I just crouched there like a stone, frozen in a horrifying moment that stretched into all eternity, and then I watched helplessly as my trembling hands slid the cover off, as my arms reached out with love, as Dad slipped silently away. Miss Lilly told the tale.

> *I never planned*
> *in my imagination*
> *a situation*
> *so heavenly...*

We climbed back up the ladder to the aft deck, where Geoffrey joined us with a silver tray holding several big tumblers of clear liquid over cracked ice.

"Boodles." Delsie smiled painfully. "Your dad's favorite brand of gin. So here's to him, and here's to Uncle Bud."

As we lifted our glasses, one and all, the band brought the music to a sweet conclusion while Miss Lilly sang the final phrase.

> *...and stars fell on Alabama that night.*

Then the members of the band put their instruments aside, stood silently, and joined us in our toast.

I looked around as the last rays of the sun winked out. It was as though I were floating in a dream. All those boats, all those lights, all those people; all come to say goodbye to Dad and Uncle Bud on a calm, deep blue sea. They would have liked that. A deep blue goodbye.

The ceremony appeared to be over, but then an indistinct little sound, a murmured *tink-link*, began wafting across the water. At first, I wasn't really sure if I heard it or not. Then it grew in intensity, and grew, and grew, and then it was behind me and around me too. I turned slowly, and realized that everyone had drained their tumblers, and had·raised their arms high, rattling the ice in their glasses in a final, elegant salute.

Delsie had managed it perfectly. She'd given me the release that I'd needed so badly, and she'd replaced the horrible images of Dad's death with splendorous memories of his passing. Oh, I snuffled quite a bit more, and my eyes were red and puffy, but mostly I felt a sense of wonder, as though one life had ended with dignity, and another were about to begin.

8

Geoffrey woke me up at dawn the next morning, just as I had asked him to, and placed an ordinary cardboard carton on the nightstand beside my bed.

"I had to find an all-night grocery, Miss Jean," he said. "Now, let me see. Half a dozen clipboards, a bag of rubber bands, two rolls of three-quarter-inch Scotch invisible tape, and a black Sharpie pen. Was that everything, Miss Jean?"

"Yes," I said as I yawned and stretched. "Thank you very much, Geoffrey. I appreciate all of the trouble that you went to."

He opened the drapes and tied them back, flooding my stateroom with fresh morning light. "Oh, it was nothing, Miss Jean. Really. May I assist you in some way?"

"No, I don't think so. Thank you just the same. My, but that's a beautiful sunrise this morning. Isn't it lovely? So pale and clean. Like a lemon daiquiri."

"Oh, yes, ma'am. A lemon daiquiri sunrise. Clear and bright. A gorgeous day. Good sailing weather. Perhaps you'd care for some decaf, and a basket of my cinnamon-pecan swirls? I can whip some up in a jiffy."

"No, thank you," I repeated. "I think I'll just wait until breakfast."

He returned to the cardboard carton, picked it up gingerly, removed each and every item, inspected them as though they were something foreign, then laid them on the nightstand as if he were arranging a formal table setting.

"A little fruit perhaps?" he suggested. "I have some nice fresh kiwi and papaya, and there are seedless red grapes left over from last night. I might even find a pineapple if I look hard enough."

"Later, thanks."

"Tea? I can brew a fresh pot."

"No."

"Well, all right then. Just buzz me if you need anything. I'll be in the galley."

He stepped out into the companionway, and pulled the door almost closed. I could see that he was trying to think of one more bit of friendly repartee which might gain him access to my secret, but he couldn't invent anything plausible to say, so the latch finally clacked into place.

Geoffrey's curiosity was eating him alive, but I had two important things that I wanted to do alone, so I pulled the plastic bag from under the bed, dumped its contents on the covers, and pressed Memory-12 on my cell-phone.

I breezed through Coast Guard protocol, and then the patch clicked.

"L'Ouverture," barked the voice on the other end.

"Good morning, Commander. It's Jean Pearson," I announced as I started fussing with the riot of paper on my bed.

"Ah, good morning, Doctor. I am glad that you called. I wanted to tell you that the funeral service was lovely."

"You were there?"

"Under cover; in mufti. With a few of my very best people in what looked like just another pleasure craft. We took photographs of virtually everyone who attended, surreptitiously, of course, with telephoto lenses and infrared film. It's a tried and true investigative technique. Arsonists often linger to watch the infernos that they set, and murderers have been known attend the funerals of their victims, so if we photograph the crowds at similar events, occasionally we get lucky."

"And how's your luck running? Anything new?"

"Unfortunately, no," he sighed. "There were a great many small vessels at the service, most of them filled to capacity. I am sure that we could have issued a dozen citations for overloaded watercraft, lack of adequate flotation devices and so forth, but that was not our mission. We were there merely to observe, and we saw nothing overtly suspicious. However, one vintage boat did attract my attention—a 1938 Chris-Craft Custom Runabout, meticulously restored—because there was only one person on board. Sigmon Curlee."

"Is that significant?"

"Not in itself, no. But I ran a criminal records check on him, and it turns out that he was something of a rowdy in his younger days. He was arrested twice in July of 1973 for assault and battery, and assault with a deadly weapon. It seems that he resented the attention that another fellow was paying to a certain JoBeth Tadlock. The first time he tried to settle the matter with his fists. That approach evidently failed, because then he dented the other fellow's skull with a monkey wrench. As a consequence, Mr. Curlee served 6 months of an 18-month sentence at the Indian River Correctional Institution. He was also suspected in the sinking of the other man's fishing trawler. Somebody boarded her one night and opened the sea cocks, causing her to flood and sink while tied to the pier. But Mr. Curlee was never charged. Miss Tadlock gave him an airtight alibi. And you, Dr. Pearson? Have you discovered anything new?"

"Not, really. We've confirmed that Dad and Uncle Bud were on their way to the Keys when they were killed, but I don't think that they were going fishing because all of Dad's reels were in the shop for servicing."

"We?"

"I'm staying with a friend," I said as I sorted the paper strips according to color, "primarily because there's been so much trouble."

"What kind of trouble?"

I told him about the break-ins, and the Blues Brothers.

"Dr. Pearson," he said, "I am afraid that there is a great deal going on here that we do not understand, and I also fear that you may be in some real danger. I do not wish to see you place yourself in harm's way, so please ignore my earlier request for assistance. It was clumsy of me. The funeral is over now, so what more can you hope to accomplish here? Perhaps you should go home and resume your practice."

"You're probably right," I conceded. "My employees are worried, and I really should get back to the clinic."

"Yes. I support that idea, and to make it less painful for you, I will promise to keep you informed of any progress that we make. I am not going to let this go, Miss. I will find the assassin, eventually."

I thanked him for his kindness and dedication, said a polite goodbye, and hung up. Then came the hard part.

*   *   *

Later on, I met Delsie for brunch in the yacht's main saloon. Raul was sitting off to one side, nursing a huge toby mug of steaming black coffee. The mug was shaped like a pirate's head, complete with black beard, tricorn hat and eyepatch.

"I thought that we might hold our discussion in here," Delsie began, "just to be safe. Help yourself to whatever you want."

I fixed a cup of chamomile tea, and put a slim, almond biscotti on the saucer. A four-color AAA map of Florida lay unfolded on the table, with a long inset box showing the Overseas Highway as it snakes across the viaducts and islands, out through Florida Bay and the Keys. There were also two marine navigation charts, with a tracing paper overlay.

"Here it is, Sugar," said Delsie, pointing with a bright pink fingernail to a red-penciled circle on one of the charts. "Greene Key, off the southeastern tip of Long Key. Narrow slip of a thing. Not big enough to be labeled on the road map. It's about 125 miles from Lauderdale as the seagull flies.

A couple of years ago it was the focus of a brief ecological controversy. Raul will explain."

"I'll be happy to, Miss Delsie," he chimed in.

Raul put down his mug of coffee, and picking up a long pair of plotting dividers, which he used as a pointer.

"Until fairly recently, Greene Key was a part of Long Key State Park," he began. "But two years ago the Army Corps of Engineers conducted a survey in preparation for the building of new storm control jetties, and they discovered that Greene Key lay outside the park's perimeter, rather than inside as had long been believed.

"The original survey was done in 1903, when Henry Flagler was building the East Coast Railroad Extension out across the islands to Key West. In those days the surveyors used a theodolite—a little spirit-level telescope mounted on a wooden tripod—along with classical Euclidian geometry, and a lot of old-fashioned shirtsleeve mathematics. Their results were generally excellent, but not this time. Who knows what went wrong? The survey team may have been ill with malaria or yellow fever. A lot of the laborers were, you know. It was a difficult time to be making a living in the swamps; the same time that the Panama Canal was being built; Teddy Roosevelt's era."

He stopped to take a long swallow of coffee.

"At any rate," he went on, "the Corps of Engineers uses laser transits and laptop computers today, and the Army discovered that the southwestern geodetic benchmark, from which all of the southern boundary lines were drawn, was out of position by several inches. That error didn't affect the western property lines very much, but the line that the oldtime surveyors had projected eastward from the southwestern benchmark, using two other benchmarks for triangulation, was off by thirty-two feet on the opposite side of Long Key. As a result, the original park property line intersected Greene Key off the coast, but just barely.

"When the Long Key State Park boundaries were being set, the rule was that any outlying Key intersected by a park boundary line within a mile of

Long Key would fall under the dominion of the park. The oldtime surveyors' line touched on Greene Key, so as a consequence it became an annex of Long Key State Park. The modern laser transit, however, missed Greene Key by fifty-five feet. Therefore, Greene Key ceased to be a part of Long Key State Park. At least in theory."

"I think I understand," I interrupted him, "but how did the misplacement of a benchmark by a few inches translate into such a big error?"

"It's a matter of angles. Have you ever fired a rifle?"

"I'm a pretty good shot," I replied.

"Okay. What happens when you move the muzzle of your rifle a quarter of an inch when you're aiming at a target a hundred meters away?"

"The bullet lands a foot or two off target."

"Same principle. Surveying is a bit like constructing a series of triangles, and the benchmarks are the points. Move a benchmark..."

"And everything else is off line."

"That's right," he confirmed, finishing his coffee. "The original benchmark was misplaced, the angles were all off, the property lines got skewed, and the further the park boundary line was projected from its primary point of origin, the bigger the discrepancy became."

"So what happened?"

"Well, there might have been a real catfight over the disposition of the island, but before the environmental community got wind of the survey error, Greene Key was sold to a private development company by the State of Florida's Land Management Services Bureau. Representative Marion Baedeker from Monroe County, who chairs the Ways and Means Committee, convened a special meeting of the Emergency Revenues Task Force in Tallahassee. Citing a little-known statue from 1899, which grants the chairman of Ways and Means unlimited power to sell off excess nonagricultural state lands, he pushed a motion through the Emergency Funding Task Force Subcommittee, calling for the immediate sale of Greene Key. The whole thing was precooked, and only took about six or seven minutes from gavel to gavel. Later that afternoon, the ownership of Greene Key was transferred to a newly formed land development corporation for seven hundred and fifty thousand dollars, much to no one's surprise."

"You remembered all of that from two years ago?"

"Dr. Pearson," Raul stated with pride, "I am a life member of The World Wildlife Fund, Greenpeace, The Sierra Club, Save the Whales and Dolphins, The Florida Panther Society, Save Our Everglades, and Adopt-A-Manatee. Oh, the environmental community was outraged by the slam-bam sale of Greene Key, of course, but what could we do? The state's sovereignty worked against us, as did the fact that the issue in question was far too small to warrant a full-scale blitz by the tree-huggers. Too much outlay of enviro-dollars for too little return. No bang for the buck. And besides, we'd have been leaving the gate after the race had already been run. Then there was Florida's annual budget crisis, which was pretty severe that year. The state was being pressured by powerful business interests to divest itself of unessential real estate. Baedeker played on that, and was touted as a hero in the press."

"And he's from Monroe County?"

"Yes. The Keys are officially part of Monroe County. People often think that the Keys are an adjunct of Dade County because they run south from Miami along Highway One, but Monroe County includes almost everything offshore; every landform in Florida Bay from East Cape to Key Largo to Fiesta Key, and from there down to Key West."

"I didn't know that," said Delsie, looking at the map, "but one thing's for sure. We're on the right track."

"Lt. Okun?" I asked.

"Lt. Okun," she affirmed.

"So when do we leave for Greene Key?" I inquired. "I want to find out what Dad and Uncle Bud were searching for. I want to find out why they were murdered. But most of all, I want to find out who killed them. I want to get the bastard."

"Sunset will be soon enough," Delsie replied, picking up another piece of melba toast. "I spread the word last night that I'm taking you cruising for a week or two, Sugar. North toward Charleston; maybe even to Newport News. I wasn't all that specific. I said that we'd play it by ear. Everyone agreed that it's a splendid idea, so we have our cover story in place."

"Wonderful. But cruising? Why not drive? It's faster."

"There are a lot of reasons," she began as though making a sales pitch. "In the first place, there's luxury. Why put up with public accommodations and hotel food when we can bring this floating palace along? In the second place, security. The *Jerome* sails with three very dedicated bodyguards. In the third place, mobility. We're talking about the Keys, after all. The best routes, virtually the only routes, are by water. If we need a car, we can lease one. In the fourth place, communications. We've got a full range of commercial marine radios on board, and we have our own satellite uplink for telephones, data and fax. Daddy ran his business empire from here, so we also have a new Macintosh computer with all of the peripherals, including video conferencing. And lastly, perhaps most importantly, there's image."

"Huh?"

"We've got to project the appropriate image, Sugar. We'll do far better if we arrive on a yacht, believe me. There are a lot of fresh young women in south Florida driving Maseratis and Ferraris and such, but virtually no one commands a vessel like the *Jerome*. We're going to be asking a lot of questions, and people who have big money get answers."

"Privileges of wealth?"

"Privilege?" she said with a flip of her hair. "Privilege has nothing to do with it. Daddy taught me when I was just a pee-tad that wealth is the master key that opens all doors. Wealth isn't about privilege, Sugar. Wealth is about power. Wealthy people have money to spend, and other people, especially sales people, want that money. Most of them want it badly. So the wealthy get to call the tune, and the others have to dance. It's all in knowing which tune to whistle."

"It sounds a bit manipulative."

"Listen here, Sugar. You can take that politically correct, anti-manipulative crap and stow it. When David Copperfield manipulates rabbits, it's called prestidigitation. The masses are happily hoodwinked, they pay handsomely for it, and they applaud. When a chiropractor manipulates your spine it's called therapy. You feel better, and you pay. In my spare time this summer I've been massaging egos from Galveston to Palm Beach so that I can manipulate other people's money to build a new children's orthopedic wing in Mobile. And don't forget; someone manipulated the explosives that killed your family. The whole world is one gigantic game of mutual manipulation. I'm just playing with a pat hand."

Delsie clearly wasn't in the best of moods.

"Something wrong?" I asked.

"Thirteen hundred and seven grams," she snapped angrily, flipping a piece of dry toast across the linen tablecloth. "I've gained thirteen hundred and seven grams in the last two weeks. That's nearly three pounds, and I am absolutely determined to walk it all off. Right now. Today."

Raul rolled his eyes toward the ceiling as though he'd heard this lament a hundred times before, concocted a transparent excuse about checking the supply manifest with Geoffrey, and left without further comment.

"What about Greene Key?" I asked.

"Sugar, I need a real workout," she grumped, "and the best exercise that I can think of is to go shopping. It will do wonders for my disposition, and it wouldn't hurt yours either. We're due for some recreation. We'll go downtown first, to the specialty stores, and then we'll do every mall in greater Lauderdale. There's a cute li'l swimwear shop up in Boca that I just know you'll just adore. You brought plastic, I presume?"

"Of course."

"Good. We'll charge everything. You're in desperate need of a wardrobe, and although I'm more than happy to lend you mine in a pinch, you don't exactly…"

"Fill yours out properly?"

"Sugar, we've both got the same stuff," she cooed in that honeyed tone that only Southern women can affect. "It's just that the good Lord stretched yours out farther, and bunched mine up some."

"If that's meant as a kindness, thank you."

"Jean," Delsie confided in a tone laced with pain, "let me share something with you. When I was a little girl I wanted to grow up to be beautiful, just like my Mama. Well, I got my wish, and some sarcastic angel threw in voluptuous as well. Now I'm right good looking, as they say. I know it, I'm proud of it, and I like to flaunt it. But secretly, I've always been envious of you."

"Of me?" I said in surprise, nearly splattering the table with Clamato juice. "Why?"

"Sugar, you're tall, and lean, and refined, but not the least bit skinny. You've got the kind of legs that men can't resist, and that dash of red in your hair gives you sparkle. You've got an open face like Claudia Schiffer, but more mature, more feminine. Okay, so your hips aren't as broad as mine, your butt's a little flatter, and you wear a C cup to my D, but if I could wave a magic wand I'd change places with you in a heartbeat."

"If you're trying to solicit my sympathy, don't bother. I've seen the way that men look at you. You're gorgeous, you poor thing. You attract hunks the way blood attracts sharks."

"True enough; but the wrong ones. Let me tell you what it's like to be built this way. Most men look at me with the kind of lust that they feel for a Porsche. They love the lines, they love the design, they love what they imagine is under the hood. But they fear that the price of the ride is too high, or they fear the power of the motor, so they go away without ever opening the door. The few that do hang around are on usually on some kind of machismo trip. They want to take it out for a test drive. They want to run their hands along the fender, squeeze the upholstery, slip their gearshift into Hi, and slide around the curves in a hot sweat; then race it home, jam on the brakes and hop out. They think that they've proved something, that they've conquered something, so they leave the engine all hot and steamy, and never buy. Oh, no, Sugar, I'd trade chassis with you any time. You attract bright, steady guys, like Peter. I attract thrill-seeking, would-be race car drivers."

"Is it really that bad, Delsie?"

"You don't hear my phone ringing off the hook, do you? Did you see anyone with his arm around me last night? See any frilly cards stuck in the frame of my mirror? See a dozen roses anywhere with a note in them? I'm just eight months younger than you, and the only proposals that I got last year were so indecent that I won't even repeat them."

So we spent the day shopping, and Delsie was right. I needed everything. Raul came with us, of course. He followed us around in his custom van, and it was a good thing, too, for not only did we gain a sense of personal security, but we needed his cargo space for what soon became known as "The Great Haul." When we returned to Bahia Mar he used his electronic gate pass to gain entrance to the pier and drive down next to the *Jerome*, while Delsie parked Emillio in her reserved space in the main parking lot. Then we walked to the yacht.

It was a beautiful summer's eve. The sky was clear and blue, there was a gentle breeze blowing, children's laughter was in the air, the whole world tasted of salt, and there was the all-American aroma of burgers on the fire. It felt good to be alive. And yet, my every thought was tainted by incertitude and rage. Someone had killed my family. I wasn't sure who, or why, but I did know one thing. I wanted to get even.

9

For the second time in twenty-four hours the Jerome was slicing through the waters of Fort Lauderdale bay, negotiating Port Everglades channel, passing the John Lloyd Jetty and steaming beyond the sea buoy into the broad Atlantic Ocean. But the feeling was altogether different this time. Sadness and dread had given way to a defiant sense of anticipation.

"Raul reports that everything is in order," Delsie said as we ate dinner on the fantail. "The fuel and fresh water tanks are topped off, Geoffrey has stocked the galley with a month's worth of provisions, and Mikey says that all systems are good to go."

"So we're all set?" I asked.

"All set," she confirmed. "Raul is putting the *Jerome* on a lazy northerly track until we're over the horizon after dark, to deceive any interested parties who might be watching, and then he'll swing around to starboard and set a fast course for the Keys."

"Ever the covert operative," I commented with a shake of my head.

"Isn't he a dream?"

Delsie set a beautiful table. In the center of a slate blue linen damask cloth sat three luminous, sea green candleholders of Hungarian hand-blown crystal, which were nested in a colorful wildflower spray. The flatware was made of burnished Congolese bronze with inset ebony handles, and the bone china was a Noritake pattern aptly called

Opulence. The bell-shaped Waterford stemware was edged with gold, and the salt and pepper mills were part of an antique Castillian silver service which Delsie's grandmother had brought with her from Spain.

Dinner consisted of Portobello mushrooms and Vidalia onions sauteed in olive oil and garlic, endive and cherry tomato salad with balsamic vinaigrette, chicken limonese, steamed broccoli, French bread, and a carafe of Signorello Founder's Reserve Sauvignon Blanc '91. For dessert there were Bartlett pear halves, lightly poached in Port wine, and served with a generous sprinkling of freshly ground cloves. A melon baller had been used to remove the pith, and the resulting depressions were filled with softened Edam cheese. Bitter Brazilian coffee and butter mints followed.

"You were right," I conceded as I dabbed at my lips with an Irish linen napkin. "This is the way to travel."

"Yes," Delsie grinned, stretched her arms forward with fingers interlocked as though cracking her knuckles. "Ain't it the truth!"

The stars were coming out, and the lights of the coastline were twinkling merrily on the western horizon. It was a rare moment of serenity; a moment to be savored, and remembered.

"Raul plans to anchor off Greene Key sometime late tomorrow morning," Delsie said, "but we've got to solve a big problem first, Sugar. We still don't have any idea what we're looking for. We're not even certain that Greene Key is the right place to start. Have you had any new flashes of inspiration?"

"No blazing insights," I replied coyly, "but I do know that Greene Key is the right place."

"Oh?"

I reached underneath my chair, pulled a clipboard from Geoffrey's cardboard carton, and handed it to Delsie. On it were thirty-six strips of lined notebook paper, each a quarter-inch wide, all held in place with rubber bands and clear tape.

"What's this?" she asked. "I treat you to a starlit dinner that would tickle the fancy of any self-respecting gourmand, and you repay my superlative efforts with a gift of reconstituted office debris?"

"Do you remember the hostage crisis in Tehran?"

"Sugar, I was a mere child then," she huffed. "Fifth or sixth grade. It's not one of my strongest memories. In those days I was far less concerned with international politics than with persuading Mama to buy my first training bra."

"Well, I remember it vividly," I replied. "I watched the news every night, praying for the release of the hostages. I knew just how those people felt, being alone and afraid. I felt that way a lot when I was a child. Mom died the day after I was born, you know, and Dad never knew that I existed. No one even told me who my Dad was until I was fifteen. So I grew up as an orphan, raised by Mom's older sister, Rita, and her husband, as one of their healthy, raucous brood. In terms of age, I fit right in the middle. I was lucky, and I know that. They gave me everything that I needed. I had a loving home; good people. But I never really felt that I belonged. I felt kind of disconnected. It wasn't their fault. They were terrific. All of them. It was me. It's a hard thing to describe, Delsie, but when you're an orphan, you feel kind of vacant, almost forgotten. You feel abandoned.

"Anyway, I remember one news item in particular. Our embassy staff had put all of their official papers through shredders, in an unsuccessful attempt to destroy them, and a team of Persian carpet weavers was piecing all of those documents back together again, like some preposterous jigsaw puzzle, one skinny strip at a time. The video showed those young women using lots of clipboards with rubber bands wrapped around them to hold the little snippets of paper in place, while they figured out which shreds went together. Well, I found these strips in the wastebasket under Dad's desk."

"And now you've managed to reconstruct your father's boat maintenance list?" She squinted at the frayed document in her hand. "Sugar, how, exactly, does this help?"

"It doesn't. I also restored an advertising mailer from a video rental store, the draft of a letter to a stereo manufacturer, a dental bill for two rounds of root canal work, a fuel bill, a postcard from the library saying that a copy of *Without Remorse* was overdue, and several MasterCard charge slips—all of them worthless."

I paused for effect.

"And then, there was this."

I handed her a piece of notebook paper, neatly reassembled with transverse bands of Scotch tape. She looked at it, and frowned thoughtfully.

"If I read this scrawl correctly," she mused, "it says, *Rehm, flush accts., invest $, inquire con.* And there are three question marks. What do you suppose it means?"

"I don't know for certain, but it suggests that Carl Rehm was moving a lot of money around—investment money—flushing it through various accounts."

"Perhaps," she replied in a noncommittal sort of way. "Or it could be interpreted to mean that Rehm told your dad that his accounts were flush with funds, that he should invest some of his liquid assets, and that he should consider putting some of his money in Consolidated Something-or-other. Is this all you have?"

"No. I saved the best for last."

I handed Delsie yet another clipboard, and watched as she squinted at the heavily pleated page. Then a sly grin spread across her face as the realization set in.

"Your dad could have used a course in Palmer penmanship," she remarked as she studied his cramped scrawl, "but this mess says *green key* just as plain as day. There's the word *green*, followed by a drawing of an old-fashioned skeleton key. Then there are a lot of squiggles that are thoroughly indecipherable, and two upper case letters written in quasi-Germanic script. A few more squiggles. A line or two of curlicues. A little school of doodle fish. The word *mimosas*. More strange doodles. Another question mark."

She looked at me in a funny kind of way, and lifted one eyebrow as though she had smelled something sour.

"I think that it's a page of notes from a discussion that Dad had with Uncle Bud," I suggested. "It's certainly Dad's hand. He always liked to doodle when he was talking about something important. He said that doodling helped him to think; that he thought in pictures as well as in words."

"Go with it, Sugar," she said in an encouraging tone. "We've got nothing else to do this evening."

"The word *green* and the skeleton key are obvious enough, and the upper case letters are the initials for the name of Uncle Bud's cruiser."

"You're right!" Now we've got something to work with."

"The curlicues could represent waves, like the ocean. The fish might be a thought about their cover story. They told people that they were going fishing in the Keys, after all. Taken together, the curlicues and fish might symbolize their trip."

"Steady, girl," Deslie warned. "You're reaching."

We sat silently for a few minutes, each reviewing her own thoughts, while Delsie stared at the crinkled paper once again.

"On the other hand," she eventually offered, "the word *mimosas* is plain enough."

Then her face lit up like a searchlight.

"Geoffrey," she said, fingering a switch on the wireless intercom. "Will you look in the saloon and bring me the latest copy of *Floridays*?"

"Right away, Miss Delsie," came the cheerful reply.

Geoffrey arrived with fresh coffee and a magazine, which Delsie flipped through quickly.

"Sugar," she said as Geoffrey returned to the galley with the dirty dishes, "this li'l magazine is called *Floridays*. But it's not really a magazine at all. It's a right expensive promotional piece. Several of the premier real estate developers join forces to produce it, and the articles are actually advertisements in disguise. Here's one that you'll find pretty interesting. It's all about a wonderful new retirement community that is being built on Greene Key. Condos, clinic, cafeteria, golf course, pool, tennis courts, mini-mall, post office, ATMs, library, drug store, the works. It's called The Mimosas."

"The Mimosas?" I said. "Really? That's kind of cute. It's kind of lazy and relaxed sounding. But why would anyone want to name a retirement community after an orange juice cocktail?"

Delsie put her head back and just roared.

"Oh, Sugar," she laughed, tears streaming down her cheeks. "You're not a Damn Yankee after all. You're a Dumb Yankee."

"What did I say?"

"Jean, that drink was named for a darling li'l ol' tree. It grows wild all over the South, and it's a wonderfully dainty thing. It has skinny, dark leaves that look like long lady's fingers, and they're sort of fanned-out, like palm fronds, except that they aren't at all stiff or sharp on the ends. Mimosas are delicate, refined. The old people called them silk trees. But what everyone likes best about them is that they are absolutely covered with the most beautiful li'l ol'blossoms in the spring—all pink, and cream, and wine-colored—and they're so sheer that when you walk up to them, they kind of disappear. They're that special. The Seminole Indians claimed that Mimosa blossoms had magical powers; that they could make a person fall in love."

"That's it, then! Greene Key is the right place," I exclaimed.

"It looks that way."

"It has to be, because L'Ouverture told me that his mother was old island; that the retirement condo Uncle Bud was investigating was named for her favorite blossom, a passion flower. How many projects match that profile, and how many of them are located on Greene Key?"

"Well, only one, Sugar," Delsie replied thoughtfully, "mainly because there aren't any other projects on Greene Key. If you read the article, you'll find that The Mimosas is going to cover the entire island."

"What?"

"See for yourself."

I spent the next five minutes digesting every syllable of the promotional material about The Mimosas. Then, just as I finished, there was a loud screeching sound followed by a heavy, muffled bang.

"Raul, what was that?" Delsie demanded over the intercom.

"Checking."

We caught a brief wisp of caustic smoke, which smelled like my den after the power condenser in the television caught fire one time. It worried me, but Delsie looked more annoyed than alarmed.

"Well?" she demanded.

"Yes, ma'am," said Raul. "Mikey reports that the after portside bilge pump just quit. The motor burned out. He thinks that a cranky bearing may have put too much load on the brushes, causing an electrical short. The thermocouple must have failed as well. He won't know for sure until he takes it apart. There was some sparking down there, and some pretty nasty smoke, but no fire. There's nothing to worry about, Miss Delsie. The *Jerome* is as tight as a drum, and there are three other pumps. It's a minor inconvenience at worst."

"Minor or not," she said with obvious irritation, "I want that bilge pump repaired by tomorrow evening. And I want a brand new motor, Raul, not some ol' rebuilt piece of junk. If I learned anything at all from Daddy, it's that one never puts to sea with broken or substandard equipment."

"Greene Key is kind of isolated, Miss Delsie," he replied. "We won't find a bilge pump motor there."

"Maybe so, but Long Key is right next door, and it's only an hour and a half from there to Miami on Highway One." Delsie paused, and glanced at her watch. "It's just six minutes past eight. You have radios and cellphones. Use them."

"Aye, aye, ma'am. Right away, ma'am," he answered in crisp, military style.

She pushed the intercom key for the galley. "Geoffrey? Two tee-ninesy snifters of Courvoisier Initiale Extra, please."

"Yes, ma'am."

"Now, let's see," Delsie suggested as she flipped a thick coil of ebony hair from her face. "Why don't we repair to the upper sun deck, like proper ladies, sip our cognac, and work on our cover story for tomorrow."

10

The next morning was hot, hazy and muggy. There wasn't a breath of air stirring. Even the steady motion of the *Jerome* provided little in the way of a breeze, so at Delsie's insistence we donned our new swimwear and killed a couple of hours lounging on deck. Mine was a conservative little halter top and scoop bikini bottom, in a playful teal and pistachio print. Delsie's was a rather daring thong, made of the brightest banana yellow that modern science could devise, and against her cinnamon skin it shone like a beacon.

While skirting the anvil-shaped eastern peninsula of Long Key State Park, Raul invited us to the bridge to view something utterly spectacular. He grinned impishly when we arrived, and slowed the yacht's movement to a crawl.

"Out in the Bahama shallows," he began, "there are numerous examples of a curious phenomenon which local fishermen call a Blue Hole. A Blue Hole is a natural depression in the sea bed, where the bottom falls abruptly away in a round, vertical abyss, and the water is such an inky blue that it's almost black. Ancient maritime legends claim that Blue Holes are unfathomable, and they have become part of the modern Bermuda Triangle myth. We're about to cross over one now."

I looked out past the bow to a place where the turquoise waters suddenly turned to cobalt. Just ahead lay a mammoth circle of shadow; a virtual chasm in the bottom of the sea. Even in the tropical heat, the mere sight of it made a chill race up my spine.

"Of course," Raul assured us, "Blue Holes aren't really bottomless. Most run three or four hundred feet deep. This one, however, is a bit peculiar, in more ways than one. I chatted with some sport fishermen on the marine band a while ago, and they claim that their fish-finding sonar recorded a depth of over fourteen hundred feet. That's nearly three-fifths of a mile."

As we crossed over the lip of the abyss, Delsie and I stepped out to the end of the bridge wing and looked straight down. The sight which met our gaze was breathtaking. Beneath the buttery hull there wasn't any color at all; just deep, unending darkness. No fish cut through the water. No waves rolled across the surface. It was as though we were looking into the very gates of Hell. There was neither light nor life, and yet there was a terrifying power. The gaping maw seemed to be taunting us, beckoning us, willing us to jump overboard as it held our minds in its dark, hypnotic grasp. I felt as though I were in a trance, and I had to shake my head, violently, to break the spell.

"It's awesome," Delsie whispered, her eyes kind of wide and spacey.

"Yes, it is," said Raul. "The first time that you see a Blue Hole, you feel as though you are being sucked in. It has an unearthly way of draining your spirit. Mariners have always been a superstitious lot, and since before the days of Columbus they have refused to sail their ships across these frightful marvels."

"Before Columbus?"

"Most people don't know it, but the ancient Mayan Indians of Yucatan built large sailing vessels, and traded throughout these islands long before the Europeans arrived. In those early days the Carib Indians inhabited the Florida Keys—they were the indigenous people for whom the Caribbean Sea was named—and the Mayas told of Carib legends which identified Blue Holes as the sacred doorways to the realm of the ancient goddess of darkness. The legends claimed that whoever piloted his craft over a Blue

Hole and dared to look through its portal would be sucked into the chasm on his very next voyage, and would never be seen again."

"Oh, come on," Delsie chided him, in a tone which utterly lacked conviction. "You sound as though you actually believe this ridiculous mumbo-jumbo."

"Well now, Miss Delsie," he answered with a frown, "as Shakespeare said, 'there are more things in heaven and earth than are dreamt of in your philosophy.' All I can tell you for certain is that this particular Blue Hole is new, and that its magic is extremely powerful."

"Nonsense!" she scoffed. "If I want to be frightened by superstitious tommy-rot, I know a juju man in New Orleans who can drain the color from your hair!"

"Did you say that this hole is new?" I asked.

"Yes," Raul said. "It formed sometime last winter. It isn't even on the charts yet."

"Formed? How?"

"Most of Florida and this part of the sea lie on prodigious beds of limestone," he explained. "Limestone is relatively soft, and soluble in water. Over time, moving water erodes the more porous limestone, and underground caverns are formed. Eventually, the roofs of the caverns grow thinner, weaken and collapse. That's how Florida's infamous sinkholes emerge. The backcountry is literally pockmarked with them. Every year or two you see an item in the news about a sinkhole that has opened up, swallowing a house or a section of highway. Blue Holes are basically sinkholes that form on the bottom of the sea."

He pushed the throttle forward slightly, increasing our speed as we passed over the opposite rim of the crater, and I was relieved to be sailing on radiant, turquoise waves once again.

"In another forty-five minutes or so we'll be arriving off Greene Key," said Raul. "They don't have docking facilities for a yacht this large, and there isn't a channel deep enough for the *Jerome* either. According to the charts, we'll have to anchor about a mile and a half offshore."

"Is the Zodiac ready?" asked Delsie.
"It's trailing behind the swim board now."

*   *   *

An hour later the three of us were pounding through the waves in the Zodiac—a rubberized, black, inflatable boat driven by a 75hp Evinrude outboard motor. Raul was at the helm, smiling happily. Delsie and I were wearing light cotton sun dresses, hers misty rose, mine cornflower blue. We were holding our newly purchased Gucci sandals in one hand, and were using the other to keep our straw hats from blowing into the water. We must have made a comic pair, bouncing along on the inflated rubber tube that served as a seat. When Raul finally cut the boat's speed, we almost fell on our noses.

Raul had called ahead to announce our arrival, so a boyish administrative assistant was waiting to greet us.

"Please don't step in the water," warned the jovial young man who hailed us from a new wooden pier. "This cove is full of spiny urchins. They're kind of hard on the toes."

We had the minor misfortune of arriving at extreme low tide, so stepping up onto the dock proved something of a challenge. Our young host didn't seem to mind helping us, though, and I got the firm impression that he liked what he saw as he pulled us up to dock level.

"Miss Delsie," Raul said. "If you don't mind, ma'am, I'll be going back to the *Jerome* now, to help Geoffrey with the chores. Do you see that little flagpole at the far end of the dock?"

"I know, Raul," she replied with the bored, huffy air of a dilettante. "Run the li'l ol' flag up the pole when we're done, and you'll putter back in and pick us up."

Raul simply nodded, and motored away without comment. He was part of the act, too.

The deeply tanned administrative assistant led the way, and he showed us to an electric golf cart covered by a gold-fringed canopy.

"My name is Gary Ibsen," he said with boyish enthusiasm. "Welcome to Greene Key, the most convivial spot in the ocean. If you'd like, I'll be happy to give you a tour of the island before you meet with Mr. Finnegan."

It sounded like a good idea, so we spent the next uninspiring hour weaving along a gritty track that paralleled the shore, looking at signs announcing where The Mimosas' unbuilt facilities would eventually stand, and listening to the inane twaddle of Gary, our personal tour guide. According to him, Greene Key had once been a botanical paradise, a shrine for Native American cult activity, a refuge for the survivors of a storm-wrecked Spanish treasure galleon, a haven for pirates, a smugglers' den, a base for Confederate blockade-runners, a landing spot for Nazi saboteurs, and NASA had once considered Greene Key as the location for an emergency homing beacon to guide the Space Shuttle, should it lose power on takeoff and have to coast in for a water landing. Apparently, Gary subscribed to the same rigid code of ethics as the volunteer docents who give those stuffy tours in art museums: 'If you don't know the facts, make some up.' He did possess one redeeming virtue, however; a large, plastic Igloo cooler stocked with half-liter bottles of icy Poland Spring water.

While riding along, I couldn't help noticing Greene Key's wonderful diversity of flora and fauna. Clustered along the limestone beaches were impenetrable tangles of black mangroves, behind which stood elegant pal-mettos and royalpalms. Shimmering among the wind-blown grasses were dense clumps of goldenrod, orchids, sandwort and coralroot. Double-crested cormorants roosted in immense colonies along the shoreline, and there were also large numbers of white ibis, great blue herons, egrets and wood storks. Sharp claw marks in the ground hinted at the presence of raccoons, and it didn't take much imagination to envision that the waters were teeming with loggerhead turtles, snooks, tarpons, carditas, barracudas and manatees.

Then I saw something that turned my stomach. It wasn't the skeletal remnants of a fish or bird, where some predator had eaten its fill in nature's supremely choreographed dance of death and renewal. It was a dynamited lagoon, shattered limestone, the gentle earth scarred by bulldozer tracks, hundreds of sun-rotted eggs from a disrupted rookery, and a big, shiny sign announcing the site of the Mimosas' coming marina. The dredging of the boat channel, Gary told us proudly, would begin in two weeks.

"Where is everything?" Delsie finally asked in exasperation.

"Everything?" Gary responded.

"Everything," she bawled. "You know. The pool, the health spa, the mini-mall. I could really use an ice cold avocado salad right now, with white raisins and cashews, and I need to buy some different nail polish. The stuff I brought with me doesn't match my dress like I thought it did in the store. And besides, I left it open, and now it's too ookie."

She was playing her role to perfection.

"I'm afraid that most of the amenities aren't in place just yet," Gary replied. "The causeway to Long Key was only completed a few months ago, but the first twenty-four condominium units are now in place. They're all finished and ready for occupancy. Well, almost, that is. The water main is in, and the electrical and communications conduits are done, but the sewage pumping station won't be functioning until November."

"E-yewww!" Delsie squealed. "Whatever do y'all do?"

"We use Porta-potties," said Gary.

"E-yewww!"

There was a little more chit-chat, but as Delsie's supposed personal secretary, I kept out of it.

We finally arrived atop the island's tallest hill, some eighteen feet above sea level, where Gary showed us into a double-wide mobile home which served as The Mimosas' executive office and visitors center. In other words, we found ourselves in a construction trailer. Gary then introduced us to the Acquisitions Director, Sean Michael Finnegan, a rail-thin, balding, middle-aged man, who wore an open-neck vanilla shirt, several gold chains, a pea green gabardine suit and jade Hushpuppy shoes. Finnegan appeared weary and careworn, as though he'd been in sales too long, but his eyes were keenly focused, in an unhealthy kind of way, and his lips never quite closed. He reminded me of a caged boa constrictor at dinnertime, just waiting for the mouse to drop, except that he had the worst case of sunburn that I had ever seen on a redhead. It actually hurt to watch him move.

Finnegan invited us to sit on a reproduction Louis XVI brocaded settee, served up chalices of Bartles & James strawberry wine coolers, and offered an oviform sweetgrass basket of Pepperidge Farm Goldfish.

"Well, what do you think?" he asked.

"Dreadful!" replied Delsie. "Positively dreadful."

"Oh, you musn't be so hard on us, please," Finnegan laughed, searching for an angle. "We've only just begun construction. But it won't take long now that the road's in. Everything's modular, you see. The condominiums and townhouse suites are being made of pre-stressed, pre-fabricated concrete, like the hotels at Disney-MGM. They're as solid as Gibraltar. Virtually indestructible. There's a lot of experience in pre-fab construction here in South Florida. The units are being built up in Ocala, and they're shipped here by truck. All of the finishes and furnishings are pre-specified, so the building inspections are a breeze. And the amenities will start going up in another month or so."

"I'm looking for a comfortable place for Mama and Daddy," mewed Delsie with the most vapid expression she could muster. "Daddy says he wants to spend his winters down here. He says that the desert is too cold."

"That's perfect," said Finnegan. "If you pre-buy a suite for them right now, you'll get your choice of location, floor plan, level and view. Here, why don't we take a look at the scaled miniatures."

We stepped over to a felt-covered plywood table where two architectural models were on display. The first showed the layout of the entire island of Greene Key, complete with every condo, sidewalk and trash can. The second was a mockup of a condominium structure, with the back cut away so that you could see all of the furnishings. Miniature light bulbs glowed in the tiny fixtures. There were even little people watching television, and others playing cards at a dining room table. It was the most detailed doll house that I had ever seen.

"What do you think now?" asked Finnegan.

"I don't like the wallpaper in the dining area," whined Delsie. "It's too... I don't know... motel-looking, or something."

Finnegan was obviously an experienced salesman. He simply ignored Delsie's comment and cruised right on.

"Well," he beamed, "that's no problem, little lady. If you pre-buy now, you can pre-select all of the finishes. Wallpaper, carpets, window treatments, the works. You can even put in special requests for personal window styles and such. Why, I had a woman in here just yesterday who was dead set on having a big bay window and paneled wooden doors. She ordered them, too. Superior Court Judge Holloway requested an extra-wide picture window for his bedroom, so that he'll have a view of the golf course, even when he and his wife are having breakfast in bed. Yes, ma'am! You can set up your parents' condo any way you want. Here, let me give you some complimentary brochures, a video tape, and a map."

He reached into a cabinet, and handed Delsie a genuine cowhide valise that was fairly bulging with printed materials. There were drawings, floor plans, and all of the usual sales gadgets, along with a thermographed menu from one of the soon-to-be-built gourmet restaurants. There was even a booklet of discount coupons for the soon-to-be-built mini-mall.

"Have you sold any yet?" asked Delsie through a yawn. "Mama and Daddy like to party a lot. They don't want to live like hermits."

"See those twenty-four units out there?" Finnegan bragged. "That's Phase I, and it's all sold out. Being furnished right now. And those people

got a great deal, too. You can count on it! There will be eighteen phases of
condo construction in Mimosa Village, and more to come in Mimosa
Gardens. And you can get a great deal for your parents now, too, because
we've lowered the prices on pre-sales."

"How much for the biggest suite?"

"The Presidential? The pre-sale price is a mere $1,352,000. And your
parents would own their unit, of course. It's real estate, just like any townhouse or condo. They can sell it, bequeath it, whatever."

"I like it," said Delsie. "You got any gum?"

"Gum?" I don't know. "Let me see."

He got up and hustled to the other end of the trailer, where a pair of
small rooms served as offices. One of the office doors was closed, and we
could hear voices coming from inside. Finnegan disappeared through the
other, which had a neatly lettered sign marked *Sales*.

"Well, what do you think?" whispered Delsie.

"Are they kidding about the price?" I asked.

"Not in Florida, they're not. Lots of elderly people with real money
come here to retire. They're easy marks, so there's an expression in the
business community: You've got to fleece the old sheep, because mutton is
too hard to chew. Quaint, isn't it?"

Finnegan came back with two packs of gum—an open pack of
Doublemint, and a fresh pack of Big Red. Delsie selected the Big Red, and
dropped all of the wrappings on the floor as she crammed two sticks in her
mouth.

"May I see a specimen purchase contract and deed?" she slurred.

"Yes, ma'am." He'd seen dim-witted rich girls before, and he was sure
that he could sell this one.

Delsie looked at the paperwork, read all of the fine print, out loud,
slowly, under her breath, asked an endless string of questions about terms
like *co-op, franchise, regime fees,* and the like, and then she asked Finnegan
for a pen. He had it out in a flash. She took it, clicked it open and shut,
open and shut, open and shut, and finally drawled, "I don't kno-ow."

"What can I help you with?" Finnegan asked eagerly.

"Well, I like brand name merchandise," said Delsie as she stuffed the specimen contract and deed into the complimentary valise. "So, who's building this big ol' place? Anybody I ever heard of?"

"Oh, of course," Finnegan said with a sense of urgency. "The Mimosas is being built by some of the finest companies in the state of Florida. The general development group is EPDI. That's Escorbilo Property Development, Inc. And the general contractor is Rodriguez & Schulman."

"Uh-huh. What about financing?"

"You want to finance your purchase? No problem."

"Oh, that's silly," Delsie laughed, spraying a light mist of saliva. "I don't need to finance anything. Daddy covers all of my checks. What I meant was, where does *your* financing come from? You're not going to run out of money and walk away before the job is done, are you? There was a lot of that going on along the Gulf Coast several years ago."

"Oh, no, ma'am. The financial backing for this project is underwritten by two of the largest banks in south Florida. That means that the banks are guaranteeing every one of the loans, which means that the investment bankers, their accountants and lawyers are watching things very, very carefully. Everything is being done strictly by the book. And the banks are both local businesses. No outside interests allowed. No corporate raiders to mess things up. No interstate banks to reassign resources in order to impress the banking czars. Nothing can go wrong. There's a whole lot of commitment on this project. Believe me. Oh, yes, ma'am. The Mimosas will be south Florida's premier retirement community when it's completed."

"Okay, you sold me," Delsie declared with a smile.

"Great!" replied Finnegan.

But before he could manage to say another word, Delsie stood up and stuck out her hand. "Thanks for your time. I'll be in touch."

"But I thought you were going to buy," stammered Finnegan.

"Well, Daddy taught me that it's always best to sleep on big decisions overnight. This is a big one, so I've got to follow the rules."

She started moving toward the door.

"Yes, ma'am," he flustered. "But you should know that I'm authorized to offer a six percent discount on pre-sales if you sign today.

"Oh, piddledy," giggled Delsie. "Why, that's only about $44,000! What's that between friends?"

"But the sample contract and deed," he protested. "I'm afraid that I can't let you take them. Company policy."

Delsie had the door half open.

"Why, Sean Michael Finnegan," she mewed, putting her index finger under his chin and tickling him lightly. "I thought that *you* were the company."

"But..."

She'd just put one foot outside when the office door at the opposite end of the trailer banged open, and five hot, steamy men emerged. Three of them were complete strangers, but one was Carl Rehm, and the last was Lt. Okun.

*   *   *

"Well, Miss Delsie, Dr. Pearson, what a pleasant surprise!" Rehm hailed us as he walked across the trailer and offered his hand. "I had heard that you ladies were sailing to Savannah."

"Change of plans," Delsie answered without missing a beat. "Daddy called just after we set sail last night, and he asked me to take a look at this project for him. He read about it in *Floridays* magazine. He and Mama miss south Florida something awful, Mr. Rehm. They truly do. So Daddy has decided that he wants a place down here that they can winter in. Since we were taking the *Jerome* out anyway, we decided to swing by here before heading north."

"Well, I can certainly understand that," Rehm agreed.

"And what are you doing here?" asked Delsie.

"I'm reviewing the monthly construction audit. The bank has a significant bit of venture capital invested in The Mimosas. It's a very solid project, and the management is excellent, but you know how cautious we bankers are."

Everyone laughed politely at that, and then Rehm turned to me.

"So tell me, Dr. Pearson, how are you enjoying life aboard the *Jerome*?"

"Doctor?" said Finnegan in amazement. "But I thought..."

"Oh, it's just lovely, Mr. Rehm," I replied, cutting Finnegan off. "It's a delightful way to end a very demanding trip. My friends will all be jealous of my tan when I get home."

"You're going home?" asked Okun.

"Of course," I said without smiling. "I came here to bury my dead, and that's done. Mr. Rehm has offered to take care of any extraneous details for me, and I have a veterinary practice to run, after all."

"You wanna sell your papa's boat?" Okun pressed.

"Oh, my word," I sighed as though the idea were too much for me to manage. "Well, I'm sure that Mr. Rehm will be able to handle that for me, too. Won't you?"

"If you wish," Rehm replied.

Having run out of social niceties, we offered a few hurried goodbyes, and then Delsie and I climbed into the golf cart while Rehm and Lt. Okun watched our every move from the stoop. Gary pulled away smartly, and launched into some moronic piffle about how they were trying to preserve the unique ecosystem of Greene Key. It was nonsense, of course. I wanted to grab him by the ear like a spoiled little boy, and drag him to the dynamited lagoon, and make him sit among all of the broken, rotted eggs, and ask him to explain his vision of conservation. But his diatribe kept us from having to say anything until we had put a little distance between ourselves and the construction trailer.

As soon as we disappeared around a clump of groundsel-trees, Delsie spit her gum out, and pulled a large cell-phone from her bag.

"It's an Iridium," she said when she saw the confused look on my face. "No need for those ugly cell-phone towers. This one's satellite direct."

Pulling out the antenna and punching a number on the speed-dialer, she waited for a moment or two and said, "Flag's up."

Then she put the phone away and looked at me.

"Well, Sugar, what do you think of this project?"

"Aunt Rita took me to Sunday School every week," I said, "and I can't help remembering the parable about the foolish man who built his house on the sand. It ends with the verse, 'and the rains fell, and the floods came, and the wind blew and beat against that house, and it fell; and great was the fall of that house.'"

"Translation?"

"I paid attention to the specifics. The construction trailer is located on the highest spot on Greene Key. That's only eighteen point three feet above mean sea level. And the island is basically a sand bar on a limestone/coral shelf. The substrata is probably uneven, and the shape of the island is determined by wave action, currents and drifting sand, so its margins are always in flux. I'll bet that if you dig down twenty feet or so on the west end, you'll find that whatever goop lies underneath pumps pretty good, like quicksand. Greene Key is fully exposed to the Atlantic, it has no protection at all, and it's right in the middle of Hurricane Alley. So, what do you suppose will happen to The Mimosas when the next Hurricane Andrew hits? Those lovely, pre-fab concrete condos may hold up to wind and rain—in fact, they're probably some of the sturdiest structures on the coast—but they're being erected on sand! According to the schematic diagrams, and judging from the site preparation for Phase II, there are no reinforced concrete piers under any of those condos. So what will hold them level in a hurricane? What will keep them in place?"

Delsie smiled at me. "Sugar, I've lived through hurricanes. Even Andrew's nasty ol' winds wouldn't have moved those condos."

"Not the winds," I insisted. "The water. The flood surge. The gargantuan waves that hurricanes produce. When Hurricane Hugo hit the coast at Charleston in 1989, the flood surge was twenty-seven feet above sea level. It swept completely over the barrier islands, wiped them clean, and ran a hundred miles upriver. So what do you suppose will happen to this little island when a wave like that hits? Did you ever stand at the edge of the surf and let the waves undercut the sand beneath your toes? Your feet sink and your ankles twist, you lose your balance and you fall. Well, that's precisely what will happen here. The foolish man built his house on the sand, and great was the fall of that house."

"Hey, girl!" said Delsie. "I thought you were a veterinarian. Where did you learn so much about architecture?"

"From my husband. Peter was a civil engineer; remember? When we were in college, he thought that going to look at a construction project was a hot date. You know the old story. If you want to capture a man's heart, you have to show an interest in what he does. You'd be surprised how much I know about hydraulics, and placing concrete."

"Placing concrete?"

"In the trade you don't *pour* concrete, you *place* it."

Gary pulled the golf cart to a smooth halt at the dock, and he fell all over himself trying to help us board the skiff. Raul was waiting, with the outboard running and the Zodiac's bow pointed out to the sea. I kept glancing backward as we jumped aboard, and I really wanted to talk to Delsie, but with the roar of the motor, and the slapping of the waves against the rubberized hull, and the wind in our ears, and both of us trying to keep our balance while bouncing through the chop on that inflated rubber seat, we didn't say another word until we were back aboard the *Jerome.*

*   *   *

We returned to the yacht, and found a beat-up aluminum workboat tied to a cleat beside the swim board. It was filled with greasy rags, dirty cardboard, and rusted bits of equipment.

"Mechanic from Long Key," Raul stated. "He responded to the CQ that I radioed last night, and found a bilge pump motor in Newport. Should be about done."

"Good," said Delsie. "I want to get under way as soon as possible."

"Yes, ma'am. Just as soon as he's gone." Raul headed for the bridge.

Delsie and I didn't say another word until we got to the saloon, but as soon as the door shut behind us my pent-up frustration exploded.

"What is Carl Rehm doing here?" I blurted out.

"I don't know, Sugar," Delsie replied thoughtfully. "He said that he's here to review the construction audit. It sounds reasonable to me."

"But Delsie, he's a Trust Department lawyer!"

"Okay, so it's somewhat less than plausible. Boy, he sure shook you up. It was written all over your face."

"It wasn't just Rehm! Did you hear what Finnegan said? Judge Holloway owns a condominium at The Mimosas. He's the one who appointed me executrix of Dad's and Uncle Bud's estates; overnight, and at Rehm's request. So where does a Superior Court Judge get that kind of money? How can he afford to live here? And the general contractor for the Mimosas is Rodriguez & Schulman. R&S. When Raul rescued me from the Blues Brothers, the bumper sticker on their car read R&S. Then there was Lt. Okun. What is he doing here? Investigating a major crime wave at the soon-to-be-built mini-mall?"

"Who knows?" Delsie said with a shrug. "Maybe he's a bag man for the Sheriff."

"Bribery?"

"Why not? It appears that a whole lot of influential people are involved in this project. Finnegan indicated that inspections are no problem, so somebody is undoubtedly greasing a few palms, and Representative Baedeker must have received some form of consideration for ramrodding the land deal. Most politicians aren't exactly selfless, you know. Ecological impact statements had to be approved, and permits had to be obtained in order to build the causeway and marina, because currents and tidal patterns will be disrupted. So we have local, state, and federal involvement here, to say nothing of the financial interests of some very influential construction companies. And then we have to consider the investment concerns of two of south Florida's most powerful banks."

"You're right," I replied with disgust. "It's really no coincidence that Lt. Okun is here. But Carl Rehm? I don't trust him."

"Your father did."

"And Dad's dead! Rehm tried to convince me that the explosion on Uncle Bud's cruiser was caused by a gasoline leak, but Sigmon Curlee told me that he had notified the bank's insurance division about the conversion to diesel a week or so before the accident happened. They're both tied up in this somehow."

Once again, quiet tension filled the saloon.

"Sugar," Delsie finally sighed, "the repairs to the *Jerome* are almost done, and we'll soon be under way. It's been a long and tiresome afternoon for both of us. Why don't you freshen up and meet me on the sun deck in half an hour?"

"Oh, Delsie. I want to talk this through right now. I want to make some sense of it."

"Listen," she said like a big sister. "We both need a break; a little stress relief. Let's go below, to each her own, and do all of the things that will make us feel perky and feminine again. Then Geoffrey can pamper us, and we can talk all of this through at our leisure. We've got the entire evening to work on it if we have to."

"Oh, all right. That really does sound pretty good."

Precisely thirty minutes later, after a quick rinse in the shower, and having donned a fresh peach and cream check short set, I grabbed my purse and headed topside. Delsie didn't arrive for another half an hour, and by that time Geoffrey had plied me with two delectable Margaritas, homemade salsa with cilantro, hot corn chips, and an offering of his own—chilled snow crab legs. I was feeling pretty mellow, lying on a padded rope chaise, staring at a sunset that blazed with fiery purples and reds, when a haunting line of Bruce Cockburn's poetry drifted up from my subconscious.

> *Sunset is an angel weeping,*
> *holding out a bloody sword.*
> *No matter how I squint I cannot,*
> *make out what it's pointing toward.*

The corn chips started to curdle in my stomach, and the ethereal lights took on a disturbing quality. Were the flaming streaks in the sky really angels? Were they bearing omens? That prickly sensation suddenly returned, as though I were being watched once again, but this time the feeling was accompanied by something even worse. Something with pointed teeth and fetid breath. Something with malice and intent. I squinted at the sunset. I tried to make out the sword. I searched for a sense of direction.

There was an abrupt thump as Delsie tossed her Mimosas valise on the deck and sat down beside me.

"Feeling better?" she asked.

"A little," I said, "but I'm doing precisely what L'Ouverture warned me against. I'm playing private eye."

"Want to quit?"

"No way!"

"Good. Raul reports that everything is all right now. The repaired bilge pump is working like a charm. The mechanic left shortly after we came aboard, and Mikey says that he was a very knowledgeable guy. He taught Mikey about a new industry standard for wiring electrical bilge pump motors. I don't understand electrophysics all that well, but it had something to do with electrostatic discharges from the bilge water in steel hulls, and installing a ground wire from the motor housing to the extractor mouth to counteract the static buildup. He showed Mikey how to do it, so

Mikey updated the other three bilge pump assemblies while the mechanic replaced the damaged motor. Mikey said that the guy was a lot of fun to work with. I caught a brief glimpse of him when he left. Young, sandy-haired fellow. He would have been kind of cute, except that one of his ears was mangled."

Somewhere between watching the bloody sunset and finishing that second Margarita, my brain must have gone numb, because it took me several seconds to react.

"His ear?" I demanded, lifting my head.

"He was missing an earlobe, Sugar; like from an accident or something."

I jumped to my feet and glanced around. There were three separate canopies on three different decks, but since it was evening, the crew had furled them tight, and lashed them to the bulkheads. I ran to the bracket on the port side of the sun deck, inspected it, and found nothing. Then I ran to starboard. Nothing again. I charged up the ladder, two rungs at a time, to the aft upper sun deck where the band had performed. No wires. No nothing.

"What are you looking for?" yelled Delsie.

I waved her off as I slid down the ladder, ran aft, and dropped three steps to the fantail. Those brackets showed no signs of tampering either, so I started to relax a bit.

"Don't mind me," I hollered with false bravado. "I'm occasionally given to fits of groundless paranoia, that's all."

Then I saw it.

The sun deck canopy was extremely large, and the thick aluminum poles that supported it were organized in four groups, two on each side of the yacht. When not in use, the crew collapsed those at the rear into fat bundles, which they lashed to the deck, inside the rails by the scuppers. It had gotten pretty dark out, so I knelt on the deck and felt around the brackets with my fingertips. My first sweep found nothing, and then my pinky got caught on a wire. A single insulated wire. The fact that the copper was shiny told me that someone had stripped the insulation from it that afternoon.

I jerked the wire loose and tossed it over the side, but it got snagged on the hinge of a service port and just hung there, flapping in the breeze.

I looked up, saw that we were running parallel to the beach, a mile or so off Long Key State Park peninsula, and a dark sense of dread overwhelmed me. Glancing forward, I then saw something that filled me with absolute terror. The sea just ahead was darker than midnight, and even in the twilight gloom I could still make out the rim of that horrid Blue Hole. It looked like an open grave, and I could sense the cold, bony finger of death beckoning.

Running over to the rope chairs, I picked up my purse, stuffed it into the Mimosas valise, grabbed the wireless intercom and pressed the button marked *Bridge*.

"Raul," I barked, "this is Jean Pearson. There's a bomb on board. No time for explanations. Abandon ship. This is no drill!"

"Do you trust me?" I demanded, unlatching the gangway gate and pulling it open.

"With my life," Delsie replied.

"Good answer."

I grabbed Delsie by the wrist, jerked her to her feet, and her eyes grew wide in alarm as I leapt overboard, dragging her out into space. The fall wasn't long, but far worse than I had imagined, because we both landed awkwardly and hit the water with a horrible wallop. We went under briefly, and entered a directionless world where there was neither up nor down; just the sizzling of a jillion angry bubbles, and the thundering of the yacht's big propeller as it rumbled by.

"Jesus, Joseph and Mary!" Delsie sputtered as she surfaced in the boiling wake of the *Jerome*.

We both looked up to see the yacht's stern speeding away from us, further and further away, over the lip of the crater.

Delsie coughed, and gagged, and tried to get rid of the water that had poured up her nose, belching a combination of Margaritas and salsa. Then, staring at me with real venom, she screamed, "Just what the bloody hell was that..."

But Delsie never finished her question. She was cut off in mid-sentence as a tremendous, thundering explosion threw sharp spray in our faces. White-hot, nuclear lightning seemed to rend both sea and sky, and then there was another explosion, and another, and another, as the *Jerome's* four fuel cells went off in a chain reaction. The underwater concussions were brutal, slamming into us like a series of sledgehammer blows. They battered our bones, turned our insides to jelly, and drove the air from our lungs. It became impossible to breathe, difficult to move. Shock paralyzed our nervous systems, and Delsie started sinking like a dead mackerel.

The valise had filled with air when we had jumped, and it provided a little bit of buoyancy, so, holding onto it with my left hand, I grabbed Delsie's hair with my right, and pulled her back to the surface.

"Breathe!" I ordered, starring her in the eye. "Breathe, damn it! Come on, breathe!"

She took a few pitiful sips of air, gagged and puked, then started panting like a retriever. Looking over her shoulder, I watched the nightmare unfold.

The *Jerome* didn't last very long at all. Accompanied by the shrieking groans of twisting steel, it rolled belly up, revealed a gaping wound in its side, and then quickly sank by the stern. Down, down, and further down it moaned, into the bottomless pit. Its red emergency lights were still burning as it sank, and they glimmered like ghosts in the distance, shrinking smaller and smaller, weaker and weaker, until they were swallowed by the ancient goddess of the gloom.

Nothing at all remained except some random bits of flotsam, and a large stinking carpet of oil.

"What... hap... happened?" Delsie finally managed to cough.

"A... bomb," I replied.

"Who?"

"One-ear."

"How... do you know?"

"Because, a boat yard flunky... missing his right ear lobe... was the last person to work on Uncle Bud's boat... and then he took a bus down to the Keys."

"But why us?"

"Because we're getting close."

I heard a funny noise just then—kind of a wet *pop* followed by a slurping sound —and I saw a shadow in the darkness about eighty meters away. It was the Zodiac. It had broken free as the *Jerome* had gone down, and had bobbed back up to the surface.

I pointed to the inflatable. "Can you swim?"

"No... problem," she answered gamely.

"Good. Then you can help me. My backstroke is okay, but I'm not going to get very far dragging this damn valise."

"Raul?" Delsie suddenly whispered as the horror of the moment settled in. "Raul! Geoffrey!! Mikey!!!"

It was one of those moments of frailty of which I will always feel ashamed, for I couldn't think of a single comforting thing to say.

"Come on," I finally rasped. "Let's get the hell out of here. We have five scores to settle now."

11

Climbing into the Zodiac proved to be a bigger trick than I had imagined. For one thing, there was an ebb tide running, which constantly pulled the boat away, so it took us a good twenty minutes to close the gap. For another, Delsie was injured more seriously than I had thought. The underwater concussions had bruised her abdomen, and having no warning of the leap from the *Jerome*, she had landed badly, on her side, striking her head. A small stream of blood was trickling from her left ear. I helped her aboard first, holding onto the side of the uncooperative rubber craft with one arm, and letting her kneel on my shoulders. With what appeared to be her last ounce of strength, she lurched forward and disappeared into the boat. But after a minute or two she managed to sit up and grab me under the arm, so I held onto one of the rubberized oar loops, and swung my leg over the side. It was like mounting a greased mule in the middle of a river, and I just hung there for a while, half in and half out. Then disquieting thoughts about Delsie's bleeding ear and hammerhead sharks made the adrenaline flow again, and I pulled my other leg into the boat. When I finally tugged the valise in after me, we both collapsed.

A cavalcade of stars was twinkling overhead in colorful profusion, there was a playful, sweet-smelling breeze, and the strobe lights of several airplanes winked lazily across the sky. It was a typical summer night at sea, except that we were injured, covered with fuel oil, and half drowned.

The current carried us northward for several minutes before Delsie patted the valise and spoke.

"Do you really think that there's anything in here that will help us to get the bastard?" she asked.

"Well, there's one piece of paper that should prove useful," I replied.

By now a number of small boats had converged on the Blue Hole. Some of them were running searchlights, and all were picking through the debris. They appeared to be a mile or two away, but it's extremely hard to judge distances over water at night. Lights are generally a lot further away than they seem.

Delsie hoisted herself to a sitting position. "Let's see if we can get the outboard running, and head in," she suggested.

"No way," I countered sharply. "We'll drift a while longer. I don't want anyone to suspect that we're out here."

"Why?" she cried. "I'm hurt, I'm exhausted, and I'm thirsty. I want to be found. I want to be rescued. I want to be fussed over."

"What difference will that make? You're dead."

"Sugar," she said with a worried look, "did that explosion loosen your gray matter? I'm perfectly alive, so to speak."

"No, you're not," I insisted. "As far as our would-be killer knows, you and I are crab bait at the bottom of that hideous Blue Hole, and I want to keep it that way."

"But why? What are you thinking?"

"I'm thinking that persons unknown have been trying to frighten me, intimidate me, threaten, kidnap and murder me ever since I arrived here. And I'm also thinking that if they believe us to be dead, they'll stop trying. That should buy us some time."

Delsie groaned, and slumped back down dejectedly.

Not ten seconds later I heard the heavy growling of a powerful inboard engine. It grew louder and louder, and then a racing boat shot past us at terrific speed, about fifteen yards seaward. Instinctively, Delsie and I propped ourselves on our elbows, and peered over the edge of the dull, black inflatable. The speedboat's stern displayed no running light, and it disappeared from view as suddenly as it had approached, leaving nothing but a greenish, phosphorescent wake to mark its passage.

"Man!" exclaimed Delsie. "That was too close. That damned fool nearly ran us over."

"No lights, and flying like a bat out of hell in the dark," I commented. "Probably a drug smuggler."

"Not unless they've taken to using antiques. That was a wooden boat. An old mahogany runabout."

"Chris-Craft?"

"Maybe." She just stared at me, her mouth hanging slightly open. "Okay, Sugar. I agree with you. We go underground. But what will we do for money?"

"I've got some cash in my purse, I have a few travelers cheques, and I also have some plastic. We'll manage."

"But we'll need transportation."

"Not to worry," I replied with such raw determination that I hardly recognized my own voice. "Do you know these waters, Delsie?"

"More or less."

"Can you make out where we are?"

She threw her arm over the side of the raft and lifted her head.

"About a mile or so off Lower Matecumbe Key, just north of Channel Two."

"Is there a highway near a beach?"

"There's a shell beach of sorts at each end, where the viaduct bridges come and go, but there are always people fishing at those spots. And then there's the boat traffic, too. It's unpredictable, but frequent. We'd be spotted for sure. However, there's a small cove about a mile ahead that's not far from U.S. One. You can see the headlights from the traffic on the highway if you look. I don't recall ever seeing anyone fishing in there, probably because that cove is so shallow. I went there with friends from school once. We anchored a small ski boat, looking for a place to party, and got hung on the bottom when the tide spilled out; had to get out and tow the boat into deeper water. It's only a hundred yards or so from the road. It should be okay."

"Good. Let's drift past the cove, then start the motor and run back up, slow and easy. That way, if anyone should notice us we'll be coming from a direction opposite the wreck."

"Look who's going covert now!" she sniffed.

"I'm a quick study."

"And what will we do then, Mata Hari? Thumb a ride?"

"Not exactly," I declared as I reached into my purse and pulled out my cell-phone. "We're going to ride in air conditioned style."

I pressed the power button on my Motorola digital phone. Its integrated circuit boards were encased in a waterproof plastic gel, so it hadn't shorted out, and the diodes lit up right away. That was a relief. Then I fished around in my purse until I found a soggy bit of cover stock. Straining to read the number by the yellow-green glow of the diodes, I punched it in, pressed *Send*, and waited. My first three attempts ended in failure, but on the fourth I must have connected with a relay tower somewhere, because there was a chorus of high frequency chirping and dinging, and then, after three rings, someone picked up the phone.

"Chello-o-o!" came the cheerful greeting.

"Is this the Road Warrior?" I inquired.

"Dat you, Mees?" Norman replied. "You need a leeft?"

"I sure do. A real long one. And I think that it's high time for Benjamin Franklin to meet Ulysses S. Grant."

"Me too! Time for a family reunion."

"Norman, it's going to be an all-night ride, and a big reunion."

"I like big families," he said.

"Okay, but one thing first. Stop somewhere, and buy a dozen beach towels. Big ones. And a dozen bottles of cold spring water, too."

"O-chay. Just tell me where you are."

I told him to go to the south bridge on Lower Matecumbe Key, and to wait there for another call.

"No problem," he said.

As if to reassure me, the last thing that I heard before the line went dead was the sound of squealing XGT Extra Wide tires.

*   *   *

Delsie had been right. The cove was only a hundred yards or so from U.S. One, but she'd neglected to mention that a mangrove swamp covered half of the distance. We had to proceed by dead reckoning, because once we were in the mangroves we couldn't see a thing; not even the stars. But we could hear just fine, and it was obvious that we were not alone in that miniature jungle. Soft grunts and snorts and scratchings and hoots and swishings of all kinds echoed in subsonic symphony through the trees, as the unseen terrors of the night moved above, beside and beneath us. Demonic creatures of all kinds surrounded me, and every time I moved I imagined that I was stepping on a snake, or an alligator. I felt something slippery glide past my hand as I groped for a branch to hang onto, and I cringed every time that I walked through a spider web. My left hand clutched Delsie's right like a pair of Visegrip pliers, because we were afraid that if we lost contact with each other in that dreadful darkness we'd never get back together. I was terrified of all the monsters that my imagination conjured up, but my eyes couldn't see a thing. I was a ripe, juicy morsel in a world filled with predators, and I knew it. Then I remembered that during a backpacking trek through the Montana wilderness of Glacier National Park, a ranger had told me that the best way to keep Grizzly Bears at bay is to make lots of noise, so I talked, and I sang, and I yelled, and I whistled, and I made every kind of sound that I could manage. But my feeble display of bravado did nothing to lessen the feeling that I was being watched, by a thousand pairs of hungry eyes, every inch of the way.

We had abandoned our Gucci sandals during the long swim to the Zodiac, so when we finally collapsed in the sawgrass not far from the highway, after two horrific hours, we found that our feet were bruised and bleeding. Nevertheless, the moment of redemption came when Norman answered his cell-phone on the first ring. I told him to start driving north, slowly, with his roof light on, and to pull well off the road when he heard a stick hit the side of his car. He didn't like the idea, but he complied.

Parched, aching, and with my skin on fire from the fuel oil that covered nearly every inch of my body, I sat propped up on my elbows in the litter-strewn grass—among faded Pepsi cans, cigarette butts, candy wrappers and blue plastic urinals—and I was pummeled by the boiling gusts of exhaust-polluted air as the traffic pounded ceaselessly by. Longhaul trucks. Minivans. SUVs. Sedans. They all had specific objectives. Normal destinations. They were racing to places sane. To homes, and restaurants. To shopping malls, and multiplexes. To a world that I had known, but to which I no longer belonged. And I didn't even know why.

*   *   *

"Mees!" Norman cried in genuine anguish when he watched us hobble toward his cab. "Oh, my sainted mother!"

I hadn't realized how dreadful we looked until I got a glimpse of Delsie in the lights of a passing semi. Covered with coagulated gunk from head to toe, she resembled one of those unfortunate sea birds that get slimed in oil tanker spills. Worse yet, her feet were caked with blood.

Norman hurriedly covered his back seat with towels, and then helped us to climb inside, giving each of us a big, cold bottle of water.

"You need a hospeetal," he declared.

"No," I insisted, emptying the first bottle. "No hospitals. Nothing public. Just find a safe place where we can clean up."

"Trouble with the law?"

"Could be."

"O-chay. I've got a cousin, lives outside of Homestead. Way back in dee woods. Very private. Hees wife, she ees a practical nurse. Preetty good, too."

"Great," I said. "Let's get started."

We'd only gotten about twelve miles or so, and were coming off the bridge onto Plantation Key, when Norman cried, "Look out, now! There's a roadblock ahead. Cops! Heet looks like a license check, or maybe they search for DUIs, or maybe for smugglers, or sometheen."

"Or maybe they're looking for us," I grimaced.

"Queeck," said Norman. "There are not many cars ahead of oos. Fold dee back seat down, and crawl inside dee trunk."

"Is there room?" asked Delsie.

"Do we have a choice?" I replied.

We had just managed to cram our injured bodies into the tiny cargo space when Norman flipped the seat up hard to latch it in place. Then the taxi ground slowly to a halt. A minute later I heard the sound of hard leather shoes crunching on the roadway.

"Le'me see your license and registration, boy," a gruff voice demanded.

There was a moment of silence while Norman handed over his papers.

"This your cab, boy?" asked the officer.

"Yes, sir," replied Norman.

"You own it?"

"Yes, sir."

"Kinda far from home, ain't ya, boy?"

"Yes, sir."

"What you doin' out here tonight, boy?"

"I took a crazy man fishing, sir."

"Fishing?"

"Yes, sir," Norman lied. "A crazy-ass rich man. Peecked him up in downtown Lauderdale. He had a three-piece suit, and one of those leetle fishing poles, like keeds feesh weeth, and he paid me a brand new hundred dollar bill to drive him out to dee Keys. He said that he was fed up, that he couldn't take it any more, that you have to say dee hell with it once in a while."

"He's right about that, boy," said the cop. "Show me the hunert dollar bill."

There was another delay while Norman fished a bill out of his wallet.

"I don't like these new hunert dollar bills, do you, boy?" asked the officer. "Don't like this extry big pitcher of that Damn Yankee Franklin."

"They all spend the same," replied Norman.

"Looking for another fare, boy?"

"Why, sir?"

"Why?" sniggered the lawman. "'Cause you got your roof light on, boy; that's why. You spectin' to find another hunert dollar fare out here?"

"Well, you got to bait dee hook to catch dee fish," Norman replied bravely.

The officer chuckled again.

"Got anything in your trunk?"

"Just a good-looking woman and a case of beer." Norman laughed.

"You messing with me, boy?" the officer growled.

"Yes, sir. I mean no, sir."

"You better not be, boy. Now move along. You're holdin' up traffic."

"Yes, sir. Uh, my hundred dollar bill, sir?"

"Your fine, boy. For driving around Monroe County with your roof light on, when your permit is for Broward and Dade only. You know the rules, boy. You can haul 'em in here, but you can't haul 'em out."

"Yes, sir."

"Now git. And turn that damn roof light off."

"Yes, sir."

Norman drove away slowly, and it was several minutes before he pulled the seat release.

"Whew!" said Delsie. "I'm glad that's over."

"Maybe it's not," I replied.

"Why?"

"Because that was Khaki-pants."

"Okun's sidekick? Are you sure?"

"I'd recognize that smarmy voice anywhere."

"So they're leaving no stone unturned!" Delsie whispered in alarm.

*   *   *

For the next hour or so we rode in silence, crouching low in the brightly lit spots so that no one would see us. Eventually, we turned off Highway 997 and drove down an old shell road, coming to a stop in a grove of baldcypress trees near a cinder block house. The solitary, yellow porch light was barely strong enough for me to make out the Spanish moss which hung from every limb, or the motley pack of underfed dogs which charged out to greet us—an old black Lab, a Toy Poodle, a Sheltie mix, and an odd assemblage of canine spare parts which looked vaguely like an Australian Shepherd. The dogs barked loudly while circling the taxi, until a big, shirtless man emerged from the whitewashed house, rattling off a rapid-fire string of indecipherable Spanish. The dogs lost interest, and drifted off.

"Chico! Que pasa?!" cried Norman, only now getting out of his car.

"Paco!" replied the homeowner with a happy burst of laughter. "Maria! Maria! Ees Paco!"

A petite and obviously pregnant young woman emerged from the house, dusky arms waving high, toothy mouth smiling. She ran over to join the men, and there was a brief celebration as the three of them embraced excitedly. Then Norman led his cousins over to the cab.

"Theese ees one of my friends," he indicated, pointing to me, "and theese is her friend."

Pointing to our hosts he said, "Theese ees Cristobol de la Torre, who we call Chico, and theese ees his lovely wife, Maria."

Maria walked toward the cab window to say hello, and froze.

"Madre Mia!" she exclaimed, crossing herself. "You are hurt?"

"Yes," I said. "Both of us."

Yet another rapid-fire exchange took place in Spanish, during which Norman explained what little he knew of our plight. Maria crossed herself two or three more times as the story progressed, each time inhaling with an audible gasp. She then stepped up to the cab with authority and opened the door.

"Por favor," she said, "you will come inside. We will feed you and tend to your wounds, and you can wash in our tub. Mi casa, su casa."

"Thank you," I replied as we limped toward the porch.

"Muchas gracias, mi amiga," added Delsie.

"Where are my seex little nephews?" hollered Norman as we entered the house.

"Five of them are asleep in the back," said Maria, "and if you wake them I will chase you out with the broomstick. The seexth piqueña," she added with a smile, rubbing her ample stomach, "is to be a niece. Just theese morning we saw the zonogrammes."

"Aye-yi!" complained Norman. "There goes my baseball team. Who will play shortstop now?"

"Little girls play now as well as boys," Maria scolded. "You wait. She'll be a 300 hitter. You will see."

Chico gave us each a glass of white rum while Maria awakened her 14-year-old sister—who was visiting from Miami and spoke no English—and she ordered the girl to help Delsie with her bath. I heard Delsie squeal when she stuck her feet in the water, and I winced at the thought of what was facing me.

"Norman, we need a few things," I said, sitting down slowly at the kitchen table. "If I give you some travelers cheques, will you go to town and pick them up?"

"Yes, Mees," he replied.

Maria gave me a paper bag and a pencil, and I made out a list of clothes, toiletries, cosmetics and other essentials.

"Here," I said to Norman, handing him a pile of soggy $100 cheques. "If we can dry these out, one is for you, to make up for what that SOB stole tonight. The rest are for supplies. I'll backdate the checks by a couple of days, and make them all out to cash."

Without saying a word, Maria took the cheques from Norman, opened an old, wooden ironing board, laid the damp paper between folded layers of cotton dishtowel, and went to work with a flatiron. She had them all dry and smooth in no time.

"Paco," she said to Norman, after I'd signed all the cheques. "You take half and shop for the blonde woman at Wal-Mart. Chico, you take the other half and shop for the dark woman at Kmart. Theese way no one notices that you are buying for two women. Ees o-chay?" she asked, looking at me.

"Perfect," I replied as the men disappeared into the night.

"Now, let me see your feet," said Maria.

She lifted them up, one at a time, and laid them on a folded towel atop another chair.

"Aye, yi!" she exclaimed when she saw the soles. "I will have to wash and dress them. Eet will not be too bad. Wait. You will see."

She went into the living room and returned with what appeared to be an oversized fishing tackle box, but when she opened it up I was pleased to see that it was brimming with fresh medical supplies. After taking my temperature, blood pressure and pulse, she rummaged in the bottom of the box, withdrew an aerosol can, and directed a frosty spray at my feet.

"Ees Ethyl Chloride," she explained. "Eet will take some of the sting out, but not all."

She set to work without another word and washed my feet, half way up my calves, with a stiff scrub brush and Dial antibacterial soap. She found a number of small lacerations, but none deep enough to warrant stitches, and finished by massaging my feet with an antibiotic ointment comprised of Bacitracin, Neomycin Sulfate, and Polymyxin-B Sulfate. Then, as an added precaution, she applied a thin layer of petroleum jelly, "to keep the soap and water out when you bathe," she explained.

It was a very professional and thorough job, and I thanked her.

Delsie looked a thousand percent better when she emerged from her bath, even though she was wearing one of Maria's old housecoats. "Your turn, Dr. Pearson," she said.

Maria's sister, whose name was Sarita, did a wonderful job of washing the fuel oil out of my hair. I almost felt human again when I limped back into the kitchen, smelling of pine soap, with one towel wrapped around my torso, and another wound around my head.

I had a brief discussion with Maria, and she put Sarita back to work, removing all of the soggy papers from the valise and my purse, and drying them out in the microwave oven, one or two sheets at a time. A microwave works by exciting the water molecules in food, making them vibrate so quickly that they get blistering hot, so when the microwave converted the water in the papers to steam, they became dry, if somewhat wrinkled. The genuine cowhide valise, and my Ferragamo purse, went into the clothes drier. Shriveled would best describe their condition when they finally emerged.

"Dr. Pearson," Maria said with a frown, "please look at theese."

She had done a beautiful job of treating Delsie's feet, but the oyster shells in the mangrove roots had cut two deep lacerations in the ball of Delsie's left foot; deep enough that they would require sutures.

"I sometimes sew up leetle cuts on dee farm worker's hands," apologized Maria, "but theese wounds require more skill than I have."

"Do you have a syringe and some local anesthetic?"

"Si," she replied shyly. "Some 12cc syringes, and 22 gauge needles. Also, I have some 2% Lidocaine."

"Sutures?"

"Some 3-O Nylon on PS-2 needles."

"Excellent. You did a splendid job preparing the patient, Maria. Will you draw up the Lodocaine while I scrub?"

"Si, Señorita Doctor."

"Oh, terrific," groaned Delsie. "Here I lie, bludgeoned and bleeding, no more than an hour away from the finest medical facilities in south Florida, and I'm going to be sewn up by a doggy doctor."

"Consider yourself fortunate," I quipped as I washed my hands in a dark brown Betadine solution. "I have to be better than those ER docs, because my patients bite."

An hour later Delsie was comfortably asleep on the sofa, her foot sporting two lovely spiral sutures, and I was getting dressed in the colorful cotton outfit that Norman had so painstakingly picked out for me—an unpleated skirt with a bold, printed design of blue Hydrangeas and red Poppies, a sheer lilac blouse with a deeply scooped neck and puffy sleeves, and bright orange sandals. I looked like a refugee from a Mariachi band. On a higher note, the men had returned with gym bags filled lip gloss, toothbrushes, hair dryers, eyeliner, and all of the other things that I had requested.

"What now, Mees?" asked Norman.

"How do you feel about driving to Tallahassee tonight?" I asked.

"O-chay. Up I-75?"

"I don't know. Maybe we should use the old state roads. Highway 19. I want to be as inconspicuous as possible."

Norman looked at me thoughtfully, then turned and had a long exchange with Chico, in preposterously overheated Spanish.

"I hev made other plans," he finally announced with great pride. "I am going to rent Cristobol's peeckup truck, and he uses my taxi until we return. No one will notice you in a truck driven by an hombre like me, and you will be more comfortable, too, I theenk. Theese way we can take I-75 all the way to I-10, then I-10 to Tallahassee. No towns, no stoplights, no local cops."

The thought of bumping along in a pickup truck all night, from one end of Florida to the other, left me feeling ill. But Norman was so proud of his plan that I didn't have the heart to argue.

"Okay," I said. "Let's go."

Maria and Sarita got Delsie dressed in a chic, aqua, Grecian-looking gown that Chico had picked out, and then we walked outside, very, very slowly. To my everlasting surprise, Chico's pickup turned out to be a new GMC Sierra Club Cab; an extended, four-door model with reclining bucket seats up front, and a full bench seat in back. It was a monster truck, and, as things turned out, it was just what we needed.

Maria said a long prayer for our safety. I gave her a lingering hug, and a kiss on each cheek, and promised to come back and visit one day soon. Chico blessed his truck several times, in English as well as in Spanish, using an odd assortment of hand signals that I'd never seen before, while Delsie crawled up onto the broad back seat, nestled into a huge pillow and promptly fell asleep. Norman took his station behind the wheel, and I rode shotgun with the puckered cowhide valise and its cargo of salvaged documents on my lap. It took me a little while to get used to the idea of riding way up high as opposed to hunkering down in the back of Norman's cab, but by the time we turned west on the Everglades Parkway I was feeling so calm that my eyes started to get heavy.

"Go ahead and sleeep, Mees," Norman said as he reached into the back seat and handed me a pillow.

So I pushed at the little buttons until the motorized seat assumed a comfortable position, adjusted the lumbar control, nestled my head in the pillow against the doorpost, and dozed in and out of uneasy dreams about giant black sea monsters and screaming buttermilk yachts. And every now and then I awoke with a start, certain that I'd heard Raul calling my name. It was nearly sunup before I got any real sleep.

12

Delsie woke up about mid-morning, complaining that her feet hurt, which they undoubtedly did. Mine were certainly painful. Maria had given us a paper envelope containing half a dozen 50mg Demerol tablets, but not wanting to give Delsie any more medication until she had something solid in her stomach, I asked Norman to find an out-of-the-way place for breakfast. He promptly took the old US-90 exit off Interstate 10, and we ended up at a little Mom & Pop eatery on the banks of the Suwannee River. It was a lovely spot, with moss-covered live oak trees bending over a lazy stream, and we decided to eat outside, on a terrazzo-covered patio bedecked with potted cacti. There was a wholesome, provincial serenity about the place, and there was also music of a sort, for the pianissimo of bumblebees thrummed a lilting counterpoint to the melodies of a dozen species of songbirds, as dirtdauber wasps buzzed noisily about. Our only other company was a pair of sleek, powder-green lizards that chased each around a nearby tree trunk in tense, scratchy sprints.

"What now?" asked Delsie as she devoured a platter of fried eggs, country ham, and hominy grits with redeye gravy.

"We should do a little digging into the corporate records of Escorbilo Property Development," I answered.

"Shall we stay in a hotel, or lease an apartment?"

"What?"

"Listen," she said with a protracted sigh. "When I was interning with Prentice, Cottrell, Heath and Krone prior to taking the Bar exams..."

"The Bar exams?"

"Why, yes, Sugar. Didn't your father tell you? When I finished my double major in Business and History at the University of Alabama—Business because Daddy insisted; History because I enjoyed it so—I decided to read for the Law, as they say, because both Business and History are considered prerequisites. I can be one hell of a litigator when I need to be. Some yeh-hoos from Philadelphia tried to play corporate raider with one of Daddy's autonomous subsidiaries last year, and by the time I got through with them they owed us seven million, and were indicted on securities fraud. At any rate, I did a heap of research on a convoluted corporate pyramid scheme one time, so I had to spend several weeks with the good folks at the Florida Department of State's Division of Corporations, working my way through mountains of filing forms, applications, records, et cetera, ad infinitum, ad nauseum. Oh, I know the whole, gruesome routine, Sugar. It takes time. Lots and lots of time. And if we're looking for something shady, it will take us even longer."

"I'm impressed," I said with genuine appreciation.

"You should be."

"But there's just one problem. We can't spend a lot of time on this, because we're dead."

"Oh, yeah," she said softly, memories of the previous night bringing tears to her eyes. "I forgot. We went down with the *Jerome*."

"Madre de Dios," whispered Norman. He crossed himself slowly and then kissed his thumbnail.

"So what can we do?" I inquired of the sky.

"Well," sniffed Delsie as she wiped her eyes on a paper napkin, "I certainly can't waltz into DivCorp's central office. Word of our disappearance will be out soon. If even one clerk recognizes me—and I worked with dozens—then this li'l ol' game is up, Sugar. So I reckon I'll have to teach you everything that you'll need to know as we drive along. But don't worry. You won't have to remember very much, because everyone who does research at DivCorp carries tons of legal pads. We'll pick some up on the way. You can write everything down, carry the pads with you, and you'll look perfectly normal."

"You don't think that I'll stand out in the crowd?" I asked delicately, with a quick glance at my attire.

"Sugar, they have a massive phone bank call-in line at DivCorp, where they get over five hundred telephone calls per hour. The walk-in traffic isn't quite as formidable, but once you're in the building no one will have the time to notice your idiosyncrasies. And besides, this is Florida, where nobody looks out of place. Just be sure to take cash for the copying charges."

"That reminds me. We've got a little bit of cash right now, but we'll need to get a whole lot more."

"Why? We can use plastic, can't we?"

"I don't think that's a good idea. We shouldn't risk accessing my MasterCard or VISA accounts, because every credit card transaction in the United States is reported instantaneously to two monstrous data banks in Florida."

"They are?"

"Yes. We use one of those electronic card verification machines at the clinic. I learned from an account rep that there are two computer centers here in Florida which record virtually every credit card transaction made in the United States, and then break all of that information down demographically to provide marketing data for advertisers and business planners."

"That's scary."

"It certainly is, and in our predicament, it's even worse. If our pursuer is as clever as we think, then he'll put a trace on my accounts. Any business person can do it. The numbers are on the billing records at the hotel, along with a score of other places where we went shopping. The killer wouldn't have very much trouble identifying them. If I were to use my accounts this morning, he'd not only suspect that I'm still alive, but he'd be able to pinpoint exactly where we are."

"Terrific!" spat Delsie.

"Right. But I think that I may know how to fool them. At least for a while. I've got an old American Express card that I use exclusively for business trips. The card is in my maiden name—I never got around to changing it—and the monthly bills go directly to my accountant."

"So the supercomputers won't know that it's you."

"I hope not. Especially if I get just one big cash advance."

"You go, girl!" Delsie looked as though she were coming on line again. "DivCorp is located on East Gaines, and there's an American Express office over on North Monroe, which crosses Gaines. It's convenient, and this will keep us anonymous for a little while longer. Let's go there first, withdraw a pile of cash, and then we can start the records search."

"Sounds good."

We finished our breakfast with sticky slabs of homemade pecan pie, and washed it down with chickory-flavored coffee. Thirty minutes later, having stopped in Madison for gasoline, legal pads and mechanical pencils, Delsie started dictating a complicated research outline, and I began scribbling it down just as fast as my hand would fly.

*   *   *

The Florida Department of State's Division of Corporations occupies a massive glass and concrete bunker in a sprawling government complex at the heart of downtown Tallahassee. Housed in that vast labyrinth are literally millions of copies of regulations, applications, fee receipts, corporate name registrations, annual reports, reinstatements, certificates and more, occupying thousands and thousands of steel file drawers, overseen by hundreds and hundreds of employees. But I got lucky. I found an angel.

Smiling DivCorp staffers, who were polite, courteous, and severely overworked, forwarded me from office to office, until I found myself standing in a zigzag maze of yellow ropes and plastic stanchions, at the tail end of an interminable line of bored people who were waiting for assistance. There were ten or twelve clerking stations at the service counter, and not too long after I got there a young man at the head of the line was called forward by a retirement-age woman with a bright red nose and runny mascara.

"May I help you?" she sniffed, a damp hankie in her hand.

"Yes, ma'am. I'd like to know if..."

But before he could finish his question, the old woman burst into tears.

"Um..." he stammered. "Is there something I can do for you, ma'am?"

"No," she sobbed. "There's nothing anyone can do. My dearest friend was killed in a boating accident last week, and we've just learned on the news that his only niece is missing somewhere off the Keys, and is presumed drowned."

The young man looked positively shell-shocked.

"Excuse me," she cried. "Someone else will have to help you." She brushed through the gate at the far end of the counter, and disappeared down the hall. I glanced casually around. None of the other clerks paid the slightest attention to her, so I walked along the corridor to the Ladies' Lounge, and stepped quietly inside. There she stood at the far end of the room, leaning against a porcelain sink, crying her eyes out.

"Dear me." I tried to soothe her. "Would you care to talk about it?"

"What good will talking do?!" she fumed. "He's dead, his best friend is dead, and now his niece is gone, too. Oh, I hate boats! Wicked, ugly things. They make you so sick you can't stand up, and when they're not fouling the air, they explode and kill people."

Her sobbing was completely out of control by this point, so I took a brush out of my purse and fussed with my hair, waiting for the squall to subside. When it eventually did, I looked at her and offered a few well-chosen words.

"Were these relatives of yours?" I asked.

"He and I were soul mates," she sniffed. "I knew the friend that he died with, too, of course, but I'd never met his niece. She held their funerals the day before yesterday. I understand that it was just lovely, but I didn't attend. It was on a great big yacht, you see, out in the middle of the Atlantic. I was just too shy, I guess, and I don't like boats, and I was afraid that they wouldn't understand; that they might not accept me."

The tears started again, but not as hard as before, and after a while I said, "I'm sure that they would have been very touched by your sorrow. He must have been very well loved."

"Oh, my, yes. Everyone simply adored him. He was a great big teddy bear of a man, but oh, so smart."

"He certainly was," I smiled, taking the next step, "and he was talented, too. I'll really miss his incomparable Chili. That stuff was nearly lethal."

"Oooo-eee. He gave me a thermos of it once. It was the hottest thing that I ever tasted."

There was a long pause as it dawned on her that we were talking about the same person, and then she said, "Did you know him too?"

"Can you keep a secret?"

She nodded her head vigorously.

"I'm his missing niece. I'm Dr. Jean Pearson. And his boat didn't explode on its own. The Coast Guard told me so in strictest confidence. Someone put a bomb on board. He and my Dad were murdered, you see, and the assassin tried to kill me last night, too."

"Haaw!" she gasped, her soft hazel eyes springing wide. "I knew that there was something fishy going on. I just knew it." Then her eyes narrowed. "How do I know that you're telling me the truth?"

So I showed her my Ohio driver's license, an old snapshot of Dad and Uncle Bud on the houseboat, and my part-time University staff identification card. She studied them carefully, asked me the name of Uncle Bud's boat, and then hurried me off to a drab little conference room. Locking the door behind us, she sat close beside me at a worn formica table, and we told each other everything.

Her name was Miss Ida Mae Knechtle, and she'd been Uncle Bud's sweetheart, although he may never have known it. According to her, they had been intimate friends for years and years, and whenever he'd needed to research corporate status reports and the like, he'd work with Ida Mae, because he'd claimed that she was the most competent records clerk in the world.

"Ida Mae," he'd supposedly said, "when God made you, He broke the mold to prevent all the cherubs from crying their eyes out in jealousy."

"Yes," she reported, "your uncle had been working on a complicated research project in recent weeks. Some kind of real estate deal, or development, or something of that sort. There was some State entanglement, too, somehow. I really can't remember exactly what it was about, dear. Can you wait here for a minute?"

I said "yes," and she scurried out the door. A minute or two later she returned, carrying one of the biggest fishnet bags that I had ever seen.

"Here," she declared with a smile, withdrawing a battered steno notebook from the bowels of the bag. "Occasionally he'd call me to check on some new angle or other after he'd gotten back home. It's so terribly difficult to backtrack on things after a couple of days. The memory fades quickly, you know. So I started keeping a diary of all of the things that we'd look into together, and then it was never a problem to assist him if he called and needed more information.

"Now, let me see, dear. Oh, yes. He was here three weeks ago. He was looking into a development project called The Mimosas, and he wanted to know about all of the companies involved. Land acquisition. Deeds. Titles. Corporate names. Annual reports. Names of registered agents. Fictitious name applications. Filing fees. UCC information. Certificates of Record. Certificates of Status. Yes, that was it. It took us two or three days to follow all of the paper trails and copy all of the necessary records, but then he called me again several days later. He told me that when he'd

gotten home he'd stumbled over a hawser, whatever that is, and that he'd
dropped his packet of papers overboard. The ink had bled, and the
papers had been ruined. He apologized over and over, and he asked for
replacements.

"Let's see now. He asked about the title transfer of Greene Key, from
the State to private hands. I didn't have any of that documentation here,
so I had to call a friend over at Legislative Archives. She's such a dear. Her
father was a Colonel on Omar Bradley's staff during the Second World
War. She faxed me copies of... oh, let me see, now... the minutes of an
Emergency Funding Task Force meeting... that's a subcommittee of Ways
and Means... then we found the transfer papers... and I mailed everything
to him two days later."

"So all in all," I stated rather than asked, "it took three or four days to
get the material together."

"Well, yes. If you include the Legislative Archives material."

"Ouch!" I was anything but happy. "There goes the ball game. I can't
pretend to be dead forever. I'll have to resurface in another day or so, and
I wanted to use that time to study the records."

Miss Ida Mae's eyes twinkled with devilish delight.

"Well," she proposed, "if you had a friend at DivCorp who knew the
ropes, who knew which strings to pull, and who had a record of the
paperwork that your uncle had asked for, then you could have those
records by, oh, I should say, late this afternoon."

"Do you really think so?"

"Sweetie, every record in this place is time- and date-stamped, and then
coded by document number and location prefix. I always write those registration numbers in this little pad of mine, just in case. Now, my friends
will leave me alone today because they know that I'm upset. I'll just tell
them that I'm working on an old records audit, and I'll spend my time
expediting this request of yours. There's no harm done, dear. Yours is a
legitimate request, after all. It would have to be done by someone sooner
or later."

"Oh, thank you, Miss Ida. What time shall I meet you back here?"

"Here?" she scoffed. "Nonsense, my dear! You will meet me at my house at four o'clock sharp. We'll share a nice cup of tea, and I'll show you what I've managed to pull together. Mr. Pringles will be so happy for the company."

"Mr. Pringles?"

"The most beautiful tabby you've ever seen."

She gave me her RFD address, and a hand-drawn map. I thanked her profusely, but all I got in response was a series of "tishes" as she hurried me out the door.

When I returned to the government parking lot I found that the truck was gone. Panic started rising from my kidneys like a flood, but I soon discovered that Norman had moved into the spindly shade of a palm tree. Delsie was sound asleep on the back seat, and Norman was snoring heavily in front. They made quite a pair. The princess and the pauper. The old guard and the new masses. I just stared at the two of them, lying in that mammoth apple green pickup, and I suddenly realized how ridiculously conspicuous we were. Between Norman's lavender snakeskin boots, denim shirt and Stetson hat, Delsie's diaphanous Aphrodite gown, and my stylish Cinco de Mayo festival ensemble, we looked as though a renegade carnival had just blown into town.

"Norman," I said, shaking his arm gently and waking him. "A lot is happening, and I want to be able to react quickly, so it's time that we looked for another change of clothes."

"What she said," yawned Delsie.

"Aye-yee," complained Norman. "Fweemen always want to change dee clothes. O-chay, Mees. We go."

"By the way," I probed as he started the big engine, "we haven't discussed your fee yet. How will you figure our bill?"

"Well, there's the rental on Chico's truck, and gasoline, and my loss of eencome from peecking up fares in Lauderdale, so..."

"How does a thousand dollars a day sound?"

"Yes, Mees." He brightened right away. "Ees a very fair price. Where do you want to go shop? Fwe can do eet!"

An hour later, Delsie and I were both garbed in faded Guess jeans and silk shirts. She wore a pair of Teva sandals, and a straw cowgirl hat which the sales clerk had bent in "goat-roper style." I was just happy to find a pair of white Nike Airs. Then we stumbled across a hometown barbecue house where we ate a late lunch of spare ribs, French fries and coleslaw, and where we looked more or less like everyone else.

13

Miss Ida Mae Knechtle lived six miles south of Tallahassee on an old farm that backed up to the Apalachicola National Forest, and over-looked Lake Munson. It was a beautiful location; the kind of building site that most families dream of but never possess; the kind of real estate that greedy developers fight over so they can slap up shoulder-to-shoulder ticky-tacky houses that will satisfy no one but the mortgage bankers and tax assessors; the kind of home that almost makes you wish that you had grown up in another era.

The antebellum house was set well back from the road on a slight rise. Its narrow, white clapboards and slate roof spoke of strength and determi-nation. Its arthritic brick chimney testified to age and mortality. Most of the outbuildings were there, although in various states of disrepair, the great barn slouching like a tired old hassock, never again to shelter prized Hereford steers. Rusted chicken wire rattled dryly in the windows of the henhouse. Weeds obscured what remained of the stone-lined well. It was a stately, tired plantation in its dotage, and I was glad to make its acquain-tance before it passed away.

Norman parked the pickup by the front door, and left the keys dan-gling in the ignition.

"Who steals it here?" he asked when I raised an eyebrow.

A thin stream of gray smoke was curling away from the chimney top, and I wondered if Miss Ida were still cooking on a cast iron wood stove as I climbed up the creaking plank steps. There was neither bell button nor knocker, so I started to rap on the paneled door, but then I saw that it was ajar an inch or two. How trusting, I thought as I pushed the door open.

"Hello! Miss Ida? Yoo-who! Anybody home?"

I heard a faint coughing sound coming from the kitchen area, so I walked back in that direction, calling out as I went, past aged photographs in dusty frames, an army of Windsor chairs, and the all-but-faded memories of lives and times gone by. The faint scent of old-fashioned eau de toilette hung in the air, but it was nearly overpowered by the odor of fresh smoke. Delsie was right behind me, and we collided with a jolt when I stopped short in the kitchen doorway. There lay Miss Ida, sprawled on her back, legs akimbo, her eyes fluttering strangely as she stared up at the ceiling, her beautiful silver hair rumpled in a dark, spreading pool of red. A blood-stained skillet lying on the floor made it clear that she had been attacked.

I knelt down gently beside Miss Ida, as Delsie hung onto the door frame, trying not to faint. Meanwhile, Norman produced a wicked-looking stiletto, and switched it open with no-nonsense authority.

"I'm sorry, dear," whispered Miss Ida when I took her hand. "I was so looking forward to our tea. I tried to stop him, but..."

She inhaled hard and caught her breath sharply. Then her eyes flew wide, her body went rigid, and finally she relaxed, slowly and completely, as her very last breath rattled out like a snore.

I put my fingers on the hollow of her neck, searching for a carotid pulse. No throbbing. No pumping.

"Is she...?" winced Delsie.

"Yes. She's dead."

Miss Ida's eyes needed closing, but before I could do it I heard the sound of a car starting up nearby. I sprinted down the hallway and out the front door just in time to see a rickety Nissan Stanza pulling out from the far side of the woodshed. Without thinking, I jumped into the pickup truck, started the big V-8 engine, and dropped the transmission into low. The sedan had a head start, but as it sped around the long circular drive, leaving a thickening stream of dust, I cut across the grass to intercept it. I must have been out of my mind. I really don't know what possessed me. I just kept accelerating, and shifting, and aiming for the side of that damned little Stanza, until the body of the car filled my windshield.

The impact was terrific, and then everything seemed to happen in slow motion. The pickup had one of those oversized front bumpers made of framing lumber, and the right edge of the bumper struck the Nissan where the driver's door latch met the frame. The Stanza's front door caved in, throwing the driver across the seat as the truck pinned the sedan against a massive yellow pine. I didn't see anything at all after that, because the airbag inflated with an explosive bang, saving me from smashing face first through the windscreen. The truck bounced back a foot or so, jammed itself into the sedan once more, and the airbag deflated like a spent balloon.

Some things are born of habit, I guess, because I found myself turning off the ignition and setting the handbrake before crawling out of the truck. My legs were a bit wobbly, and my stomach was queasy, so I took a quick personal inventory. Everything seemed to be working the way it should. No double vision. Nothing broken. But there was blood dripping in a continuous stream from my chin, and I soon discovered a nasty abrasion running down the length of my nose, and another on my chin, where the steel mesh of the airbag had scraped the skin off. Otherwise, I appeared to be in good working order.

The stiletto still gripped in his hand, Norman came sprinting up beside me, with an expression of fearful concern on his face.

"You o-chay, Mees?"

"I think so," I answered, working my jaw from side to side, and wishing that my ears would stop ringing.

I took a few slow, tentative steps, and then we checked on the driver of the sedan. It was Khaki-pants, and he was in a very bad way. The impact hadn't tossed him across the front seat as I had thought. He'd been wearing his 3-point safety harness, and the webbing had cut through his gut from navel to spine as the dislodged door had pushed him through it; like cheese being forced across a wire. He just sat there, in the middle of the car, mouth agape, eyes wide open, holding a glistening wad of pink intestines in his hands.

"He'p me, boy," he managed to squeak, moments before breathing his last.

Delsie came hobbling up just then, took one quick look in the car, fell to her knees and started retching.

"Are you going to get sick on me too?" I asked Norman.

"No, Mees." He walked around to the other side of the car. "At home I used to kill dee hogs and make dee sausage. Why ees thees so different?"

He reached through the broken side window, and removed something from the floor. It was Khaki's wallet. Fishing through it, he removed a crisp, new one hundred dollar bill, and stuffed it into his shirt pocket.

"Cerdoso!" Norman spat with contempt, employing the Spanish word for *pig* with great ferocity. Then he tossed the wallet back where he'd found it.

We helped Delsie limp to the front porch of the farmhouse, where she sat down heavily in a shaded spot on the steps. Norman offered to look after her while I returned to the kitchen.

Although Miss Ida had been boiling water for our tea on a propane range, a door on the front of the cast iron woodstove was hanging open, and a nest of orange embers glowed within. I peeked inside the sooty chasm, and it didn't take long to establish that Khaki-pants had reduced Miss Ida's hard work to a pile of feathery ash, so I watched dejectedly as the last of the ash crinkled up and fell through the grate. Then I kicked the heavy iron door closed, as hard as I could.

"Damn!" I cursed. "We were so close!"

Turning around, I saw that Miss Ida was still staring at the ceiling. Nothing of any real importance could be done for her now, but out of respect for the customs of her generation, I closed her dull, vacant eyes.

"Feeling better?" I asked Delsie, who was holding a cold washcloth to the back of her neck.

"A little, but the score now stands at Badguys six, Goodguys one, and I think we just fumbled the ball."

"We're not finished yet," I insisted, "but we'd better figure this thing out fast. Norman, how's the truck?"

"Dee bumper frame ees a leetle bent," he shrugged, "and the right shock absorber ees soft."

"Is it drivable?"

"Oh, yes. But eet won't look very good. Eet will be a leetle low on the right until dee shock absorber ees replaced."

"Can you fix it?"

"No problem."

"Okay. I want you to drive back to Chico's as soon as it gets dark. Buy a new shock absorber and whatever tools you need somewhere along the way. Pay for them with cash, throw the receipt and packaging away, and repair the truck as best you can before you get to Chico's. There's no point in getting him involved in this mess. The less he and Maria know, the better. Drop the truck off, but don't hang around and visit. Drive your cab back to Lauderdale right away, and pick up a few fares. Talk to the doormen at the hotels. Buy gas and food at places where you'll be recognized. And buy some lottery tickets, too. They're time-stamped. Make everything look nice and normal, just in case you need an alibi."

"Ees good, but what about you, Mees?"

"Yes, Sugar," carped Delsie. She spit into the grass. "What about us?"

"We're going to borrow Miss Ida's car," I announced. "I doubt that anyone will miss her until tomorrow. By then we will have dumped the car somewhere."

"Oh, that's wonderful," Delsie complained. "We've just graduated from simple snooping and prying to felonious manslaughter, conspiracy, and grand theft auto. If we keep this up, we'll make the FBI's Ten Most Wanted list in no time."

"Listen," I snapped at her, "do you want to stay here and try to explain this to the authorities, or do you want to take a shot at resolving things?"

She just stared at me with a look of disgusted resignation.

As dusk fell Norman climbed into Chico's pickup, and turned south. Then Delsie and I got into Miss Ida's antique black sedan, and headed east through the backcountry toward I-75.

"How old is this heap?" asked Delsie. She was squirming around on the cracked vinyl cover of the lumpy front seat, trying in vain to get comfortable.

"This old heap, as you call it, is a true classic," I replied. "It's a 1949 Mercury Coupe, with a flathead 8-cylinder engine. It's the same model that James Dean drove in *Rebel Without A Cause*."

"Well, then it's perfect. So where are we off to, my rebel-without-a-cause partner in crime?"

"Oh, I've got a cause, and we're going back to the Riverside Hotel, where we'll find hot showers, plush towels, fresh linens, soft beds, room service, and the key to some much-needed answers."

Delsie started to say something, but screamed instead as a wild-eyed bundle of fur, teeth and claws came hurtling over the seat and landed squarely between us. Seeing nothing familiar, the glowering animal arched its back and raised its tail in a ritualized preamble to attack. It hissed, and it threatened, and it showed its needle-sharp fangs.

"Well, hello there, Mr. Pringles," I cooed, as I reached down carefully and scratched the fur on his chest.

He relaxed then, began to purr heavily, and as though looking for a home away from home, he curled up beside my hip and drifted off to sleep.

"The poor dear must have run away and hidden in the car when Miss Ida was attacked," yawned Delsie.

Then she, too, let her weary eyes close as the vintage Merc thundered through the pinewoods like some archaic, mythical warbird, its four-sixty air conditioner working like a breeze.

*   *   *

It was just after four a.m. when I parked the tired old car on an unlit street beside the Grove Drug Store. The drive back to Lauderdale had been tedious, the coupe having neither CD, cassette player nor radio, and the ravenous engine had forced me to stop at convenience stores twice, each time for gas and oil. I was bone weary, and ready for bed.

"What are you doing?" asked Delsie as we got out of the car and stretched our aching legs.

"Huh?"

"The keys, Sugar. You left them in the ignition."

"Uh-huh."

"But somebody will steal it."

"That's the general idea. With the prices that they pay for vintage cars in Miami, some entrepreneur ought to have it down there by noon. They'll take it to a garage, lose the license plates, grind the serial number off the engine block—they didn't have Vehicle Identification Numbers in 1949—run it through a detail shop, put slipcovers on the seats, and voilà! It's gone without a trace."

We made a quick stop in the drug store, bought a big canvas beach bag and six different kinds of cat food. Then, when we exited via the corner door, I pointed up the empty side street.

"Damn, that was fast!" remarked Delsie, as I wondered which drug dealer would become the new owner of Miss Ida's classic Merc.

The lobby of the Riverside was as quiet as a chapel. There was absolutely no one in sight, so I pulled the room key out of my purse and rang the little bell that sat on top of the reception desk.

"Si? I mean, hello," came the sleepy reply from the office.

Two minutes later I rang the bell again.

"Si, si. I am coming," said the little man who stumbled around the corner, stifling a yawn with his fist.

Showing him my room key number, I asked if I had any mail. He looked at me as though I were insane, heaved the pregnant sigh affected by overworked peons the world over, pulled a couple of tightly folded manila envelopes from a pigeonhole, and handed them over with obvious contempt. Fortunately, he was too sleepy to notice Mr. Pringles, who was poking his head out of the beach bag that hung beneath my left shoulder.

My fourth floor room was just the way I had left it. Thick, shamrock green carpet. Burgundy damask wallcovering. Mahogany veneer wet-bar. Soft, canopied, king-sized bed with flowing drapes. Broad French doors which led to the private balcony.

"I feel like I've been time-warped," said Delsie as she dropped her gym bag on the floor. "First that dreadful old car, then that rundown, pitiful excuse for a pharmacy, and now this... this... Sugar, I'm way too tired to play guessing games, so tell me the truth. Where are we exactly? 1935?"

"Only the ambiance," I answered tiredly, removing a dark brown bottle of my favorite Mexican beer from the mini-bar. "The amenities are all thoroughly modern. Why don't you try the jacuzzi? Your legs will love it."

"Does this shrine to Humphrey Bogart have room service?"

"They offer a superb, 24-hour selection," I groaned as I plopped down in an overstuffed recliner.

Delsie snatched up the phone, pressed the kitchen number, and waited. When someone finally answered, she started barking orders in the irritated tone of a wealthy woman who is used to getting her way.

"Two African lobster tails with drawn butter, two Caesar salads, a chilled bottle of Dom Perignon—I don't care which year—and something dark, heavy, and sinfully chocolate, preferably with fresh raspberries. Figure a 30% tip on the bill, and charge it to the room. Fifteen minutes will be fine. Thank you."

She turned to me as she dropped the handset back on the cradle and, with an exasperated look in her eyes, said, "Sugar, I'm going to take a shower, so for the next fifteen minutes you're on your own."

As Delsie started running the water, I checked the voice mail. There were three messages from Angie, telling me that everything was all right at the clinic, and asking me to call her at the office whenever I got the chance. There was also a message from Carl Rehm.

"It was good to see you at the Mimosas this afternoon, Dr. Pearson," he'd said. "I'm in the car now. Just leaving there myself. Long drive home. I know you won't be receiving this for several days, but I'd like to talk with you as soon as possible. I've had another thought about your father's trip to the Keys. Perhaps we could meet somewhere and discuss it. Please give me a ring when you get back from your cruise. Bye now."

His voice was pregnant with insecurity and tension.

I flipped on every light in the room to chase the banshees away, and lowered the air conditioning to suck the stuffiness out of the place. Then I turned my attention to Mr. Pringles. Even the best of cats are finicky creatures, and after a stressful day I had no idea what he might feel like eating, or if he'd even eat at all. So I decided to let him make his own selection. I opened three different cans of cat food—Lamb Brisket, Salmon-Trout and Beef Stroganoff—and I set them all on the floor. Mr. Pringles sniffed at each one in a noncommittal sort of way, turned his back disdainfully, rolled around in the middle of the carpet for a couple of minutes, slowly returned to the open cans, nibbled tentatively, and devoured all three.

Meanwhile, I took a thin sip from my bottle, and stared with disbelief at the beer. Another good thing ruined! Why is it that when you find a superior product made by a small and diligent concern, some profit-driven conglomerate of MBA idiots buys it up, expands the manufacturing process, waters down the goods, and leaves you with yet one more example of New Age nothingness? I stepped over to the wet-bar, ran the beer down the drain and shook my head. I was beginning to sound just like Dad.

The shower stopped running, and a minute later there was a knock on the door.

"Room Service," came the muffled announcement from the hallway.

Too tired to think, I said, "Just a minute, please," removed the safety chain from its bracket, and turned the deadbolt. But when I unlatched the door it burst open in my face. A slick, meaty hand caught me by the nape of the neck, and another one clamped itself over my mouth. It was Lt. Okun.

I tried to cry out, but I sounded like a ventriloquist under water.

"Enough," growled Okun, sharply increasing the pressure on my mouth. He smiled at me like a sadist pouring kerosene on a cat. "Hell, you're jus' like your daddy; ain't you? You think you can go around everyone; think you're smarter than everyone; think you're better than everyone. Well, he wasn't, and you ain't, neither. Now you're coming with me, little lady, nice and quiet like. If'n you don't, I'll break your neck like a twig. Understan'?"

I nodded my head a fraction of an inch, and then shards of porcelain filled the air. Delsie had heard the commotion and come to my rescue, bashing Okun in the back of the head with a heavy celadon table lamp. For a split second I thought that he might shake the blow off. Then his beady little eyes rolled back into his skull, and he fell forward.

Finding myself trapped on the bed beneath three hundred pounds of rancid blubber, and thoroughly unable to either breathe or extricate myself, I looked to Delsie for help. But she just stood there, stark naked, gazing out the door.

"Put it here," she said to the incredulous porter who pushed the service cart into the room.

She pulled on a house robe, signed the tab, said a polite, Southern, "Thank you, kind sir," and gently closed the door. Then, tugging at one of Okun's stubby little legs, she shifted his position until his own dead weight dragged him to the floor. His head hit the carpet like a hammer.

"Thanks," I gasped. "Now let's get the hell out of here."

Fortunately, Delsie hadn't washed her hair, so she dressed quickly while I stuffed Mr. Pringles back in his beach bag. Okun was breathing shallowly, and we didn't know who else might be lurking in the hall, or in the lobby, so we took our stuff, stepped out onto the balcony, and climbed four stories straight down the steel fire escape ladder. It was one of those times when not looking down was precisely the right thing to do. The New River was rolling lazily by, and hustling along the famed Riverwalk, we moved past ghostly restaurants and lifeless shops until climbing an exit stairway beside the Broward Center for the Performing Arts.

"What now?" asked Delsie as she sat on the edge of a concrete planter and inspected her feet.

"Cab?"

"Not Norman!"

"No. They may be watching him."

There was a kiosk with several pay phones nearby, so leaving Mr. Pringles with Delsie, I flipped through the yellow pages, found what I wanted, and called a taxi. Then I found a second listing, and tore that page out of the book.

Ten very long and anxious minutes later, a Comet Cab arrived.

"Where to, ladies?" asked the grizzled female driver.

I looked at the crumpled yellow page.

"Fifteen Twenty-three Old Dixie Highway, Oakland Park."

"Now don't y'all worry none, ya hear?" said our driver as the cab picked up speed. "Everything's going to be just fine. Believe it. I know the score, and I know the way. Been there myself a time or two. Just you remember, girls, the sun comes up new every morning."

"What is she talking about?" asked Delsie. "Where are we going?"

"To the battered women's shelter. Where else?"

"Good Lord," moaned Delsie. "Last night I was living in the lap of luxury. Then I got blown out of the water, and lost my friends, and tonight I end up in a shelter."

"Yes'm," agreed the driver sympathetically. "We've all been there, girl. Sure enough."

The sun was just creeping over the horizon, hot, red and angry, when we arrived in front of Hope House. The driver wished us well, and after watching a 10-minute video which explained the philosophy of the shelter, the receptionist showed us upstairs to a daisy-wallpapered bedroom with a pair of twin beds.

"We always eat breakfast together," said the young attendant who helped us to get settled, "but since you ladies are arriving so late, we'll let you sleep until ten or so. Then you'll have an opportunity to take a hot shower and eat brunch, after which you'll have separate interviews with an intake counselor. We'll explain the rest in the morning."

She turned to leave, but stopped and glanced back.

"As a general rule," she smiled sweetly, "pets are not allowed. But I must have been pretty sleepy, I guess. I never did see that cat. You're safe here. Get some good sleep."

She stepped into the hallway, and closed the door quietly behind her.

"Now listen, Sugar," Delsie insisted, "I'm as hungry as a bear, and so are you, although you may not care to admit it. So let's not talk anymore, or plan anymore, or even think anymore. Let's just eat and go to bed."

With that, she reached into her gym bag and withdrew three big, crinkled wads of aluminum foil. The first held an assortment of soft corn muffins, bread and rolls. The second contained two cold, but absolutely delicious lobster tails. The third consisted of a smashed Fallen Marquis Chocolate Torte, complete with fresh red raspberries. And in her typically stylish way, Delsie had also brought a bottle of Dom Perignon '79.

I don't know who enjoyed that mini-feast more—Delsie, me, or Mr. Pringles.

14

Delsie and I got up a little after nine. Exhausted though we may have been, we were just too wired to sleep any more, so we decided that a three-hour respite would simply have to do.

After bracing, cold showers, and a breakfast of sourdough toast, grapefruit halves and black coffee, one of the counselors informed us that instead of having separate intake interviews, we'd be meeting with the program director together. It would be a difficult session, we imagined, for if we shared our story and asked for asylum, one could legally construe that Hope House was harboring two fugitives, which is precisely what we had become. On the other hand, if we did not tell the whole truth, we would be manipulating honest people who had dedicated a good portion of their lives and fortunes to a just, and often dangerous, cause. Neither of those options was palatable.

"Good morning," the director said with a polite but cool smile as she invited us into her office. "Won't you ladies please take a seat?"

Hope House had once been a sizable private residence, and the director's office was capacious, to say the least. At one end, surrounding a tiled fireplace that arched out into the room, there were three love seats arranged in a square horseshoe. We each took one, and I opened my mouth to say something, but the director held up her hand.

"Before you divulge anything at all," she began, "please allow me to
state our position in regard to your case. Hope House exists to aid women
in distress. In a more specific sense, it aids women who are the victims of
physical, sexual, or emotional abuse. In most cases, such abuse takes the
form of domestic violence, perpetrated by a spouse, or boyfriend.
Therefore, the overall intake profiles of our clients are generally consistent,
and you ladies don't fit."

I stiffened, waiting for the blow.

"For one thing," she continued in a resolute tone, "battered women
usually appear alone, or in some cases with children. They never appear
on our doorstep in pairs, much less at the hour when you two arrived.
For another, ninety-seven percent of the women who appeal to Hope
House for assistance have a high school education or less. Based on staff
observations made both when you arrived and while you ate breakfast, I'd
probably be safe in assuming that you have college degrees of some sort,
and quite possibly post-graduate training as well. Then there's the matter
of diet. The last time that anyone ate lobster tails and chocolate cake in
this venerable house was somewhere prior to 1965. Therefore, I must
conclude that neither of you meet the profile of either our clients or our
program."

Delsie glanced at me with the wan expression of an eight-year-old who
had just been caught playing with her mother's makeup. I knew just how
she felt. A knot was forming in the pit of my stomach, too.

"Nevertheless," our host went on, "I am not suggesting that you aren't
in some kind of difficulty, or that you do not require some form of assistance. You clearly are, and you clearly do. Now, if I take what I've read in
the newspapers this morning, and add it to your enigmatic appearance,
and if I've drawn the proper conclusion, then the two of you are in a very
tight spot. This, however, is not the proper place for you to either hide or
work through your problems. Your continued presence could prove an
embarrassment to Hope House; a most undesirable outcome which we
would all regret deeply, I am sure. So here is my proposal, ladies.

"First of all, no one actually stays here at Hope House. That is the community's impression, but it is inaccurate. In point of fact, this facility serves as a clearing house only. We run a double blind system, you see, for the physical and mental security of our clients. Once a woman has been taken in by our organization, she is moved to one of six safe houses in the greater Fort Lauderdale area, none of which is known to the public. In this way, we put a great deal of space between our clients and their potential persecutors. At present, we have a two-bedroom safe house available, and our volunteers are stocking it with a 24-hour supply of foodstuffs even as we speak. The utilities have been turned on, and there is a telephone, should you need one. The house is yours to use until noon tomorrow, at which time a crew will arrive to clean it up and lock off the utilities.

"To avoid discovery in transit, you will use our standard exiting procedure. In fifteen minutes a volunteer will escort you to the garage, where you will get into a small commercial van driven by yet another of our volunteers. We have a great many of them, and they are all highly dedicated and discreet. You will sit on the floor of the van until you reach the safe house, whereupon you will go directly indoors. Is this agreeable?"

"Thank you," I said. "We appreciate your kindness, and..."

The director put her hand up again. "A simple thank-you will be quite sufficient. Hope House has seen far worse than this, and survived without a scratch. From here on I enjoin you to say nothing except *thank-you* to our staff. In this way, should anyone ask about you later, we can truthfully report that you told us nothing."

Delsie and I nodded in agreement, stood up, shook hands with the director, and then a counselor led us back to our room. There we found a very pleasant young woman, who was holding Mr. Pringles on her lap while brushing his fur.

"I took him out in the back yard and let him walk around a little bit," she stated shyly. "I thought that he probably needed to... you know. I figured that you might want him to take care of that now. It's beginning to cloud up."

"Thank you," I replied, keeping my pledge to say nothing more.

We packed our things, and the counselor escorted us to the garage, where we found the director waiting.

"Is there anything else that we can do for you?" she asked as we prepared to leave.

"I don't wish to be presumptuous," I replied, "but would it be possible for us to make one stop along the way? I really need to take care of something at the Post Office on South Federal Highway. It's a matter of the utmost importance, I assure you."

The director raised an eyebrow and looked at the volunteer driver, who shrugged good-naturedly, and we were soon on our way.

*   *   *

There was no waiting line in the lobby of the Post Office when we arrived, so I walked right up to the counter.

"Good morning," I said. "I'm administering the estate of my uncle, who passed away recently, and I'd like to make arrangements for his mail."

Opening one of the envelopes that I had picked up at the hotel, I withdrew two documents and pushed them across the countertop.

"Here is a copy of his certificate of death, and here is a court order naming me as the executrix of his estate."

The clerk ignored my claim of legal authority and hollered, "Hey, Fred! I got a lady here what wants to pick up some dead guy's mail. Does she hafta fill out some kinda form or sumpin?"

"Nah," yelled Fred in response. "Only if she wants his mail forwarded."

"I only wish to pick up whatever is in his box right now," I informed the clerk.

I wanted to get this over with as quickly as possible.

My gregarious postman, who appeared to be a transferee from the Bronx, read my paperwork very carefully. Then, smiling at me he said, "Okay, dare. Everytin's in order, but how do I know dat it's you?"

"What?"

"I need to see some ID, lady. I need a picture ID. A driver's license. Sumpin like dat. You know?"

"Oh, damn," I replied a bit too loudly.

I'd been so preoccupied with sorting through the envelopes and legal documents that I had neglected to bring my purse in with me.

"I'll be right back," I said.

Certain that time was running out, that I'd bump into a group of friends from Dad's marina, that a news crew would film me while doing a story on the Elvis stamp, that a mirthful cadre of Congressional aides would detain me while celebrating the ten billionth visit by a postal patron in Lauderdale, I ran out to the van and retrieved my license.

The wind was beginning to blow, and ominous gray clouds were darkening the landscape as I ran back into the Post Office.

"Wait here," the clerk smiled after glancing at my driver's license photo.

My heart stopped cold every time another person entered the lobby. The fear of discovery had my adrenaline flowing, and my eyes kept darting around the room. I felt as tense as a flagpole.

Five minutes later the clerk returned with a milky, corrugated plastic box, with **U.S. MAIL** stenciled on the side in dark blue letters. It was filled to overflowing with all sorts of envelopes and catalogs.

"I'll let yous borrow da box if you bring it back," he teased.

"Oh, I promise," I grunted as I took the heavy crate, and waddled toward the door.

Then all of my fears turned real.

"Dr. Pearson? Dr. Pearson, is that you?" a male voice called out from the other end of the lobby.

I bolted for the exit.

"Dr. Pearson! Dr. Pearson!"

Banging through the door, I charged out of that Post Office like a halfback on fourth down and three to go. People jumped out of my way as I scrambled across the parking lot at full tilt, or nearly full. For a woman carrying thirty pounds of mail in a stupid-looking plastic box, I was doing pretty well.

"Dr. Pearson!" the voice called insistently. "Stop!"

My pursuer chased me through the parking lot as the first fat drops of rain began to splatter on the pavement.

Delsie slid the side door of the van wide open, and I dove in headfirst, pushing the mailbox ahead of me to create momentum; and before my knees hit the floor the van was moving.

"Go, go, go!" Delsie yelled as the van zoomed out of its parking slot.

"Miss Jean!" the man bellowed as he sprinted behind the van. "Come back here! Come back!"

The rapidly accelerating van pounded across a concrete strip in the parking lot, banged over a curb or two, and slammed onto the highway. It leaned over at an alarming angle when we skidded into a tight turn, and made a deafening racket as the heavy-duty differential ground furiously away, spinning at least half the tread off the tires. Then we fishtailed several times while switching lanes.

Trying unsuccessfully to regain my balance, I ricocheted off the sidewalls and rear doors before Delsie managed to wrestle the sliding side door shut. When she finally got it latched in place she looked as though she had just faced Cerberus, the three-headed hound who guards the gates of Hell.

"Sheez! That was close!" yelled Delsie. "I thought that I was going to fall out of this thing! Who was he, Sugar? Did you get a good look at his face? Did you recognize him?"

"I didn't have to see him. I've heard that voice often enough this week. It was Carl Rehm."

"Your husband?" inquired our driver, who'd gotten caught up in the excitement.

"Worse," I frowned. "That was my lawyer."

Delsie looked at me with a worried expression. "So the jig is up," she said with a shake of her head.

"Yes, it is. Rehm will talk to the clerk, he'll find out whose mail I picked up, and he'll know for sure."

"So we'll have to crack this thing today."

"Right. Today."

"Sugar, what about this van?" Delsie asked, reviewing our situation and seeing the weak link. "Do you suppose that he got the license number?"

"Shoot, girls!" laughed our driver. "It won't matter if he did get the tag number. I borrowed this van from my hubby's vending machine company. Do it all the time. He's got over forty of them, so there's really no problem. I'll just bring a box of doughnuts with me to occupy the dispatcher when I get back. Then I'll access the sign-out register in the computer, make a few random adjustments, and instantaneous data mayhem! They've got the DP Blues. By the time they can figure out who, or when, or which one, and by the time anyone gets around to talking to me, it will be Thanksgiving at least. By that time, I won't remember a thing. Let me see. What day was that anyway? Was that the week of the Girl Scout cookie drive? The church bake sale? The March for Life? The Loaves and Fishes food bank drive? I'm afraid that I won't be able to help them very much."

"Okay," I declared. "We've got the first team blocking for us, and we've heard the two-minute warning. It's time to even the score."

"I'm with you, Sugar," Delsie said bitterly, "but we're down by five.

"Yeah, but one touchdown will do it."

Delsie lips curled into the most diabolocal smile that I had ever seen. "Then let's give them the ol' flea-flicker," she growled, "in honor of Raul and the boys. Let's mow the bastards down."

15

The safe house was pretty much what I had imagined; a bungalow tucked into an older residential neighborhood, which was bordered on one side by a wooded recreational area named Snyder Park, and by Interstate 595 on the other. The main runway of the Lauderdale airport rumbled with jet traffic just beyond the Interstate. It was a damp and dismal scene, but the house had two window air conditioners, a modest supply of low-fat food, some bottled drinks, a copy of the morning paper, and roach motels in every closet. One of the volunteers had drawn all of the curtains shut, and some caring soul had left a shallow cardboard box filled with Kitty Litter on the kitchen floor beside the back door. The good folks of Hope House had thought of everything.

"Shoot!" said Delsie, as she sat down and flipped through the *Sun-Sentinel*. "I guess we're famous now, Sugar. Look at these headlines: *Missing Heiress Believed Alive; Wanted for Questioning in Double Homicide. Veterinarian Also Sought.* We must have left fingerprints at Miss Ida's. I see that they dug up one of my old society page photos. Not too bad, although the dress is out of style. But Holy Hannah! Where did they get this mug shot of you; from your high school yearbook?"

I looked over her shoulder. "Oh, that's a publicity still that Peter took when I opened the clinic. Angie must have supplied it."

"Is that all you have to say?" she stormed. "In case you haven't tumbled to it, Sugar, we're wanted by the law. We're in very deep trouble. Mama and Daddy are probably going bonkers right now."

The storm had renewed its assault, and the rain was coming down in buckets. It drummed heavily on the roof, and banged through the downspouts in slapping-clacking surges. It might have been a bad day for the beach set, but the storm gave me a sense of empowerment, a feeling of immunity. I walked into the living room, picked up the ugly postal box, carried it into the kitchen and set it on one of the cane-bottomed, bentwood chairs. But before I could reach for its contents a piercing scream shattered every nerve in my body.

"Eeeik!" yelled Delsie. "Oh, my Gosh! Listen to this! Listen to what it says in the paper!"

"The only confirmed survivor of the destruction of the Jerome *has been identified as Raul Bautista Alberdi, who served as captain of the sunken yacht."*

"Raul's alive?"

"Yes. Shut up and listen, Sugar."

"Local sport fishermen, who rushed to the aid of the sinking vessel, found Mr. Alberdi unconscious in a fuel oil slick, and plucked him from the water. His inflatable life jacket had kept him afloat.

"'Mr. Alberdi is alive today because he used an approved flotation device,' commented Lieutenant JG Brandon Cole, a Public Information Officer at the Key West Coast Guard Base.

"A Coast Guard Sea King air-sea rescue helicopter flew Mr. Alberdi to the Trauma Department at Fishermen's Hospital in Marathon, where a spokesperson reported his injuries as 'minor abrasions and contusions, first-degree facial burns, and mild smoke inhalation.' He regained consciousness yesterday morning, and is listed in good condition. The hospital expects to release him early today."

"Oh, I'm so glad," I sighed.

Delsie dissolved in a flood of tears, and I bent over to hug her. The next thing I knew we were both crying, and then Delsie snuffled proudly and said, "That's enough of that, Sugar. Let's get to work."

We spread Uncle Bud's mail out on the kitchen table, dumped the junk back in the plastic box, and searched through the larger pieces. Finally, Delsie found an oversized manila envelope boasting the return address: Florida Department of State, Division of Corporations. She ripped the envelope open, and the scent of eau de toilette filled the air. It came from a sweet little handwritten note that Miss Ida had penned on creamy personal stationery, underneath which lay an orderly stack of legalistic gobbledygook.

Thirty minutes later, we had sorted the jumble into several stacks.

"All right, Sugar," Delsie said. "Let's see if we can establish a chronology, and I'll try to flow-chart these documents."

So I started calling out the names and dates on the various papers, while Delsie noted them on a yellow legal pad. After two or more hours of painstaking work, she had managed to construct a complex diagram, which looked as though someone had arranged a brood of baby tarantulas on the page, and stomped them flat.

"See anything interesting?" I asked.

"No. Do you?"

I shook my head in exasperation.

"Okay," Delsie prompted. "Let's walk this thing through. The purchase contract states that the condominium community to be known as The Mimosas is being built by Escorbilo Property Development, Inc. Escorbilo has a plethora of contracts, subcontracts and partnership agreements with various and sundry construction firms, for innumerable projects including the completion of the causeway, fresh water mains and sanitary sewer systems, communications trunks, et cetera. In addition, there are other corporations, like The Mimosa Gardens Operating Fund, which will be responsible for the maintenance of the condominiums themselves and/or the common areas, such as streets, sidewalks and parkways. Evidently, everything on Greene Key, with the exception of a few commercial plots which are being set aside for things like the shopping mall and marina, will be part of an entirely private and autonomous residential community, rather than becoming a formally incorporated public township. So far, so good. It's all been done before, and it works pretty well, as long as the residents possess sufficient funds to pay for the cost of upkeep and services."

"The price of the condo units should serve as a screening mechanism, separating the haves from the have-nots," I suggested.

"Precisely," she affirmed in the emotionless tone of a law school professor. "The contract makes it clear that the condominium purchasers will be the sole owners of their individual villas, and that they will all be the co-owners of commonly held property, with the exception of the shopping mall and marina, which are being held separately by the Escorbilo Mercantile Development Corporation as a commercial venture, in fee simple. In other words, buy a condo and you not only own a home, but a fractional portion of all common areas such as the golf course and beaches."

"It sounds pretty democratic. But is it legal?"

"Absolutely. In fact, it's a very sweet deal if one wishes to live in an exclusive enclave and have some true measure of community control. The owners, you see, each have a fractional percentage actual ownership in Greene Key. Therefore, The Mimosas, as a community, will be run along the lines of a traditional town meeting. It's a larger and significantly more expansive version of the co-op buildings which are so popular in New York City. The owners establish the rules, by direct vote or by proxy. Everyone shares the responsibilities and the expenses, and everyone has a share in the decision-making. Communities like this have sprung up in Arizona, Massachusetts, even Kansas. Risk management can be a concern, because opportunists can sue enterprises of this magnitude for big bucks, but the major underwriters, like Chubb and Lloyd's, have established both legal and reinsurance mechanisms to handle such contingencies. Therefore, this appears to be a very sound project, in principle at least."

"No sign of fraud, embezzlement, or double-dealing?"

"None that I can see. Unlike a lot of financial undertakings, this one looks as clean as a whistle. The annual reports look good at any rate. Of course, we don't have the benefit of reviewing the actual financial audits, or even the corporate tax returns, but there aren't any complicated false fronts in evidence, and there aren't any of the usual holding company entanglements. It's pretty much as Rehm described it when we ran into him on the island. The condominiums are being sold as the project moves along, which keeps traditional financing at an advantageous minimum while assuring that cash flow is normalized. Everything is being done by permit and by statute. It looks really good."

"Dad used to have an expression," I mused. "He said that anything that looks too good to be true probably is."

Delsie got up and pulled the blinds open on the back door. The rain had tapered off a bit, and it was drizzling outside, grim and bleak. She sighed and let the blinds fall back in place, startling Mr. Pringles, who was napping on top of the refrigerator.

"Well," she said, "let's look at it from the other end."

I took a couple of bottles of Snapple pink lemonade from the refrigerator, opened them, handed one to Delsie, and we sat down again.

"All right," I began. "According to the minutes of the Emergency Funding Task Force of the Ways and Means Committee, dated Monday January 24, 1996, a motion proposed by the Honorable Marion Baedeker, acknowledging the recent survey results by the Army Corps of Engineers as placed in evidence, and calling for the sale of Greene Key by the Chairman of the Ways and Means Committee of the State Legislature of the sovereign State of Florida, pursuant to paragraph 3 of the Excess Non-Agricultural Lands Disposal and Disbursement Act of 1899, was passed by acclamation, in a unanimous voice vote and without dissent, and was entered as such into the record."

"What about the sale itself?"

"We've got a photocopy of the bill of sale somewhere. Here it is. Monday January 24, 1996. Property described as... blah, blah, blah, a full page of surveying measurements, blah, blah, blah, otherwise known as Greene Key, sold by the Land Management Services Bureau of the State of Florida to Escorbillo Property Development. The sums paid, the names, the official seals and stamps, are all listed as if this were an 18th century royal grant from King George III."

Delsie's face curled into a funny expression. "Sugar, have you got a copy of the deed there?"

"Yes, here it is. There's a letter attached to it as well. It says that the certificate of ownership—it's not an actual deed per se—is a lawful, legally binding instrument, but that Greene Key will hereafter and forever fall under the jurisdiction of Monroe County, and that as soon as the State's Attorney General notifies the Attorney for Monroe County and the Monroe County Tax Assessor of the jurisdictional transference, the transferee can obtain a proper deed without encumbrance or further expense."

"And what is the name of the owner of Greene Key, as listed on that temporary certificate?"

"Escorbillo Property Development."

"Let me see those papers."

Delsie pored over the bill of sale for Greene Key, inspected the certificate of ownership, reviewed the specimen sales contract for The Mimosas, and compared the three of them several times. Then a crafty grin lit her face.

"Bingo, Sugar," she said with confidence. "We've just found the trap door that leads to the mysterious secret passage. Your Uncle Bud undoubtedly found it, too. That's why he and your Dad were sailing down to the Keys on a fictitious fishing trip. They were going to do a little digging and scratching, just like always."

"Do you mind letting me in on the secret?"

"Listen closely," Delsie explained. "First, it's a matter of strictest legality. The company names on the bill of sale and certificate of ownership in regard to Greene Key, and on The Mimosa's sales contract for its condominiums are truly and substantially different. One signifies a formal corporation, and uses the word Incorporated. The other does not. Therefore, the two entities listed are not the same company."

"But couldn't Escorbilo Property Development have been incorporated, or had its request for incorporation formally approved, after the official transfer of Greene Key had taken place? Raul said that the sale was a hastily done deal, after all. It may have taken time to get the official corporate charter filed and stamped."

"Yes," she said thoughtfully, sifting through the papers. "In point of fact, you're right. The Fictitious Name Application for the alias Escorbilo Property Development wasn't submitted until February 7th, 1996. That would provide a good explanation for the difference if anyone, like your Uncle Bud, got curious and started asking questions. But then there's also the spelling."

"The spelling?"

"Sugar, you really must study Spanish one day. The first company name has two Ls: E-s-c-o-r-b-i-l-l-o. The second has only one L: E-s-c-o-r-b-i-l-o."

"Couldn't that be a simple copying error?"

"Ordinarily, I might buy that, but in this case the names are Spanish sounding, and in Spanish there's a big difference between a single L and a double L, because a double L is pronounced like a Y. For example, the scouring pad trade name Brillo would be pronounced Bree-yo in Spanish. Therefore, with a double L, Es-core-bil-o becomes Es-core-bee-yo."

"And this is a big difference?"

"Legally, yes. When one files a Fictitious Name Application in order to secure a unique name for a business, and when the name is rendered in Spanish, DivCorp requires that the name be given in English as well. The reason for this is quite sanguine. To forestall confusion, the State wants to avoid having two different corporations chartered under the same name, even though the names are in different languages. As an example, DivCorp will not approve the corporate name Rio Blanco if there is already a firm doing business under the name White River; and they will not approve Old Homestead if there is already a company named Rancho Viejo. The only exception to this rule comes in the use of family surnames, which often cannot be translated anyway. Therefore, Escorbillo and Escorbilo could be, and in fact probably are, two separate corporate entities."

"Which means?"

"Which means that I smell a land scam. A big one."

Delsie reached for the telephone on the wall, but I stopped her.

"Thanks to Carl Rehm, the police probably know we're back in town. Hard-wire phones are easy to trace. It's virtually instantaneous. When you call 911, for example, a computer monitor in front of the Police dispatcher provides a full screen of information which identifies your telephone number, the subscriber's name, and your exact location. It even displays a street map showing the position of the nearest squad car. So use my cell-phone. The best that they can do is get a fix on the cell tower nearest our location, and that's about a two-mile radius, over eight square miles."

Delsie took the cell-phone without a word, entered a number from one of the documents, and called the Florida State Division of Corporations. That phone call took forever. She asked question after question about corporate names, certificates, reports, filing dates and more. When she finally flipped the phone shut, she looked exhausted.

"I think that I may have gotten farther than your uncle did," she said. "There are, indeed, two different business entities in the State of Florida. Escorbillo, and Escorbilo. The trick is that Escorbillo is a DBA."

"A DBA?"

"In most states you have two basic choices when you start a small business," she explained. "You can form and incorporate a company, or you can simply use your own resources, taking significant financial risks, but avoiding a lot of legal requirements, in what is commonly referred to as a sole proprietorship. A kid who mows lawns is running a sole proprietor-ship, as are most wallpaper hangers and pet sitters. However, the State of Florida offers a third option, a DBA; short for *Doing Business As*. A DBA is recognized as a legitimate business, and DivCorp will register a fictitious name for a DBA, but a DBA is not a formal corporation. Therefore, a DBA doesn't have to file annual reports or audits, like a corporation, so DBA records are scanty."

"And?"

"Although DBAs are not required to report the names of their owners or partners, when filing a Fictitious Name Application someone with a permanent address must be listed as the agent of record. The agent of record can be the owner, his or her attorney, or CPA, or anyone at all."

"And the agent of record for Escorbillo is...?"

"Jefferson Davis Okun."

"Lt. Okun?"

"The very same."

"Lt. Okun owns Escorbillo Property Development?"

"Well, there is no true ownership with a DBA, because there are no real assets. Okun probably doesn't own one percent of either Greene Key or The Mimosas. More than likely, he's just an errand boy."

"Okay. I understand all of this, but how does it add up to fraud? Where's the swindle?"

"If I had to guess, I'd say that it's the ol' South Carolina shuffle. It's a perfectly legal con game that's been played for years on the Grand Strand around Myrtle Beach. Some shyster buys a piece of beachfront property. He leases it to another company for the purpose of development. Condominiums go up, promotions are run, a real estate firm is brought in to sell time-share condos. People buy a week's worth of condo ownership for next to nothing, and are assured of summer vacations at the beach in perpetuity. Then a management firm is hired to run and maintain the condo property, and everybody ends up happy.

"The developer makes good money, the advertising firm charges fat fees, the real estate company rakes in commissions by the score, the management group has ongoing employment, and the bankers get their pound of flesh at every turn. Then thirty or forty years roll by, and the shyster who bought the land in the first place produces his original contract and announces that the lease is up. By law, improvements made on leased real property become the actual property of the land owner at the termination of the lease. In other words, everyone who made mortgage payments for condominium ownership in perpetuity finds that he or she owns absolutely nothing. The shyster then becomes the sole owner and landlord."

"So what you're suggesting is that The Mimosas is being built on land that is leased, and that the condo owners may wake up one sunny day to find that they are no longer elite members of the landed gentry, but the latest additions to America's homeless population."

"It looks that way."

"Then whoever killed Dad and Uncle Bud did it to prevent them from putting all of this together," I declared with growing hostility.

The rain had picked up again, and between the skittering clouds and the late hour it was getting pretty dark outside. I started to turn on the overhead light, but that itchy feeling was back. Someone was stalking me again, and my instincts warned that it was safer to talk in the dark.

"Isn't it time to call in the cops?" I asked.

"Which ones?" Delsie asked scornfully. "The cops who want to arrest us for the killing of one of their own, which is every officer in Florida, or the cops who are tied to the land fraud scheme and want to make us disappear? We can't prove anything yet, Sugar. All we have are some Xeroxed documents, some well-founded suspicions, and someone else's cat."

Blustery gusts of wind were throwing sheets of rain against the side of the house, and greenish-white lightning flashed every couple of minutes.

"I think it's time to force the rats into the open," I growled.

I reached for my cell-phone and touched a number on the speed-dialer. A distant phone started to warble, and was picked up on the second ring.

"Hello, Mr. Rehm? It's Jean Pearson. I'm sorry that I ran away from you at the Post Office this morning, but I'm in terrible trouble. Someone has been trying to kill me. I think that the police are involved, so I can't call them. I don't know who to turn to. I really need your help, Mr. Rehm. Can you meet me at Dad's boat in thirty minutes? I need to talk to you. I'm really confused. I don't know what to do. I've got to go now. Bye."

I heard him start to say "Of cour...," but I hung up.

"What are you, nuts?" Delsie exploded. "What makes you think that Rehm will come alone? And if you've got to confront him, why do it at your Dad's houseboat? It's so confined there. Why not meet him in an open place, in a public place?"

"I'll tell you why," I said with unbridled venom. "Because that boat is a floating arsenal, and I want some firepower. There are pistols tucked almost everywhere. In the closet. In the medicine cabinet. In a holster beside the bed. I'm sick and tired of people chasing me around, and I'm fed up with being a victim. We're going to get there first, grab a couple of guns, wait for Rehm and then get a few solid answers. It's time to face this thing head on, Delsie. It's time to nail these people, and I'm going to even the odds. Speaking of which..."

I punched another number into my speed dialer.

"It's Jean Pearson," I announced.

"Thank God you're alive," replied L'Ouverture. "Where are you?"

"Never mind that. Can you meet me at my Dad's houseboat in an hour? Dad and Uncle Bud were killed because they discovered a big land scam at Green Key, and my attorney, Carl Rehm, is up to his neck in this thing. I'll have Rehm on the boat with me, along with enough documentation to give the prosecution a running start. Come and get him. He's all yours."

"Yes, but listen..." L'Ouverture tried to say. But I hung up on him, too.

"Why the delay?" asked Delsie. "Why not have L'Ouverture arrive with us? It would be safer."

"Because Rehm is a lawyer. He won't volunteer a single thing on his own. Not if L'Ouverture is there. He's far too shrewd for that. But I'm no cop. I'm a private citizen, and I'm also a fugitive, so I won't have to play by the restrictive rules of legitimate law enforcement. I won't have to recite the Miranda warning, and I certainly don't have to respect Rehm's civil rights. I'll just point Dad's M2 submachine gun at him, put a few rounds in the deck if necessary, and he'll sing like a canary. You'll be an independent, third party witness. Even if he claims that his statement was made under duress, we'll still have the information. Game, set, and match. Then we'll turn him over to the Coast Guard."

Delsie started to say something, but a ferocious bolt of lightning hit nearby, and the booming peal of thunder drowned out her words. Then her expression turned to one of abject terror as she put her left hand over her mouth, smothered a scream, and pointed with her right.

"The front door!" she gasped. "Look at the front door!"

There was a plastic window blind hanging over the big rectangular pane of glass which comprised the top half of the entry door, and with the next bolt of lightening I saw it, a flashing silhouette. Someone was standing on the porch. It was an obese, dangerous, hulking man, and he was holding a massive revolver in one hand while trying the door latch with the other. It was Lt. Okun, without a doubt.

I jerked Mr. Pringles off the refrigerator, tossed him into the beach bag, and threw the strap over my shoulder. Then Delsie and I hobbled out the back door during the next barrage of thunder. The downpour was terrific, a perfect black squall, and we lost sight of the house before we'd gone fifty feet; but we kept limping along anyway, right through the madly swaying trees of Snyder Park. When we finally got to the opposite side of the woods, we found ourselves crouching in someone's back yard.

Thinking of Norman, I rummaged through the beach bag.

"Oh, shit!" I cursed. "We left the cell-phone on the table."

"Now what?" asked Delsie as we huddled beneath a tree.

Delsie had obviously popped her stitches during the race through Snyder Park, because the puddle in which she was standing was stained with a growing cloud of crimson.

I looked around for shelter, for an escape route, fearful that our pursuer was hot on our trail. At the far side of the yard there stood a decrepit, free-standing garage which sat well back from an untidy clapboard house. Someone had used an old row boat oar to prop the overhead door open, and a light was burning inside.

"Come on," I whispered, leading Delsie across the yard to the corner of the building.

There were two young boys in the rickety garage, about ten or twelve years old. They were playing a madcap game of Ping-Pong on an old closet door supported by two sawhorses, using badminton racquets for paddles while beating a golf ball back and forth. A piece of 2x6 served as the net. It was a squalid little retreat, piled high with broken lawn equipment and worthless trash of every description, but on the far side of the garage sat a shiny, brand new S2 Thunderbolt Buell American Motorcycle. With a 91hp 1203cc V-twin engine, it was a real hog. There were tools and greasy rags lying on the floor, and it looked as though someone had just serviced the bike. Best of all, the key was in the switch.

Waiting until the next flash of lightning, I said, "Hi, guys," as Delsie and I strode in and disrupted the festivities.

The boys didn't know what to make of two soaked-to-the-skin females who had appeared out of nowhere in a brilliant flash of lightning, and they retreated to the back of the shed.

"Do you know how to ride one of these?" I asked Delsie, pointing at the bike.

"I've never been on one," she admitted.

"Well then, I guess that it's my turn to broaden *your* horizons, Cupcake. Here, put on a helmet."

"Hey!" yelled one of the boys. "You can't do that. That bike belongs to my brother, the Animal. He'll kill you if you even touch it. He'll tear your face off. He just went to the house to get a six-pack. He'll be back any minute. Hey, I'm warning you, lady. You better leave it alone!"

"Well," I yelled as I kicked the starter and revved the engine, "you tell the Animal that Thelma and Louise said thank-you. Tell him to take a good look at this morning's paper. Tell him that we're running from the law. Tell him that when this is over he'll have a new legend to share with his buddies. And be sure to tell him that he can pick up his bike, and five hundred bucks, at the Bahia Mar security desk any time he wants. Got it, kid?"

The boy nodded his head in amazement as Delsie straddled the seat behind me, put her arms around my waist and hung on. Twenty seconds later we were roaring down 4th Avenue, heading for the Brooks Memorial Causeway.

16

I left the key to the Buell S2 Thunderbolt with the gray-haired security officer at the marina's main gate, along with a Bahia Mar envelope containing five hundred dollars in cash for the Animal. The guard wasn't very happy about my request, but I tipped him handsomely because dealing with an angry biker can be an unpleasant, even hazardous, experience. Then Delsie and I trudged along the docks beneath the pinkish glow of the sodium vapor lamps.

Nothing in this world is more forlorn than a yacht basin when it rains. There was absolutely no one in sight. No parties, no music, no barbecue grills. The only sound was the steady thrumming of windblown rain on wood, Fiberglas and canvas. It struck me as ironic that those people who profess to love the romance of living on the water, who tell tall tales about braving mountainous waves, who claim to have survived turbulent squalls, ferocious gales and Category Five hurricanes, invariably run for cover and batten down the hatches when the first gentle drops fall from the sky.

But more important things occupied my mind. I was certain that some-one was stalking me, and my fears began to multiply when I saw a soggy figure huddled under an orange and black golf umbrella beside the board-ing ramp of Dad's old houseboat. It was Carl Rehm, and he was in a decidedly unpleasant mood.

"Well, you two have certainly stirred up a hornets' nest," he said. "Everyone in Florida is looking for you."

"It was absolutely unavoidable," I replied as I undid the spring latch on the railing, and pushed the gateway open.

"Did your father tell you why he was going down to the Keys?"

"No."

"Your Uncle Bud?"

"Absolutely not."

"Then you are truly your father's daughter. He came to me ten days or so ago; asked me to liquidate most of his CDs, and some overnight paper that we were holding for him. He said that he wanted to be flush; that he wanted the funds deposited to his consolidated accounts. Then he started talking about retirement, and he asked if I knew anything about condominium investments. It sounded rather cheerless coming from an inveterate boatman. He was a dyed-in-the-wool wharf rat, all barnacles and brine, and it saddened me to hear him talking about running aground; about apartments with electronic entry pass cards, and pools, and groundskeepers. Eventually, I mentioned The Mimosas, and that seemed to please him."

I unlocked the Schlage double safety latch, and slid the heavy glass door open. Delsie stumbled out of the downpour and into the lounge, while Mr. Pringles leapt from the beach bag to the deck. Belatedly, I tried to turn off the alarm system, but the keypad wouldn't respond to my touch. The numerical display was dead blank. Flicking a wall switch up and down, I found that the overhead lights wouldn't turn on, either.

"Damn," I cursed, drawing the wrong conclusion. "The storm must have knocked out the power."

Taking Delsie by the hand, I led her to the yellow vinyl couch, and wrapped her in a woolen blanket. She was shivering uncontrollably, the combination of fatigue, anxiety, wetness and motorcycle riding having taken its toll.

I wanted to get my hands on one of Dad's guns, but Rehm was blocking my way to the head, his left fist holding the now tightly rolled umbrella, his right stuffed deeply into the bulging pocket of his olive drab trench coat. He presented a solid and imposing silhouette, an overtly threatening barrier that I would have to outmaneuver.

Straining to see his face in the darkness, I said, "So Dad's visit tipped you off."

"Tipped me off? Hardly. I'd known your father for years; played poker with him two or three times a month. When he asked about retirement condominiums he had that keen expression in his eye, like when he was on the prowl, and his nostrils flared just a little when I mentioned the Mimosas. That was always his tell. That's how I knew when he was holding three of a kind against my straight, and that's when I realized that he was onto something."

"And you just couldn't take any chances."

"Of course not. It's an awful lot of money. Some very prominent people are tied up in this thing. It was up to me to protect their interests, so I called the hit squad."

"The assassins," I growled through nearly clenched teeth.

"They've been called worse," he said with a quirky little laugh. "The auditors."

"Who?"

"Given your father's reputation, if he suspected that there was something funny going on at The Mimosas, then I needed to get on top of it, and fast. But the audit didn't reveal anything even remotely out of line, and your father was killed in the accident, so I figured that I'd misread him, and forgot about it. There's no point in looking for trouble when there isn't any, after all. But then the two of you showed up at The Mimosas, and I started thinking. There's a curious smell about that project, but I can't quite put my finger on it."

"You don't know?"

"Know what?"

"But... what about the gasoline tanks?" I cried in exasperation.

"The what?"

I was trying to gather my thoughts, but in a flicker of lightening I saw the silvery glint of polished steel slashing downward above Rehm's head, and before I could cry out some unseen hand in the shadows cracked him hard on the back of his skull. The impact of a gun barrel on skin and bone made a sickening, wet *thwack*, like the sound of an axe splitting green wood, and then Rehm crumpled to the deck in a rag doll heap at my feet. In the terrifying silence that followed I heard the distinctive, heavy click of a pistol being cocked.

"Sit down," ordered a menacing voice in the darkness. "Do it right now or I'll kill you where you stand."

I complied without hesitation, sat on the couch, and put my arm around Delsie.

We must have been nearly as invisible to our assailant as he was to us, for I heard someone rustling in the galley. Then the microwave door clacked open, its anemic little lamp bathing us in faint yellow light; and there stood One-ear. He was leaning against the countertop, holding a snub-nosed .357 Magnum Smith & Wesson revolver in his hand, grinning in the disconnected manner of a lunatic.

Everything had taken on a surrealistic quality. The wind, the shadows, the waves, rain and lightening were all in constant, flickering motion, and I wasn't sure of anything anymore. The entire world had gone stroboscopic, loopy, and I was finding it difficult to get my bearings.

"You're going to kill us, aren't you?" Delsie asked weakly.

"Hell, lady, I've already done that once," sniggered One-ear. "I'm the guy that wired your precious *Jerome*."

"And Uncle Bud's cruiser, too," I added.

"Yup. That, too." He grinned at us. "Easy jobs, really. I used my mama's old family recipe. A few ounces of C4 plastic explosive for the primary bang, a couple of tablespoons of coffee creamer to make a dust initiator, and a little pinch of magnesium powder to give it flash. Then the diesel fuel aerosolized, and the tanks became fuel air bombs. Small primary explosion, big secondaries, and a kick-ass incendiary reaction. I used encoded detonators for safety, the boats' canopy frames for receiving antennas, and I connected them with a length of insulated bell wire. Just your basic, run-of-the-mill demolition. Nice and simple. Eminently effective. No one should have survived both the blast and the fire, but for some reason you two did. It doesn't matter, though, because I've got another shot at you now. This evening you two are going to have a little domestic accident."

"Another explosion?"

"Hell, no. A third explosion might draw undue attention. A simple galley fire will do just fine. It's raining out, you've got everything closed up, a grease fire on the stove ignites the boat, there's lots of nasty smoke, and you die of asphyxiation. Your basic fire casualty scenario. To the investigators it will look like the same ol' same ol'. Death due to smoke inhalation. Overcome by fumes and superheated gasses. Nothing sinister. Case closed."

"Won't the bullet holes ruin your plan?" I asked, standing up.

"Don't!" He pointed the pistol at my stomach. "If you force me to shoot you, I will. That's a promise. I'll simply switch to Plan B, and sink this tub in the middle of the Gulf Stream. But the difference for you will be significant. You'll have three hours of agony, gut-shot and bleeding in the rope locker. Now sit down!"

There was nothing to do but obey.

"So," Delsie hissed, "*you* blew up my yacht, you foul little turd."

"Not me," he taunted her. "I simply set the charges and gave the transmitter to the boss. He flipped the switch himself. He has a real passion for pyrotechnics. I think that he gets off on them. He just sat in a folding chair on the beach, and waited for you to steam by. Then he pulled out the antenna, powered it up, flipped the safety cover open, pushed the li'l red button, and Poof! No more *Jerome*."

"And Uncle Bud's cruiser?"

"Same thing. Hell, I was down in Long Key when the boss lit up that old piece of crap, but this job I've got to do personally. Call it an act of penance. I missed you the first time around—not that it was my fault—so I've got to make good on my professional guarantee. No customer ever goes away dissatisfied."

He started giggling like a schoolgirl, as though he'd just heard the funniest joke in history.

The lightning was flashing all around us, and I was praying that it would strike somewhere nearby. If it blinded him temporarily, if I could throw something at the door to draw his fire while diving low toward the hallway and the bathroom, I might be able to get my hands on the M2 carbine. That would even things up. If not, I could dodge into the master stateroom, and grab the Airweight .38 caliber revolver that Dad always kept beside the bed. But what would I do about Delsie? The instant I made my move, he'd shoot her for sure.

"Okay," said One-ear. He extended a grimy paw, and showed us a syringe filled with serum. "I've got a little Succinylcholine here. The doctors call it Sux for short. I like that, don't you? It's kind of sexy. Anyway, Sux is a paralyzing agent. It's used primarily in anesthesia. You'll each get a 5cc dose in the rump. It won't hurt very much. I promise. And sux works fast. A quick little pop, and in a few seconds you won't be able to move any of your muscles. They'll be kind of loosey-goosey, that's all. Flacid is the technical term, I believe. Now that ain't so bad, is it?"

He looked at us like a naughty little boy who had just convinced his sister to jump off the roof.

"Oh, yeah," he said. "I almost forgot the most important detail. It will paralyze your diaphragm as well. That's the big, flat muscle that inflates your lungs. Nothing to it, really. You'll simply stop breathing; that's all. Of course, you'll be totally awake and aware. You will see, and hear, and feel everything. You'll get that burning sensation in your chests—the one that people experience when they're drowning, or suffocating, or choking to death—but no matter how hard you try, no matter how much you concentrate, you won't be able to move. You won't be able to breathe. Oh, your lungs will shriek in agony, and your minds with seethe with pain, but you won't be able to do one damned thing about it. Then after a few agonizing minutes everything will go black."

He grinned at us and giggled a little bit more before continuing.

"The really nice thing is that Sux is completely undetectable. It breaks down into basic organic compounds rather quickly. So the Medical Examiner wouldn't be able to find it even if he knew what he was looking for. Your corpses will be found in a burned-out wreck, they will show all of the classic signs of immolation and suffocation, and no one will be the wiser."

He stared at us with the satanic smile of one who truly enjoys murder, not for the mere sake of killing, but for the insane joy of watching terror overwhelm his victims.

"Don't worry, ladies," he said "We'll still have time to party. Now get on your knees, very slowly. Lie on the deck, face down, and spread those pretty, long legs nice and wide, like good little girls."

I felt a sudden gust of wind on my cheek, and One-ear glanced nervously at the doorway. Then, his slimy grin changed into a twisting mask of torment as two heavy, muffled *whumps* came from outside. His pistachio shirt erupted in twin blossoms of red, and he just stood there for a second, mouth agape, gurgling cherry foam. Then his beady little eyes rolled all the way back in his head as he crashed heavily to the deck.

Turning to look at the door, I saw a gloved hand holding a Model 1911 .45 caliber semiautomatic pistol with a big, fat silencer. It started moving forward as one tall hoss of a man stepped through the doorway.

"Dad?" I heard myself whisper.

"Raul?" pleaded Delsie.

But it was neither my Dad, nor Delsie's SEAL. It was L'Ouverture.

*   *   *

"Am I ever glad to see you!" I gasped as I tried to clear my head. "Delsie, this is the Coast Guard Commander that I told you about."

L'Ouverture checked One-ear's neck for a carotid pulse, found none, scooped up the .357 revolver, and put it in his pocket. Then he examined Carl Rehm.

"He's out cold," L'Ouverture announced as he straightened back up.

Delsie was shivering violently, and crying, from shock rather than from fear, so I hugged her close.

"It's all right," I tried to console her. "He's dead. We're safe now. It's all over."

"Well, not quite," said L'Ouverture. "We still don't know what this was about."

"Like hell we don't," I snapped. "It's about a humongous real estate fraud at Greene Key. It's about graft, public corruption, conspiracy and murder."

"An interesting speculation," L'Ouverture commented dryly, "but how do we know all of this?"

"We followed the paper trail," I explained, "but we still don't know who's behind it. Not completely anyway."

Delsie was shivering uncontrollably now, and her teeth were chattering, so I stood up to fetch another blanket. But L'Ouverture waved his .45 at me.

"Please, sit down," he said in a commanding tone. "You ladies have been very resourceful, but unfortunately, you will not be around to tell anyone."

"What do you mean?"

"Surely, Dr. Pearson, you cannot imagine that I would let a pair of dilettantes ruin my plans."

"*Your* plans?"

"But of course. Greene Key is mine, you see."

Delsie looked at him with a mixture of hatred and incredulity.

"I don't believe you."

"Such a small imagination," L'Ouverture said, shaking his head. "The United States Army Major who conducted the storm control survey for the Corps of Engineers told me all about the misplaced geodetic benchmark over drinks one night in Key Largo. He viewed it as a minor technical adjustment, but I saw the error for what it truly was—a once-in-a-lifetime opportunity.

"A few days earlier I had intercepted a Cessna Skyhawk which was attempting to fly a shipment of cocaine across the Everglades to a strip near Devil's Garden. The pilot was a young man named Kurt Rodriguez. He is the only grandchild of Representative Marion Baedeker, and the old man was absolutely heartbroken. So I made a deal with him. I arranged for the disappearance of certain material evidence, making it impossible for the United States Attorney to prosecute Mr. Rodriguez. Then I restored the shipment to its intended recipient, in exchange for a liberal finder's fee, of course, and Greene Key became mine."

"So you own Escorbillo Property Development?"

"Escorbillo was operated for a brief time by Lt. Okun. It is now a defunct DBA. No one will file with the Division of Corporations to renew the fictitious name, and in time Escorbillo will disappear from the record."

"Let me see if I've got this straight. You stole the cocaine that you'd confiscated from the plane, ensuring that there would be no prosecution of Rodriguez, then sold the coke to a drug lord and used the proceeds to fund the purchase of Green Key?"

"Precisely. That way everyone got what he wanted. Everyone made out very well indeed. With a substantial amount of untraceable cash in hand, I lent the purchase money to Lt. Okun. He purchased Greene Key from the State of Florida, and was to repay me in regular monthly installments of principal and interest. Our arrangement stipulated that, should he fail to make even one scheduled payment, Escorbillo would be in default, and Lt. Okun would forfeit his collateral."

"Which, or course, was Greene Key."

L'Ouverture nodded.

It had gotten completely dark outside. The rain had tapered off somewhat, and the lightning was now less frequent. L'Ouverture still held his gun on us, but he used his free hand to light a thin, black cheroot. Coils of bluish smoke drifted toward the ceiling.

"Lt. Okun defaulted on the loan as planned," he continued, "and Escorbillo was forced to relinquish its collateral, but by that time two events of critical importance had taken place. The formal deed to Greene Key had been recorded by the Clerk of Monroe County, establishing a clear title and the legal right of ownership by Escorbillo, and Okun had signed a 20-year lease of Greene Key to Escorbilo Property Development. Escorbilo, of course, assumed financial responsibility for the payment of all Greene Key property taxes, and immediately set out to develop the island."

"And who is Escorbilo Incorporated?"

"A partnership of Representative Baedeker's cronies. The Honorable Marion Baedeker is a silent, ex officio partner. He owns six percent of Escorbilo, and he never had to put up a dime. His grandson makes out rather well, too. Kurt Rodriguez is half owner of the general construction firm, Rodriguez & Schulman. Even the drug lord is benefiting. Benjamin Schulman is his brother-in-law, and he is laundering significant amounts of capital by flushing it through a wide variety of subcontracting accounts on the company's books. Some of the money is also used to offset short term bank loans, and to stabilize cash flow. It is an ingenious way of transforming drug money into legitimate assets."

"And Lt. Okun?"

"Ah, Lt. Okun, is a man given to corruption. Law enforcement officers do not enjoy very lengthy careers, you see. Most of them are pensioned off by age fifty, and government benefits are anything but generous. Lt. Okun will exercise his thirty-year retirement option next summer, and then he will be hired as the Chief of Security for The Mimosas, at something like

$50,000 per year. The lease of Greene Key to Escorbilo gave him a $100,000 head start."

"That's pretty damn slick," Delsie said scornfully. "You have total ownership of Greene Key, but your name doesn't appear on any public documents. Someone else is funding the development of the island, and they'll make a tidy profit, too. Another party is covering the operating costs and taxes, and they're more than glad to do it. Everyone reaps a windfall with virtually no risk at all, and meanwhile, without any real expense or effort on your part, you've got the deed to the entire island locked in a safe deposit box somewhere, along with all of the documentation necessary to step forward in twenty or thirty years and claim legal ownership of every improvement made to Greene Key. By any conservative estimate, and adjusting for inflation, the island should be worth several billion dollars by then."

"As I said," he smiled, "everyone makes out very well indeed."

"Except for the people that you killed," I shot back.

"Yes," he said with a face that was nearly sad. "It is a most unfortunate cost of doing business. The irony of it saddens me. Your uncle was a great friend to my family, and he helped us all to become quite successful. We owed him a great deal. But when my mother saw an advertisement for The Mimosas in *Floridays* magazine, and asked him to look into the condominium project for her, I began to worry. Your uncle and your father had a well-deserved reputation for exposing the most obscure conspiracies and alliances, and I feared that they would ruin my scheme. So I had Lt. Okun and one of his deputies follow your uncle's movements. When your uncle announced that he was going to sail to the Keys, after having visited the Division of Corporations in Tallahassee, I decided that he had to be stopped. The same, of course, is true of you as well. So now you will do a little housekeeping for me, and then we shall take a brief trip together."

"Where?"

"Somewhere they will never find you."

*   *   *

L'Ouverture was using Federal Hydroshock hollowpoint bullets in his pistol, so they had done a great deal of internal damage. As a result, One-ear's corpse was lying in a huge pool of blood on the galley floor.

"Mop it up," ordered L'Ouverture. "I do not want to see even the tiniest speck of red when we leave."

Delsie nearly fainted at the sight of the mess, and the sweet, metallic smell turned her stomach, but she closed her eyes momentarily, took a deep breath, steeled herself and regained her composure. Then we both got down on our hands and knees, and started the gruesome chore using dish rags and paper towels, but blood was still seeping out of One-ear's wounds. Seeing our problem, L'Ouverture searched through the storage bins in the lounge, and found a piece of light blue, reinforced polyethylene sheeting.

"Wrap him up in this," he said, "so you will not spill blood all over the deck when you carry him outside."

Spreading the big plastic sheet on the floor, we rolled the corpse into the middle of it, and tossed the bloody refuse on as well.

Like most men, Dad hadn't kept his kitchen stocked with linens, so we soon ran out of rags. Seeing this as an opportunity, I got up slowly and started walking toward the companionway.

"And just where do you think you are going?" asked L'Ouverture.

"To the bathroom to get some more towels."

"No way."

"And what are we supposed to use for cleaning rags?"

He looked around the room, and saw a square plastic basket filled to overflowing with clothes that Dad had brought back from the laundromat, but hadn't bothered to fold.

"Use those," he said.

Delsie and I worked on our hands and knees for another thirty minutes, using dish washing detergent, Dad's tee-shirts, and a lot of elbow grease, scrubbing the last of the blood from the unwaxed tile floor. I used the time to get a few more answers.

"Who broke into my house?" I asked.

"Sandy," L'Ouverture answered, pointing his gun at the corpse. "He was very good with technical things. A very useful fellow."

"Yet you killed him. Why?"

"Because necessary as your deaths may be, I had no desire to see you suffer the sadistic ritual that Sandy was planning. He would not have been satisfied with just giving you an injection. He wanted to savor the horror in your eyes as you suffocated. And he had more carnal notions as well. Sandy liked his women to be, compliant, shall we say. But most of all, Sandy had a very big mouth, particularly when he was stoned. He was a pot-head, and could no longer be trusted."

"And the bozos who tried to kidnap me?"

"Just a couple of thugs from Rodriguez and Schulman. They were not supposed to kidnap you; just scare you. It was something of a mistake to use them, I'm afraid. They were unsophisticated muscle from the drug-running gang. But they are probably dead by now. Schulman and his brother-in-law are not known to suffer fools gladly."

"And Miss Ida?"

"Okun's redneck partner was responsible for that fiasco, but you already know that."

"Yes, but how did you know that the _Jerome_ would be at Greene Key," asked Delsie, "and how did you find us at the safe house?"

"Ah," L'Ouverture replied with a sour little laugh. "How many times have I heard smugglers ask questions like that? As I said, such a small imagination. The United States Coast Guard is a maritime police force, you see, but with full military capabilities. We operate the most sophisticated electronic surveillance systems in the world. Our P-3 Orion aircraft are in the sky day and night, sweeping the entire Florida area with hi-tech radar, so tracking the _Jerome_ was child's play. I merely watched the _Jerome_ leave port using the monitor in my office. When the _Jerome_ came about and steamed south, I called Sandy and told him to fix up a little something special. As for tracking your location on land, I used a National

Security Agency domestic communications computer link to keep tabs on Dr. Pearson's cell-phone traffic, then relayed that information to Lt. Okun. He had used standard police methods to learn about your taxi ride, and Hope House, but we didn't know which safe house you were in until you called the Division of Corporations. I got a fix on the cell tower, and there was only one safe house within range. You eluded him somehow, but by then I had posted Sandy on the houseboat, just in case, to intercept you and wrap things up."

He exhaled a long, thin stream of smoke and added smugly, "I warned you that this was no game for amateurs, Dr. Pearson."

Something primitive beneath my solar plexus went ice cold, and I had to fight the urge to lunge at L'Ouverture, sink my fingernails into his throat, tear out his windpipe. But I'd seen the damage that his .45 had done to One-ear, and I knew that I didn't have a chance of overpowering him.

We had nearly finished cleaning the floor, and I had run out of delaying tactics. Then I saw what I'd been looking for. Barely visible in the lightless crevice between the vegetable locker and the refrigerator was the rubberized grip of a pistol. Dad had stapled a black nylon holster to the woodwork, hip high, at a thirty degree angle, so that he could slip the gun free quickly, surreptitiously, without any fuss or bother.

I started wiping the face of the locker with a bloody rag, as though cleaning off splatter marks, and when my hand passed over the gun I snagged the grip with my middle finger, pulling it into the cloth. Then I crouched behind Delsie, turning the rag over as I wiped at some make-believe gore on the deck, and there in my hand was a black, Vektor CPI 9mm Parabellum compact pistol. It was a sleek, stylish, deadly little weapon. Dad had lived a dangerous life, and there had been no need to childproof the boat, so I knew that the magazine would be fully loaded; that a round would be in the chamber.

Crawling behind a butcher-block table, I gripped the little pistol firmly, put my index finger on the trigger, thumbed off the safety, popped up to my knees and aimed at L'Ouverture's chest. Dad had always said, "Shoot 'em where they're the biggest." But L'Ouverture recognized the mortal threat in the suddenness of my movement, snapped his arm around, and leveled his piece at Delsie. It was a maddening twist on the classic Mexican standoff.

"Fire if you must," he glowered, "but I'll blow her pelvis in two. You might kill me, but she'll spend the rest of her life in a wheelchair, with a colostomy bag strapped to her side."

The adrenaline rush was making my hand shake, but at that range I couldn't miss putting several rounds through the big man's heart and lungs. On the other hand, nothing could stop him from doing irreparable damage to Delsie, and that was an outcome that I simply couldn't accept, not even to save my own life.

"Shoot him!" hissed Delsie. "We're going to die anyway."

"No," said L'Ouverture. "An easy death is preferable to a painful existence. Put the safety on, and slide the gun across the deck."

Risking my own life was one thing, but I couldn't let him mutilate my best friend. So I gave in, tossed the Vektor across the floor, and watched in dismay as he pocketed that gun as well.

Then L'Ouverture stood up slowly, slid the glass door wide open, and waved at the corpse with his .45.

"Now carry him outside," he ordered, "and drop him in the skiff. Then we will all leave together."

I peered through the rain and saw a battered old Boston Whaler tied fore and aft to cleats by the stern rail. L'Ouverture was no fool. He had planned to slip in and slip out, using the rain for cover, so that no one would see him.

"What about Rehm?" I asked.

"What about him?"

"You mean that you're going to leave one of your buddies lying here on the deck?"

"That puke?" L'Ouverture roared with laughter. "He is not a part of my team. He is just a stupid bank lawyer. Not smart enough to have his own practice. Too dumb to see that they are laundering tons of drug money through The Mimosas construction accounts. The confused story that he will tell when he finally wakes up will have the police running around in circles for months. Now pick Sandy up, and haul him out here."

L'Ouverture stepped outside, and stood under the overhang while Delsie and I struggled to lug a hundred and sixty pounds of dead weight, suspended in a Saran Wrap sling. I took the lead, moving around Rehm's body, and wobbling as best I could. We had almost made it to the doorway when the plastic slipped out of my hands, and the body fell to the floor with a beefy thud.

"Here now, get a move on," L'Ouverture growled, stepping off to one side. We wrestled the body up again, and started moving, but just as I stepped beyond the door frame, Delsie tripped and fell. She landed hard on the corpse, covering herself with gore.

Just then I heard the sound of heavy feet pounding toward us along the pier. A mountainous, bearded man, with densely tattooed arms and a potbelly exposed by a too-small Jack Daniels tee-shirt was running straight at us with murder in his eye. He stopped next to the boat and squinted through the rain at L'Ouverture.

"Hey! Shithead!" he challenged. "Where's the bitch that stole my ride?"

L'Ouverture turned to confront the enraged biker, and he raised his pistol toward the Animal's face, but as he did I snatched the collapsible boat hook from its overhead clamps, pulled it down hard, and rammed it up again with every ounce of strength that I possessed. The barb slipped beneath the hem of L'Ouverture's jacket, sliced through his shirt and punctured his right kidney. The resulting pain was so intense that L'Ouverture couldn't move a muscle, or even scream. In his last conscious action he squeezed his eyes tight as waves of agony overwhelmed him, and pulled the trigger.

Whump! went the Colt before it rattled to the deck.

Still clutching the end of the boat hook, I screamed, "That's for Dad,
you son-of-a-bitch."

Then I jerked the handle up, tearing a ragged hole in his flesh.

"And that's for Uncle Bud."

L'Ouverture's eyes popped open again, and he stared at me like some
terrified beast lurking in the depths of a cave.

"And this is for Miss Ida," I concluded, pushing him over the side.

L'Ouverture tumbled into the harbor with a sickening splat, and his
dark blood mingled with the boat oil on the water, creating little, swirling
rainbows of death as his body sank slowly out of sight.

The Animal just stood there in the rain, fingering a fresh bullet hole in
the collar of his denim vest, staring first at the water, and then at me.

"Damn, lady," he said in amazement. "Next time you want to borrow
my bike, just ask."

17

Delsie had her foot treated again, this time by a board certified plastic surgeon at the Coral Springs Medical Center, and she was healing nicely. Officials from the Monroe County Sheriff's Department, the Broward County Sheriff's Office, the Fort Lauderdale Police Department, the Tallahassee Police Department, the Florida Highway Patrol, the United States Coast Guard and the Drug Enforcement Administration took our statements during seven separate interviews. I offered a heartfelt apology to Carl Rehm, which he accepted with great aplomb. Judge Holloway met privately with Governor O'Brien, as a result of which Delsie and I received full immunity from any and all prosecution arising from our actions during our week-long adventure. The authorities then arrested State Representative Marion Baedeker, Lt. Okun, Kurt Rodriguez, Benjamin Schulman and others, charging them with racketeering and conspiracy to defraud the State of Florida. A special grand jury indicted all of them, and took the unusual step of recommending that the courts deny any requests for bail. Best of all, the Attorney General negated the sale of Greene Key, attached the financial and real assets of Escorbilo Property Development, Inc., all of its subsidiaries, and Rodriguez & Schulman, established a reimbursement fund to settle claims made by those retirees who had already invested in condominiums at The Mimosas, and promised to return Greene Key to the people of the State of

Florida as a permanent extension of Long Key State Park, using confiscated drug money to demolish the causeway and fund a wildlife reclamation project.

Capt. Raul Alberdi Bautista was recuperating in style. At Delsie's insistence, he was enjoying an all-expense-paid vacation on Aruba. A recent postcard had pictured a group of heavily bronzed young men, who had apparently left their bathing suits at home, playing volleyball on a pure white beach.

Norman Alfons Nakita de Zavala was back in business, and his cousin, Maria, gave birth to a beautiful little girl, whom she named Juanita Delsita de la Torre.

Oh, yes. And the Animal invited me to join him for a Sunday afternoon picnic at his motorcycle gang's clubhouse.

*   *   *

It was another rainy night, hot and humid, and Delsie and I were lounging around Dad's old houseboat. We weren't expecting visitors, so with the air conditioning turned way down to dry out the boat, we elected to slop around in heavy athletic socks, sweat pants and shirts. My sweats were field house gray, with *Ohio State* stenciled on them in peacock blue. Delsie's were fire red, with *Bama* emblazoned across the chest in immense white letters.

"Have you arranged for a boat to take us back to the Blue Hole?" asked Delsie.

"Yes," I replied. "I visited Buz Tobler yesterday evening, over on Charterboat Row. He's got a fast little fishing-cruiser that planes well; the *YooHoo II*. Big cabin, lots of room, not luxurious, but comfortable enough. It's beamy for a displacement hull, but it has a deep keel, so it should be fairly stable. It won't rock us around too much. Dave says that if we leave at dawn we can start our run during the cool of the morning, and make it down there and back before sunset."

"And the service?"

"Your idea for a simple ceremony seems best. A few flowers on the water, some meaningful lines of poetry; that sort of thing. Since Geoffrey and Mikey were both fond of Maya Angelou, I'm reading her book, *A Brave and Startling Truth*, and marking some of the more poignant passages. It's message of hope for humanity is inspiring. Will the day after tomorrow be okay?"

"Fine."

"So tell me. Now that your insurance company has settled on the *Jerome*, what are your plans?"

"Well," Delsie sighed, "I believe that I'll drive up to Jacksonville in a day or two. There's a boat yard up there that Mr. Curlee has recommended, where they build big ol' custom yachts. I discussed the idea with Daddy, and he agrees that we shouldn't run the family business from a stock design boat; and I have absolutely no intention of living on a refurbished vessel that someone else has had the pleasure of decorating. That would be like wearing hand-me-down clothes. What I want is a thoroughly modern vessel that will suit and reflect my lifestyle. I want something passionate, bright, contemporary."

"And you'll find that in Jacksonville?"

"Probably not, but shopping for a yacht shouldn't be that much different than shopping for an evening gown. I never find exactly what I want at the first place I visit, so I'll just have to look around some. I understand that Ivana Trump is having her yacht built in Italy. I just love the Via Veneto. And have you decided what you're going to do?"

"Well, I've done everything that I can to settle the estates. The clinic is running just fine, but I've always felt more alive in Lauderdale than anywhere else in the world. I've got a thriving business in Ohio, but I'd hate to sell the boat because it would be like selling Dad. On the other hand, if I didn't live here it wouldn't make much sense to keep it. The summers are awfully hot in Florida, and I like to ski in the winter, but I've always wanted to learn how to scuba dive, and I really hate driving in the snow."

"Aesop's ass!" remarked Delsie.

"I beg your pardon?"

"Aesop's ass! Listen, Sugar. Good ol' Aesop told a fable one time about a cute li'l ol' donkey who was walking along, and suddenly found herself smack dab between two piles of hay. The poor li'l thing was hungry, so she looked first at one pile, and then at the other. They appeared to be equally far away, so she sat down to think about which one she should walk to. She got hungrier, and hungrier, but she couldn't make up her mind between this pile or that pile, that pile or this. So can you guess what she finally did?"

"What?"

"She starved to death."

"What a cheerful story!"

"Sugar, sometimes you just have to make a decision and get on with your life. Mama used to say that your life is where your heart is. Daddy's heart was always at a big, noisy party, and Mama's heart was always with Daddy. So what is your heart telling you right now?"

The Sunbeam microwave beeped just then, and I busied myself with emptying a steaming bag of Orville Redenbacher's Low Fat popcorn because I didn't have a ready answer. Delsie took her cue from my silence, switched on the big 25-inch Motorola TV, and started planning our evening's entertainment. She stood on her tiptoes, and flipped through Dad's VHS movie collection, which was stacked in the overhead bookcase.

"Yegad, Sugar," she complained. "Which macho archetype do you feel like watching? John Wayne, Jackie Chan, or Clint Eastwood?"

"It's kind of limited, isn't it?"

"There aren't any chick flicks here, that's for sure. No musicals. No romantic comedies. No copies of *Les Mis* or *Phantom*."

"Just pick something fun."

"Okay. Let's see. How about this one? *Blue, White, and Perfect. 1941. Private detective Michael Shayne tangles with foreign espionage agents who are smuggling industrial diamonds.*"

"Oh, I remember that one," I laughed as I put a big bowl of popcorn on the old sea chest that served as a coffee table. "Dad taped it off TCM one night. I had to show him how to work the VCR PLUS auto-record function."

But that was enough to trigger my memory, because I also recalled a scene from another obscure old movie that I had suffered through with Dad. In it, a small squad of Oriental harbor police board someone's private yacht, and conduct a thorough search for contraband. One of the soldiers finds a small bag of jewels hidden under a shoe rack on the floor of a stateroom closet, and the captain of the detachment confiscates the gems, warning the yacht's owner against further attempts at smuggling. Once the police leave, however, the owner laughs, and tells a friend that the secret to smuggling jewels is to hide them under something else that's hidden. With that, he pulls up a loose floor board under the shoe rack, and withdraws a large sack of pearls.

"Delsie," I asked, "would you excuse me for a minute?"

I walked into the bathroom, closed the door behind me, and locked it. The trick mirror opened with ease when I pressed the hidden spring release, and I was relieved to find that the #10 envelope was still lying on the floor of the closet. I opened the envelope and read the note again. *The smuggler's secret.*

The floor of the closet was made of one solid plank, and as I ran my hands over the walls I found no obvious irregularities. The gun pegs didn't budge when I tried to twist or pull them, and I had almost given up when I noticed that the cabinetmaker who had built Dad's mysterious closet had been very exacting in his work. The boards met flush at their seams, countersunk finishing nails held them in place, and the nail holes had been placed symmetrically, being paired with those in the opposing planks. All the holes, that is, except one. At the bottom of the plank which formed the left side of the closet there was a nonconforming hole an inch or so from the floor. Although it was the same diameter as the others, it was positioned precisely in the middle of the plank, and there

was no corresponding hole in the opposite board. But even more important, there was no nail in that hole.

Searching through the detritus underneath the sink, I found a dull ice
pick in a shoe box filled with empty medicine bottles and derelict toothbrushes. Men save the darndest things. I slipped the ice pick into the
empty nail hole, it struck a cam of some sort, and the floor of the closet
slid open a finger's width, revealing what sailors call a hidey-hole. I pushed
the board all the way open, and there sat three olive drab, military ammunition boxes. Made of steel, they had hinged lids and watertight seals
which made them perfect for storing moisture sensitive items. Dad had
used similar boxes to store his camera equipment, his spices, and his flare
gun.

I lifted the first box out of the hole, placed it on the bath mat,
wrenched the lid off, and my mouth dropped open in amazement. That
metal box was crammed absolutely full with stacks and stacks of tightly
banded U.S. currency. I dumped the money on the floor and made a
quick count. There were one hundred and twenty-five packets of fifty dollar bills, forty bills to a pack. Two hundred and fifty thousand dollars.

The contents of the other two boxes were identical to the first, and
beneath them were three more. Two held bundles of twenties, and the last
box contained a real treasure trove. In it were four Chivas Regal velvet bags
containing antique coins—silver pieces of eight, and solid gold reales—
from some unnamed Spanish galleon. And there was one more bag, this
one made of satin, holding over four hundred faceted emeralds, sapphires,
rubies, amethysts and diamonds. But best of all, in the very bottom of that
box was the last of the #10 envelopes, with the hand-lettered label *Jean*. I
opened it with tears in my eyes. The note read, *Mr. Spock*.

"Live long and prosper," I whispered.

Smiling briefly, I tried to imagine Dad watching *Star Trek*, and then I
burst into tears.

"Thanks, Dad," I wept as I put the boxes away. "Thanks for accepting
me just the way I was, thanks for believing in me, thanks for being an

adventurous, treasure-hunting eccentric, and thanks for helping me to find my life again. But most of all, thanks just for being my Dad."

Five minutes later I flopped on the couch next to Delsie.

"I've made up my mind," I announced. "I'm selling my veterinary practice in Youngstown, and I'm moving to Lauderdale."

"Really?!" She tossing the remote control aside and smothering me in a bear hug. "Oooo, I've been praying for this, Sugar. It's wonderful! I love it! What will you do? Where will you live?"

"Well, Dad and Uncle Bud left me a bit of money, enough to get started with anyway, and I suppose that Lauderdale could always use another vet. Maybe I'll work part time for a while, and let someone else shoulder the burden of running a business. As for accommodations, I guess I could live right here on the boat."

"Splendid! Will you remodel it?"

"Of course! This place always did need a woman's touch. So out with the sea chest, and in with Martha Stewart. Now let's enjoy some of Dad's cinematic favorites."

So we watched *The Shootist*, *The Protector*, and *In the Line of Fire*, and we stayed up until a quarter past three, and talked and talked, and ate bushels of popcorn and a gallon of Rocky Road, and promised to visit Jenny Craig in the morning.

Now that you've completed Jean Pearson's first novel, we'll bet that you can't wait to read about her next exciting adventure. Get a glimpse of what's to come, turn the page, and read the opening chapter of her second mystery,

DEAD ISSUE

Dead Issue

A Jean Pearson Novel

by Lori Stone

I

I wasn't her mother, but as I stumbled through the lightless alleys of New Orleans' French Quarter, the little girl that I carried on my hip kept whispering "Mama." She stared at me through glassy eyes, her head rolling feebly back and forth across my breast while I jogged awkwardly along. I could feel the sticky warmth of her blood as it dripped like rain from my fingers, and even in the two a.m. gloom I could see that her sweet little arm had been shattered by the bullet. Her face was deathly pale, and she was lapsing into shock, but I couldn't spare the time to dress her wound or calm her fears because that bullet had been meant for me.

Every instinct told me that I had to keep moving. I had to keep running; through the fog, and the garbage, and the vilest of smells; past the iron-bolted doorways and the steel-shuttered windows; along the urine-stained gutters where rats the size of gophers watched in rapt anticipation. I'd never been so frightened in my life. I'd never felt so desperately alone. And for at least the hundredth time I wondered how I'd gotten into this mess.

When I was a little girl Aunt Rita told me that I was an orphan. Later I discovered that it was only half true, of course, but maybe that's why I was the kind of child who brought home baby birds which had fallen from their nests, or gangling boys with too much acne and too little self esteem. Maybe focusing on someone else's problems made it easier to deal with my own. And maybe that's why, a few days after turning thirty, I found myself searching for an old friend's missing daughter, warding off voodoo curses, and picking through the bones of a dozen murdered children.

All I ever wanted out of life was an intelligent, loving husband, and to ride steeplechase mounts, and to breed Wirehair Fox Terriers; and I had all of that, and more. But after Peter was killed in a senseless traffic accident, I lost the horse farm that we'd bought outside Youngstown, and concentrated on my veterinary practice, ten hours a day, eight days a week. Then my Dad had died suddenly as well, and I found myself living aboard his houseboat in Fort Lauderdale. I'd been hanging out there for several months, having sold my clinic in Ohio, and was just settling in when a visit from a dear friend transformed a much needed vacation into the most harrowing weekend of my life.

                    *   *   *

It was a little after dawn on a cloudless, balmy day, and the vast marina at Bahia Mar was still relatively quiet, its abstract spider web of masts, rigging and antennas sparkling like liquid bronze in the gathering light. I was standing up on the sun deck, combing my fingers through a snarl in my platinum hair, and savoring the marshy aroma of a freshening offshore breeze. In an unrestrained moment of vanity I had clothed my slender frame in vanilla cotton shorts and a strawberry u-neck tee, to celebrate a pale layer of burn over my deepening, spring tan, and I was warding off the April chill with a steaming cup of decaf au lait. It was one of those marvelously frivolous occasions when the inner child supplants the adult, so I found myself mugging for a camera that wasn't even there. With chin lifted high to accentuate my cheekbones, and squinting at the saffron orb which floated just above the horizon, I usurped all conventional authority, as had Napoleon, and crowned myself Her Royal Highness, the Tall and Leggy Mistress of the Main, Jean the First, Princess of Quite a Lot. And I smiled at how simple things—like sun and wind, colors and coffee—can make one feel so deliciously alive. I felt cheerful, confident, exceedingly serene.

Then a dull, heavy thump jarred me back to reality. Sigmon Curlee had arrived a few minutes earlier, and was rummaging around below somewhere. He owns one of the finest custom boat yards in Florida, and I had asked him to make some suggestions about renovating Dad's old barge. The basic structure was solid enough, and the twin Hercules diesels were both in good shape, but after thirty-odd years of serving as the sporadic abode of a hard-bitten bachelor, that weary old tub had attained the rank atmosphere of a disused fraternity house. Something more than new curtains and fresh paint would be needed to make it warm and livable. What I envisioned was an efficiency townhouse on a hull.

As I was fantasizing about my dream boat, I glanced down at the dock and saw a petite, silver-haired woman holding onto the polished mahogany railing of the inswung boarding gate. She just stood there in a formless cotton print dress, weeping silently. I could see the buttery sunlight reflected in her tears, and that's when I recognized her. It was Brownie Hamilton. She was one of my Dad's oldest friends, and she'd been a real blessing to me at his funeral.

I didn't want to startle her by yelling, so I climbed down the ladder to the after deck, walked over to the gate and said, "Brownie?"

She didn't appear to hear me.

"Brownie," I repeated. "Are you all right?"

She lifted her pale, triangular face, and turned toward me slowly, like one of those little windup toys when the spring is nearly spent.

"I'm so sorry, dear," she finally whispered. "I don't mean to intrude, but I need your help."

"Of course," I said, taking her thin-fingered hand in mine. "What's wrong, hon?"

"Betty's missing," she blurted out.

That dear old woman began to cry so hard that her shoulders actually shuddered. Her lifelong dancer's posture gave way, and she looked so small and frail that I nearly started crying myself. I led her toward the lounge, but when we neared the sliding glass door she stiffened like a gazelle being forced toward a cage, so I unfolded a new pair of oak-framed canvas deck chairs, threw heavy fiesta-colored beach towels across them, and invited her to sit near the transom.

"Coffee?" I inquired.

"Black," she snuffled. "The real stuff, if you have it."

Five minutes later I handed Brownie a big mug of freshly brewed hi-test as I sat down gently beside her.

"You must be terribly worried," I probed, reaching out to hold her hand once again. "What happened?"

Brownie just sat there, sipping at her coffee, while a big curl of steam wilted the feathery lock that fringed her left temple. Then she heaved one of those great, ragged sighs that accompany the end of a crying spree.

"Well," she began, "René called at quarter 'til five. She's Betty's room-mate, you know. Sweet young thing. Puerto Rican. She apologized for calling so early, but she's an RN, too, and was leaving for her shift in NICU. That's the Neonatal Intensive Care Unit where she and Betty met. René said that Betty hadn't come home for the last two nights, that she hadn't reported for work at the clinic yesterday, that she hadn't called in sick or anything. Now, that's not at all like our Betty. She's a very responsible young woman. Anyway, René wanted to call the police, and I agreed, of course."

Brownie took a long swallow of coffee, and I held her hand more firmly.

"So how can I help?" I asked.

"Well, the dock gossip says that you're flying to New Orleans this morning."

"That's right. You know my best friend, Delsie. She's been staying at her family's home in Mobile for the past several weeks, and we've missed each other's company. So we've decided on a little reunion. She's booked a hotel suite somewhere near the French Quarter, and we're going to attend

Jazz Fest. It promises to be a fun-filled weekend of marvelous music and fabulous food.

"And," I added in a whisper, as though sharing some great secret, "from what I can gather, Delsie's got a new beau. I can't wait to join her."

"Oh, it's such a pleasure to see the two of you together." Brownie said with a weak grin. "Sometimes it seems as though old-fashioned friendship has gone out of style in this hurry-up world, but you two give me hope."

"Tell me about Betty."

"Well," she sighed, finishing her coffee, and setting the empty earthenware mug on the engine hatch cover. "Betty is an FNP, a Family Nurse Practitioner, and she works with an internal medicine group that's associated with Charity Hospital in New Orleans. So I was wondering… since you're going to be there anyway…"

"Would you like me to check with the Police?"

"Would you mind?" she asked hopefully. "I'd go there myself, dear, but Richard is coming home later today. I was washing the breakfast dishes when he had that stroke, you know. He spilled hot cocoa all over his new gray worsted slacks. But I remembered what they taught us in that First Responder course that you set up for the marina club, dialed 911, and got him to the Emergency Room right away. That miracle drug, *t-PA*, worked wonders, and he's doing considerably better now. His speech is improving, and he's pretty steady on his feet, too. But the doctors have warned me that Richard shouldn't get upset about anything; that he needs a lot of rest, peace and quiet. Lord knows, I can't tell him that Betty's missing. She's his only child, you see, by his first wife, and he thinks that the sun rises and sets just for her."

"Would you like me to talk with René, too?"

"Oh, please, yes. I would appreciate it so very much. And Richard won't suspect a thing if he answers the phone and hears your voice. I'll just tell him that you asked me to look after Mr. Pringles."

"Will you?" I asked with a conspiratorial wink.

"But of course," she replied with an impish grin. "That ol' tabby and I get along just fine, and it will save you the expense of boarding him. I'd love to have Mr. Pringles stay with me. He's such a beautiful ol' cat. I'll enjoy his company."

"Then it's a deal."

After I wrote all of the necessary names, addresses and phone numbers on a small pad of paper, and told Brownie where I'd be staying, we hugged and said our goodbyes. Then she strode up the dock, head high and back straight. I was somehow pleased to see that her dancer's legs still had a little spring left in them at sixty-something. Perhaps I was thinking of my own distant future.

Sigmon Curlee marched out of the lounge just then, his sun-burnished scalp flashing like a beacon in the warm, sharpening light. The thickly woven muscles of a professional sportsman rippled like storm waves beneath his canvas shirt and denim shorts, giving his squat but massive frame a formidable rather than fleshy appearance. Surprisingly nimble for a man of his girth and age, he moved with the effortless grace of a panther.

"Ever seen a man gut a tarpon?" he asked in a demanding tone as he wiped his brow with a big, red, Western bandana.

"I've done it myself," I said.

"Oh. Yes, ma'am," he mumbled. "I plum forgot that you were a vet."

The thunder of his grand entrance having been stolen, he just stood there like a schoolboy for several seconds, fiddling with his polished aluminum clipboard as though doing something important.

"Well now, Miss Jean," he finally snorted, trying to regain his momentum, "that's what we oughta do to this here ol' gal; gut her like a tarpon, from stem to stern, and build her up entirely new; pretty-like."

"Everything but the bathroom," I countered.

"Ma'am?" he asked in disbelief, screwing up the muscles around his eyes.

"Those big marble fixtures are exuberant, and I like them," I explained as I folded the deck chairs and lashed them to the after bulkhead with dayglow bungee cords. "I'm especially fond of that sunken bathtub, and without the full-length mirror that head would feel kind of small. Do what you wish with the rest, Mr. Curlee, but I want you to leave a little something of Dad in this boat. Somehow, the soul of a man lives in his bathroom, and I want to keep this one pretty much the way it is."

"Aw, but Miss Jean!" he complained. "There ain't nuthin' small about that head, and it's smack in the middle of everything!"

"As it should be."

"Like a cork in a dadburned bottle!"

"Why, Sigmon Curlee," I chided him. "You don't mean to tell me that you can't plan around a simple little bathroom!"

"Well, of course I can," he flustered, "but the general design of this boat won't change very much if I do. You'll be stuck with the same basic deck plan, more or less, 'cause that big ol' head will be the proberbial tail that's wagging the dog. Shoot-fire, Miss Jean! We'll be limited to stripping out the old finishes and lockers, and putting in modular stuff. Now, don't get me wrong. It will be a big improvement. It will be better looking, more efficient, even a tad roomier. Oh, yes, ma'am! It will be beautimous. But that head is a big ol' monster. It's a waste of good space."

"I like to think of it as luxurious," I said with a touch of whimsy. "When can I see a schematic?"

"Well, ma'am," he said, scratching his chin, "I can have some blue-prints—a plan view and some elevations—in a couple or three weeks."

"Good enough. I can't wait to see them. Now if you'll excuse me, Mr. Curlee, I have to get to the airport."

"Yes, ma'am," he muttered in defeat.

He stepped out onto the dock, sparked a wooden match with his thumbnail, lit a fat little stub of a cigar, and began to walk slowly away. Then he stopped short and turned around.

"Miss Jean?" he hollered with a twinkle in his eye. "Will you at least let me reposition that tub?"

*   *   *

It had been impossible to book a flight from Lauderdale to New Orleans, because only Mardi Gras draws bigger crowds than the annual Jazz and Heritage Festival, so I took Dad's old pickup, made the forty-minute run down I-95, and parked in a satellite lot outside Miami International Airport. Carry-on garment bag in hand, I made my way through the security station and down Concourse C, where I was engulfed in a tidal wave of dialectic disharmony. Nowhere else on earth can one hear so many lingual variations being shouted so forcefully, in such panic-stricken tones, and with no one apparently listening, as in Miami.

The 737 was late in departing, but our Captain assured those passengers with connecting flights that they would not be inconvenienced, and promised a "fast hop" of an hour and fifteen minutes. As it turned out, that was just enough time for me to make friends with the other passengers in my three-seat row. Sitting next to the window was an energetic young nun in traditional habit, and between us sat the most beautiful little girl that I had ever seen. Ringlets of oiled ebony surrounded a cherubic face the color of nutmeg, and her bright little eyes shone like jade. She stared at me with an expression that was both shy and plaintive.

"My?" she asked timidly.

"I'm sorry," I smiled. "What did you say?"

"My?" she repeated softly.

"You must forgive her," the nun interjected pleasantly while stroking the little girl's hair. "Bidú is an orphan from Brazil. She speaks only the dialect of the *caboclos*; the migrant peasants. It is mostly Portuguese, but with a smattering of Italian, Spanish, Indian and African. She was asking if you were her *mãe*; her mother. A family in the States is adopting her, you see, and she's eager to meet her new mama."

"How wonderful!" I exclaimed. "How old is she?"

"Oh, about twenty months," the nun answered good-naturedly. "We're not really certain. Like so many others, she was abandoned as an infant. One of the sisters found her wrapped in newspaper, in a tattered cardboard box on the steps of our orphanage in Barra Mansa."

Those precious, little green eyes had never left me.

"Mama?" the little girl inquired sweetly.

"I've been teaching her a few words of English," laughed the nun. "Let me explain things to her."

There was a brief discussion in Portuguese, of which I understood not one single word, and then we introduced ourselves. Sister Angelica was a member of the Society of Innocents, a religious order that operated hospitals, schools and orphanages for indigent children. She had majored in sociology at Northwestern, and after being called to a life of religious service, had put her education to use in the administration of an international adoption program. She said that she found the challenge of matching homeless children with childless couples a very rewarding job, and she admitted that she enjoyed delivering children to their new homes because it provided her with occasional respites from the deprivations of monastic life. I liked her. She was a real person doing useful work.

I spent the remainder of the flight sharing a sesame bagel with little Bidú. She spoke not a word, but said volumes with her eyes, and so we conversed with gestures, smiles and quiet laughter. Ours was the universal language of love and acceptance, and it warmed my heart.

"Obrigado," she whispered when the last crumb was gone.

"You're welcome, sweetheart," I replied.

Then, encircling my neck in her tiny arms, she smothered me in that uniquely powerful hug that only toddlers can bestow without inflicting serious injury, and I felt a dizzying rush of maternal emotions.

Bidú had opened a sealed door deep within me, and filled a dark, cheerless void with sparkling rays of sunshine. It was a spot that I had given up on, a space that I had thought forever dreary, because in the months before he'd died, Peter and I had tried in vain to create a baby of our own, and that dream had perished with him, leaving a deep, dusty hole at the hub of my being. Yet, miraculously, little Bidú's loving embrace had rekindled the ancient hungers, and I found myself imagining that if I ever had a daughter of my own I'd want her to be just like the priceless treasure seated beside me.

*   *   *

Just before we began our final landing approach, a flight attendant informed me that the Captain had received a radio message on the company frequency, saying that a ground hostess would meet me in the terminal. Even so, I was surprised when a pleasant young woman in a scarlet blazer hailed me just outside the plane's forward hatch, in the cylindrical wrist of the jetway tunnel.

"Dr. Pearson," she began, "my name is Marie LeBreton. Welcome to New Orleans. Do you have any checked baggage?"

"Only this carry-on," I replied as the other passengers brushed past me.

"Splendid. Would you follow me, please?"

She turned, opened a narrow service door, and stepped outside onto a slatted aluminum platform. A steep, ladderlike stairway led down to the tarmac below, and there beside a white limousine stood Delsie, my best friend.

Impeccably clothed in a cornflower sun dress which showed off her deep olive tan, Delsie's raven hair crowned a devastating figure that was straight out of *Playboy*. At five feet seven inches she was the quintessential Southern belle; her lips like ripe Bing cherries, her almond eyes sparkling with mischief. The pale angularity of her father's British lineage had been muted by her mother's Mexican ancestry, creating a delicate visage which was darkly mysterious, and positively stunning. The ancient Greeks would have made her a goddess, and even in this brave new age of agnosticism she had inspired her own fervent cult of worshipful admirers, few of whom would have guessed that this wealthy heiress was one hellaciously astute corporate attorney.

"Sugar!" she squealed when my feet touched the ground. "Oh, it's so good to see you!"

She gave me a great, crushing hug while the chauffeur stowed my bag, and then we settled into the car. After the rigid confinement of flying coach class, the broad leather cushions felt scrumptious.

"This is some grand welcome," I sighed, as she handed me a chilled bottle of Perrier. "I feel like the President."

"The airport manager is an old flame of mine," she said with a sly grin, "so those big ol' security gates open like magic. We studied together at Alabama. I blame myself that he's never married."

Blue lights flashing, an airport police car led the limo through a maze of jumbo aircraft at New Orleans International Airport, and we started catching up on all the gossip as we floated past Bonnabel and Metaire. Delsie told me that her latest love interest was a Dr. Francis Xavier Marais, Jr., but she didn't elaborate, explaining that I would meet him soon enough. Since I was new to the area, she instructed the driver to take the scenic route, so we looped around City Park, and down through the quaint old neighborhood of Gentilly on Elysian Fields Avenue. When the chocolate-red ribbon of the Mississippi River came into view I told her about Brownie's missing daughter.

"The poor dear," Delsie lamented. "She's such a sweet ol' gal. She taught me jazz dance one summer when I was just a pee-tad. I remember it well because Daddy had a dying duck fit when he saw me bopping around on stage, dressed in nothing more than tie-dyed underwear and silk scarves."

We had a good laugh over that, and then she got a bit more serious.

"Let's take care of Brownie's business right away," she suggested, "so that it won't interfere with our holiday."

I nodded in agreement, and she pressed the intercom button.

"Dominick," Delsie inquired of the driver, "isn't there a police station in the Quarter?"

"Oui, madam," came the rich Creole response. "A block south of Bourbon Street is the Vieux Carré Commission."

"Take us there, will you, please?"
"Oui, madam."

*   *   *

With its khaki, stuccoed walls and white, two-story pillars, the 8th District Police Station resembled a classical temple. Situated behind a seven-foot wrought iron fence, and approached over a black and white marble checkerboard walkway, the building was just as imposing inside. The entire structure appeared to be one large room, a sky blue ceiling loomed twenty feet above the floor, and the dandelion walls were accented by ornate ivory moldings. It looked more like the lobby of a Ziegfeld theater than a jail.

"May I help you?" asked an officer at the long service counter.

"Thank you, yes," I replied. "My name is Dr. Jean Margaret Pearson. I have just arrived in town, and I'm looking for a young woman who was reported missing earlier this morning. Her name is Betty Hamilton."

I thought I saw a slight twitch in his eyes, like you sometimes see during a bridge tournament when an opponent doubles after you've bid three hearts.

"One moment," he said, picking up the phone.

Not thirty seconds later another man walked through a swinging gate at the end of the counter. He was thirtyish, short, wiry, and sported a pencil thin moustache under an aquiline nose. A ruddy face and heavily creased forehead spoke of long hours spent out of doors, and I found his rugged good looks quite attractive.

"Good morning, ladies," he said in a flat, nasal voice filled with bayou country undertones. "Allow me to introduce myself. I am Sergeant Edouard Boudreaux of the St. James Parish Sheriff's Department. You are inquiring about Elizabeth Hamilton?"

"Yes," I replied. "She's the daughter of a close family friend."

"Please," he suggested, motioning us to a cypresswood bench, "will you take a seat?"

It was more an order than an invitation, but Delsie and I sat down while the Sergeant pulled a black Windsor chair over for himself.

"I am afraid that your search may have ended," he announced with a trace of sympathy. "St. James Parish lies up river and west of here thirty miles. It is a rural district. Yesterday evening a local catfisherman found the body of a young woman there, in the batture."

"Batture?" asked Delsie.

"The muddy flats between the levee and the river," he explained patiently. "We think that the victim may have been Miss Hamilton."

"Victim?" I asked, my stomach growing queasy.

He reached into a coat pocket, and removed a Polaroid photo.

"I apologize in advance that this will be difficult," he went on, "but you may be able to assist us. Is this Miss Hamilton?"

He turned the photograph over, and Delsie caught her breath. The picture was ghastly. Even with a badly broken nose, and mud-caked hair, and lividity staining the right side of her face a dark purple, it was clearly Brownie's missing daughter.

"Yes," Delsie flinched. "That's her."

"Elizabeth Hamilton?"

"Yes," Delsie repeated, gulping hard. "She was a few years younger than I, so she hung with a different crowd. She liked to play Frisbee on the beach. You remember her, don't you, Sugar?"

I struggled to recall a lithe, young girl in a bright orange bikini, laughing as she pranced along the surf line in pursuit of colorful flying discs, but I knew without a doubt that I would never again think of Betty Hamilton without seeing her wan, hollow-eyed, slime-streaked face.

"You said *victim*," I finally stated with a dry mouth.

"It is tragic; eh?" Sergeant Boudreaux said softly as he put the photograph away. "From all indications, she was raped and murdered. They found the body naked, and discovered no personal effects nearby, so we were not certain of the identification until just now. I am deeply sorry for your loss."

"Welcome to Jazz Fest," Delsie muttered bitterly.

"You'll make the notification?" I inquired.

"You are not family, then?" asked Boudreaux.

"We're just friends of her stepmother," I explained once again, flashing the most questioning look that I could muster.

"We moved the body here," he said, clarifying his position, "because the Orleans Parish Medical Examiner has far better facilities than we do in St. James, and because we believe that the crime may have taken place in the city. Someone probably dumped Miss Hamilton's body in St. James, or upriver perhaps, but we do not know for certain, so the jurisdictional responsibility is unclear, and we are sharing the investigation. Therefore, I do not know who will make the notification, or when, but it will not be until after the Medical Examiner has completed his report. Where will you be staying?"

"At Le Pavillon," answered Delsie. "May we go now?"

"Oui; certainly," he said, showing us to the door. "I will stop by later today with some forms for you to sign, to make the identification official."

We stepped out of the police station, into the sultry clime that is New Orleans, but I didn't feel warm, or even sticky. The cold hand of death had taken hold of my vacation, and a dank premonition chilled the very core of my soul.